Kornél Esti

Also by Dezső Kosztolányi
from New Directions

———

Anna Edes

Dezső Kosztolányi

Kornél Esti

Translated by Bernard Adams

A NEW DIRECTIONS BOOK

Grateful acknowledgment to the Hungarian Book Foundation, which
supported the translation of this book.

Manufactured in the United States of America
Published simultaneously in Canada by Penguin Books Canada, Ltd.
New Directions Books are printed on acid-free paper.
First published as a New Directions Paperbook Original (NDP1194) in 2011

Library of Congress Cataloging-in-Publication Data
Kosztolányi, Dezso, 1885–1936.
[Esti Kornél. English]
Kornél Esti / Dezso Kosztolányi ; translated by Bernard Adams.
p. cm.
ISBN 978-0-8112-1843-6 (paperbook : alk. paper)
1. Self-perception--Fiction. 2. Doppelgängers--Fiction.
3. Authorship--Fiction. 4. Psychological fiction.
I. Adams, Bernard. II. Title.
PH3281.K85E6713 2011
894'.51133--dc22   2010048874

3 5 7 9 10 8 6 4 2

New Directions Books are published for James Laughlin
by New Directions Publishing Corporation,
80 Eighth Avenue, New York 10011

I

In which the writer introduces and unveils Kornél Esti,
the sole hero of this book

I HAD PASSED THE MIDPOINT OF MY LIFE, WHEN ONE WINDY
day in spring, I remembered Kornél Esti. I decided to call on him and
to revive our former friendship.

By then we'd had no contact for ten years. What had come between us? I don't know. We hadn't fallen out. At least, not like other
people do.

Once I'd passed the age of thirty, however, he began to irritate me.
His frivolity was offensive. I became tired of his old-fashioned wing
collars, his narrow yellow ties, and especially his atrocious puns. His
determined eccentricity wore me out. He was forever getting mixed
up in escapades of one sort or another.

For instance, one day as we were walking along the esplanade
together, he, without a word of explanation, took from the inside
pocket of his coat a kitchen knife, and to the amazement of the
passersby started to sharpen it on the stones that lined the path.
Or, another time, he most politely accosted a poor blind man to
remove from his eye a speck of dust that had just gone into it. On
one occasion, when I was expecting some very distinguished guests
for dinner, men on whom my fate and career depended, editors-
in-chief, politicians—gentlemen of rank and distinction—and Esti
was also a guest in my home, he craftily made my servants heat the

bathroom, took my guests aside one by one as they arrived, and informed them that there was in my house an ancient, mysterious, family tradition or superstition—unfortunately, no details could be given—that required all guests without exception to take a bath before dinner, and he carried off this ridiculous prank with such devilish tact, cunning, and honeyed words that the credulous victims, who favored us with their presence for the first and last time, without my knowledge all took baths, as did their wives, and then, without batting an eyelid at the awful practical joke, sat down to dinner as if nothing had happened.

That kind of practical joke had amused me in the past, but now, at the beginning of my adult life, it rather annoyed me. I was afraid that sort of thing might easily jeopardize my good name. I didn't say a word to him. Nevertheless—I confess—he embarrassed me more than once.

He too may well have felt the same about me. In the depths of his heart he probably looked down on me for not according his ideas the respect that they deserved—perhaps he even despised me. He took me for a philistine because I used to buy an engagement diary, wrote in it every day, and did all the right things. On one occasion he accused me of forgetting what it was like to be young. And there may have been some truth in that. But that's the way life goes. Everyone forgets.

Slowly, imperceptibly, we drifted apart, but despite all that I understood him and he understood me. It was just that we kept passing judgment on one another secretly. The thought that we understood one another, yet didn't, set us both on edge. We went our separate ways. He went left—I went right.

For ten long years we had lived like that, without giving one another a sign of our existence. Naturally, however, I'd thought of him. Scarcely a day went by when I didn't wonder what he would do or say in this or that situation. And I must suppose that he too thought of me. After all, our past was pervaded by so vigorous and pulsating a network of veins of memory that it couldn't have been so soon forgotten.

It would be difficult to give a full account of who and what he had been to me. I wouldn't even care to try. My memory doesn't go back as far as our friendship. Its beginnings are lost in the primeval mists of my infancy. He had been close to me ever since I'd been aware of myself, always in front of me or behind, always with me or against me. I'd worshipped Esti or loathed him, but I'd never been indifferent to him.

One winter evening, after supper, I was building a tower of colored building bricks. Mother wanted me put to bed. She sent Nanny for me, because at that time I was still in skirts, and I started to go with her. Then a voice came from behind me, his unforgettable voice:

"Don't go."

I turned round and, in delight and alarm, looked at him. It was the first time that I'd seen him. He gave me an encouraging grin. I took his arm for him to help me, but Nanny pulled me away and, rage though I might, put me to bed.

From then on we met every day.

In the morning he would spring forward by the washstand.

"Don't wash up, stay dirty, hooray for dirt!"

If at lunch, despite my convictions to the contrary, I began at my parents' repeated request to spoon up the "nourishing and wholesome" lentil soup, he would whisper in my ear:

"Spit it out, throw up onto your plate, wait for the roast or the dessert."

Sometimes he was at home with me, at table or in bed, but he went into the street with me as well.

Once Uncle Loizi was coming toward us, an old friend of my father's, whom I had always liked and respected, a three-hundred-pound magistrate. Kornél shouted at me:

"Stick your tongue out." And he stuck out his own till it reached the point of his chin.

He was a cheeky boy, but interesting, never dull.

He put a lighted candle in my hand.

"Set fire to the curtains!" he urged me. "Set fire to the house. Set the world on fire."

He put a knife in my hand too.

"Stick it in your heart!" he exclaimed. "Blood's red. Blood's warm. Blood's pretty."

I didn't dare follow his suggestions, but I was pleased that he dared to put into words what I thought. I said nothing, gave a chilly smile. I was afraid of him and attracted to him.

After a summer shower I found a sparrow chick, drenched, under the broom bush. As I had been taught in Scripture lessons, I put it on my palm, and performing an act of bodily and spiritual kindness, took it into the kitchen to dry it by the fire. I sprinkled crumbs in front of it. Tucked it up in some rags. Sat it on my arm and stroked it.

"Tear its wings off," whispered Kornél. "Poke its eyes out, throw it in the fire, kill it!"

"You're crazy!" I shouted.

"You're a coward!" shouted he.

White-faced, we glared at one another. We were shaking, I with rage and empathy, he from curiosity and bloodlust. I thrust the chick at him: he could do what he wanted with it. Kornél looked at me and took pity on the little thing. He began to tremble. I pouted scornfully. While we were thus at odds the sparrow chick slipped out into the garden and disappeared.

So he didn't dare do everything. He liked to talk big and make things up.

I remember how one autumn evening, about six o'clock, he called me out to the gate and there informed me, mysteriously and importantly, that he could actually work magic. He showed me a shiny metal object in his hand. He said that it was a magic whistle, and he only had to blow it for any house to rise up into the air, all the way to the moon. He said that at ten o'clock that evening he was going to levitate our house. He told me not to be afraid, just to watch closely what happened.

At the time I was quite a big boy. I believed him, and yet I didn't. I rushed back into the apartment in agitation. I watched constantly as the hands of the clock moved on. Just in case, I went over the events of my past life, repented of my sins, knelt in front of the picture of the Blessed Virgin, and prayed. At about ten I heard music and a rustling in the air. Our house rose slowly, smoothly upwards, came to a stop at a height, then rocked and just as slowly and smoothly as it had risen, sank back to earth. A glass on the table rattled and the hanging lamp shook. The whole affair had lasted a couple of minutes. The others hadn't even noticed. Only my mother turned pale when she looked at me.

"You're having a giddy turn," she said, and sent me to bed.

My friendship with Kornél really deepened when the first pimples appeared on our foreheads, the purple springtime buds of adolescence. We were inseparable. We read and argued. I defied him, refuted his wicked ideas. One thing is certain, he was the one who introduced me to all sorts of bad habits. He enlightened me about how children were born; he once told me that adults were yellow, tobacco-smelling, bloated villains and deserved no respect because they were uglier than us and would die sooner; he encouraged me not to study, to lie in bed as long as possible in the morning even if I was late for school; he suggested that I should break into my father's drawers and open his letters; he brought me dirty books and postcards which you had to hold up to the candle; he taught me to sing, lie, and write poetry; he encouraged me to say dirty words, one after another, to watch girls getting changed through cracks in cubicles in the summer, and to pester them at dancing class with my improper desires; he made me smoke my first cigarette and drink my first glass of pálinka; he gave me a taste for the pleasures of the flesh, gluttony and fornication; he revealed to me that even in my pain there was a secret delight; he tore the scabs off my itching wounds; he proved that everything was relative and that a toad could have a soul just as much as a managing director; he gave me a liking for mute animals and silent solitude; he once consoled me when I was choking in tears at a funeral by tickling my side, at which I suddenly burst out laughing at the stupid incomprehensibility of death; he smuggled mockery into my feelings, rebelliousness into my despair; he advised me to side with those whom the majority spit on, imprison, and hang; he announced that death is eternal; and he wanted me to believe the wicked lie, which I opposed with all my might, that there was no God. My innocent, healthy nature never accepted those opinions at all. I felt, nevertheless, that it would be good to be free of his influence and finally to have done with him, only I lacked the strength: it seems that he still interested me. And then, I was greatly in his debt. He'd been my teacher and now I owed him my life, as does one that has sold his soul to the devil.

My father didn't like him.

"Where's that cheeky brat?" he burst into my room one evening. "Where've you hidden him? Where's he hiding?"

I held out my arms, showing him that I was alone.

"He's always here!" he thundered. "He's always hanging about. Always pestering you. You eat off the same plate, drink from the same glass. You're Castor and Pollux. Good friends," he sneered.

He looked behind the door, behind the stove, in the cupboard. He even looked under the bed to see if Kornél might be there.

"Now you listen to me!" he trumpeted as his rage reached its peak. "If he ever again, just once, sets foot in this house, I'll knock his block off, I'll kick him out like a dog, and you as well, and you go where you like, I'll disown you! So, don't let him into my house again. Understand?"

He paced to and fro, hands behind his back, controlling his temper. His shoes squeaked.

"He's a lazybones. He's a mischief-maker. Can't you make any other friends? He fills your head with nonsense. He's driving you mad. Do you want to be a rotten character like him? He's nobody and nothing, you know. He'll never amount to anything."

Kornél wasn't allowed to show himself. He even avoided our street.

We used to meet in secret, out of town—at the cattle market, where the circus used to pitch their marquee every summer, or in the cemetery among the graves.

We strolled, arms round one another's necks. On one such passionate walk we stumbled on the fact that both of us had been born in the same year, on the same day ,and at the very same hour and minute: March 29, 1885, Palm Sunday, at six in the morning. This mysterious revelation affected us deeply. We vowed that as we had first seen the world on the same day and at the same hour, we would both likewise die at the same hour of the same day, neither outliving the other by a single second, and in the raptures of youth we were convinced we would perform our vow with ready joy, painlessly and without sacrifice for either of us.

"You aren't feeling sorry about him, are you?" my mother questioned as I dozed in front of the oil lamp, thinking of Kornél. "It's better this way, son. He's not good for you. Make friends with other boys, honest, decent young gentlemen like young Merey, Endre Horváth, Ilosvay. They're fond of you. He's never cared about you. Just got you down, worried you, got on your nerves. How often did you suddenly wake up screaming in November? He isn't fit for you. He's got nothing going for him. He's useless, has no heart. You, son, aren't like that. You're a good boy, good-hearted, you feel things deeply," she said, and gave me a kiss. "You're not like him at all, son."

And so it was. There were no two people on the planet more different than Kornél and myself.

I found what happened a few days after that conversation all the more peculiar.

I was hurrying home from school in the midday sunshine with my books done up in their strap when someone called after me:

"Kornél!"

A gentleman in a green coat was smiling at me.

"Look here, young Kornél," he began, and asked me to take a parcel round to the neighbors when I got home.

"I beg your pardon," I stammered.

"What's the matter, son?" he asked. "It looks as if you haven't understood."

"Yes I have," I replied. "But you've made a mistake. I'm not Kornél Esti."

"What?" the man in the green coat was puzzled. "Don't play games, son. You live in Gombkötő utca, don't you?"

"No, sir. We live in Damjanich utca."

"Are you related to Kornél?"

"No, I'm sorry. I go to school with him. We're in the same class, and he sits by me in the second row. But last term Kornél failed two subjects, his work was untidy, and his behavior was bad, but I'm top of the class, good marks in everything, my work's tidy, my behavior's good, and I'm also learning French and the piano privately."

"I could have sworn . . . ," the man in the green coat muttered into space. "It's strange," he said, and he raised his eyebrows.

It also happened on several occasions that when we were out walking by the railway embankment on the other side of the woods passersby, strangers, spoke to us and asked whether we were twins.

"Look at those two," they nudged each other, "just look at them," and they laughed with pleasure.

They made us stand side by side, then back to back with our heads touching, and measured our height, putting their hands on top of our heads.

"A hairsbreadth isn't much," they assured us, shaking their heads. "But there isn't even that much difference. Isn't that remarkable, Bódi? Isn't it just?"

Later on, when we had grown up and both of us were writing, there were from time to time many things that I myself failed to understand.

I would suddenly get letters from people I didn't know, asking me to return the small amounts that they had placed at my disposal in Kassa, Vienna, or Kolozsvár, at the station, before the train left, because I'd told them that I'd lost my purse and given my word of honor to pay them back within twenty-four hours. Impolite telephone calls would accuse me of writing anonymous letters. My closest friends would see me with their own eyes wandering about for hours on end in the pouring winter rain through curving alleyways and disreputable streets, or lying blind drunk and snoring on the red table-cloth of a bar in some run-down area. The headwaiter of the Vitriol—a low dive—presented me with a bill, to avoid paying which I'd allegedly run out through a side door. Several reliable witnesses heard me in company make the rudest remarks about people of high standing, respected writers of national repute. Seconds in duels with jaunty monocles called on me, porters came with my visiting card, girls with the flower of their innocence broken unfolded before me my vows and offers of marriage. A stout, middle-aged lady from the provinces also arrived, called me *te*, and threatened me in her local dialect with a paternity suit.

Flabbergasted, I stared at these nightmare figures, who had certainly—either in my imagination or in real life—at one time lived and breathed, but were now black and dead and cold, like glowing embers after they've cooled, died down, and crumbled to ash. I didn't know them. They, however, knew me and recognized me. Some I told to go and see Kornél. At that they smiled. Asked for a personal description of him. And at that they derisively pointed at me. They asked for his address. There I couldn't really help them. My friend was most of the time traveling abroad, sleeping on aircraft, stopping here and there for a day or two, and to the best of my knowledge had never yet registered with the police. Kornél Esti certainly existed, but he was not a legal entity. So however innocent I knew myself to be of all these terrible crimes, the case against me didn't look good. For Kornél's sake I didn't expose myself to the unpleasantness of confrontation. I had to take upon myself all his debts, his tricks, his dishonesty, as if I were responsible for them all.

I paid. Paid a lot. Not only money. I paid with my reputation too. People everywhere looked at me askance. They didn't know where they were with me, whether I was right or left of center, whether I was a patriotic citizen or a dangerous rabble-rouser, a respectable family man or a depraved voluptuary, and altogether whether I was a real person or just a dream figure—a drunken, double-dealing, lunatic scarecrow who still flapped his ragged, cast-off gentleman's coat whichever way the wind blew. I paid dearly for our friendship.

All that, however, I instantly forgot and forgave on that windy spring day when I decided to call on him.

That was a mad day. Not the first of April, but not far off. A mad, excited day. In the morning there was a frost, with mirrors of ice crackling on the iron gratings round the trees and the sky a bright blue. Then a thaw set in. Water dripped from the eaves. Mist spread over the hills. A lukewarm drizzle fell. The earth steamed like an overdriven, sweating horse. We had to throw off our winter coats. A rainbow hung its gaudy arc above the Danube. In the afternoon hail fell. It frosted the trees and squashed into slush beneath our feet. The wind whistled. Whistled keenly. Whistled up on high, round the chimneys, on the roofs of houses, in the telephone wires—everything was in motion. Houses groaned, attics creaked, beams sighed, wanting to put out buds, because they too had been trees. In that starting, that revolution, in came spring.

I listened to the whistling of the wind and remembered Kornél. I felt an irresistible desire to see him as soon as I could.

I telephoned here and there, to coffeehouses, nightclubs. By late evening all that I had been able to discover was that he *was* in Hungary. I tracked him on foot and in the car. At two in the morning I learned that he was staying at the Denevér Hotel. By the time I reached it a Russian blizzard was raging around me, and the collar of my raincoat was filled with its frothy flakes.

The porter at the Denevér directed me to room 7 on the fifth floor. I climbed a narrow spiral staircase, as there was no elevator. The door of room 7 was ajar. Inside the light was on. I went in.

I saw an empty bed, the blankets thrown back in a heap, and a feeble electric light on the nightstand. I thought that he'd popped out somewhere. I sat down on the sofa to wait for him.

But then I noticed that he was there, opposite me, sitting in front of the mirror. I jumped up. He did too.

"Hello," I said.

"Hello," said he immediately, as if he wanted to pick up just where we had left off.

He wasn't at all surprised at my bursting in so late. He wasn't surprised at anything. He didn't even ask what I wanted.

"How are you?" he asked.

"Very well, thank you. And you?"

"Likewise," he replied.

He stared at me and laughed.

He was wearing a raincoat. There was snow on his collar too.

"Just got in?"

"Yes," he nodded.

I looked round the room. It was a dingy hole. A narrow, dilapidated sofa, two chairs, a cupboard, a five-day-old newspaper on the table, a bunch of wilting violets. A mask, too, goodness knows what for. Cigarette butts on the floor, yellow spectacles and quince jelly in the violin case, open suitcases. A few books, mostly timetables. No pen or paper to be seen. Where he worked was a mystery.

My father had been right. He hadn't amounted to anything. Here there was nothing but the poverty of a hermit, the liberty and independence of a beggar. I had wanted that sort of thing at one time. My eyes filled with tears.

"What's new?" he inquired.

Outside the wind was howling. The cutting spring wind whistled shrilly. A siren too was wailing.

"Ambulance," he said.

We went to the window. The blizzard had stopped. The sky shone crystal clear, as did the frosty roadway. The ambulance siren shrieked in competition with the spring wind.

Scarcely had it passed when a fire engine roared past to somewhere, its light flashing.

"Accidents," I said. "All day long bricks have been falling, shopsigns crashing down on the heads of passersby. People have been slipping and falling on the icy sidewalks, hurting their hands, spraining their ankles, bleeding. Houses and factories have been catching fire. All sorts of things have been happening today. Frost, heat, mist, sunshine, rain, rainbow, snow, blood, and fire. It's spring."

We sat down and lit cigarettes.

"Kornél," I broke the silence, "aren't you angry?"

"Me?" and he shrugged. "Idiot! I can never be angry with you."

"But you'd have good reason. Look, I was angry with you. I was embarrassed by you in front of people that mattered, I've had to get on, I've denied you. Haven't even looked in your direction for ten years. But this afternoon, when the wind whistled, I thought of you and felt remorse. I'm not young any more. I turned forty last week.

When you're not young, you mellow and you can forgive everything. Even youth. Let's make up."

I stretched out a hand.

"Oh, you haven't changed," he scoffed. "Always so sentimental."

"But you have, Kornél. When we were children you were the grown-up, you were the leader, you opened my eyes. Now you're the child."

"Aren't they both the same?"

"That's what I like about you. That's why I've come back, and now I'm going to put up with you forever."

"What's the matter with you today, that you're saying such nice things about me?"

"Well, who else am I to say nice things about, Kornél? Who is there but you that I could love and not feel jealous of? Whom can I admire in this round world if not you, my brother and my opposite? Identical in everything and different in everything. I've gathered, you've thrown away, I've gotten married, you've stayed a bachelor, I worship my people, my language, I can only live and breathe here in Hungary, but you travel the world, fly above nations, in freedom, shrieking everlasting revolt. I need you. I'm empty and bored without you. Help me, otherwise I'll die."

"I could do with somebody as well," he said, "a pillar, a handrail, because look, I'm going to pieces," and he gestured at the room.

"Let's stick together," I suggested. "Let's make a deal."

"To do what?"

"Let's write something, together."

He opened his eyes wide. Spat his cigarette onto the floor.

"I can't write anymore," he said.

"But it's all I can do," I said.

"Oh really," he replied, and gave me a hard look.

"Don't misunderstand me, Kornél. I'm not showing off, only complaining, like you. Make me whole again, like you used to. In those days, when I was asleep you were awake, when I cried you laughed. Help me now too — remember the things I forget, and forget what I remember. I'm worth something as well. Everything I know will be at your disposal. I've got a home, everything there helps my work, and it will help yours too. I work hard, I'm devout and loyal. So loyal that I can't upset anyone with whom I've exchanged a single word, not even in my mind. I'm so loyal, Kornél, that because of my old dog I won't even pet other dogs, or play with them, or even look at them. Even to inanimate objects — sometimes I ignore my fifteen excellent fountain pens and bring out a worn-out, scratchy pen which it's torture to write with, and scratch away so as to cheer it up, poor thing, and prevent it from feeling unwanted. I'm loyalty incarnate. You'll be disloyalty, instability, at my side. Let's start a business partnership. What can a poet achieve without anyone? What can anyone achieve without a poet? Let's be joint authors. One man isn't enough to write and live at the same time. Those who've tried it have all broken down sooner or later. Only Goethe could do it, that calm, cheerful immortal; when I think of him a shiver runs down my spine, because there's never been a cleverer and more fearsome man, that splendid, Olympian monster, beside whom even Mephistopheles is a worthless snob. Yes, he forgave and saved Margaret, whom the earthly judges had imprisoned, and took the mother who had killed her child to heaven among the archangels and learned men of the faith, and made hidden choirs sing his eternal defense of womanhood and motherhood. A few years later, though, when he sat as a magistrate in Weimar and had to pass judgment on a similar infanticide mother, Margaret's former champion condemned the girl to death without batting an eyelid."

"So he sent her to heaven too," muttered Kornél. "He acted consistently."

"Quite," I retorted. "Only neither of us would be capable of such vicious and divine wisdom. But if we joined forces, Kornél, we might perhaps get somewhere near it. Like Night and Day, Reality and Imagination, Ahriman and Ormuzd. What do you say?"

"The trouble is," he complained, "I get bored, bored beyond words with letters and sentences. You scribble away and in the end you see that the same words keep repeating themselves. It's all *no, but, that, rather, therefore*. It's infuriating."

"I'll see to that. All you need to do is talk."

"I'll only be able to talk about myself. About what's happened to me. And what has happened? Just a minute. Nothing really. Hardly anything happens to most people. But I've imagined a lot. That's part of our lives too. The truth isn't just that we've kissed a woman, but also that we've secretly lusted after her, wanted to kiss her. Often the actual woman's the lie and the lust is the truth. A dream is also reality. If I dream that I've been to Egypt, I can write an account of the journey."

"So will it be a travelogue?" I joked, "or a biography?"

"Neither."

"A novel?"

"God forbid! All novels begin: 'A young man was going along a dark street, with his collar turned up.' Then it turns out that the man with the turned-up collar's the hero of the novel. Working up interest. Dreadful."

"What, then?"

"All three in one. A travelogue—I'll say where I would have liked to go—and a biography in the form of a novel: I'll give details of how often the hero died in my dream. But one thing I insist on—don't glue it all together with an idiotic story. Everything must be exactly what you'd expect from a poet: fragments."

We agreed to meet more often in future, in the Torpedo or the Vitriol. If the worst came to the worst, on the telephone.

He walked me to the door.

"Oh," in the corridor he slapped his forehead. "Something I forgot. What about the style?"

"We'll be writing together."

"But our styles are poles apart. You've recently been favoring calm, simplicity, classical images. Not much decoration, not many words. My style, on the other hand, is still restless, untidy, congested, ornate, racy. I'm an incurable romantic. Lots of epithets, lots of images. I won't let you cut that out."

"Tell you what," I reassured him. "Let's meet in the middle. I'll take down what you say in shorthand, then erase some of it."

"In what proportion?"

"Five out of ten of your images will stay."

"And fifty out of a hundred of my epithets," added Kornél. "That'll do."

He slapped my hand. It was a deal. He leaned on his elbows over the banister as I went down the spiral stairs.

No sooner had I reached the bottom than I thought of something.

"Kornél!" I called up, "Who's going to put his name to our book?"

"Doesn't matter!" he called down. "Perhaps you'd better. You put your name to it. And my name can be the title. The title's in bigger letters."

He kept his word marvelously. For a year we met once or twice a month, and he always brought some new experience or novel-chapter from his life. In between, he'd just go away for a few days. I put his tales on paper partly from my shorthand notes, partly from memory, and put them in the order he wanted. That's how this book came to be written.

II

*In which, on September 1, 1891, he goes to the Red Ox
and there becomes acquainted with human society*

IT WAS THE FIRST OF SEPTEMBER, EIGHTEEN HUNDRED AND
ninety-one.

At seven in the morning, in the modest apartment overlooking the
courtyard, his mother opened the door to the longish room where
her three children slept—he, his younger brother, and his sister.

She tiptoed to the mosquito-netted bed, unfastened the rod that
held the bracken-festooned net, and gently touched the forehead of
her eldest, six-year-old son to wake him. Today was to be his first
day at school.

He opened his eyes immediately. His mother's blue eyes were
sparkling right above him. She smiled.

He was a skinny, anemic little boy, with transparent ears. He was
still feeling the effects of his last serious illness, pleurisy, which had
kept him in bed for several months that year. His heart now beat
on the right, and they had been talking about surgically draining
the fluid from his lungs when suddenly he had improved. He'd recovered, but then he'd begun to "have nerves." All sorts of weird
ideas plagued him. He was afraid of old women in headscarves, of
policemen with their plumes. He was afraid—no telling why—
that his father was going to shoot himself, and he'd suddenly cover
his ears with both hands so as not to hear the report of the pistol.

He was afraid of not getting enough air and walked from room to room, hugging various pieces of furniture so that his chest would expand with the effort and he wouldn't suffocate. He was afraid of coffin makers and death. More than once, when the lamp was lit, he'd gathered his belongings around him and made arrangements for how he was to be buried and to whom each toy was to be given, should he happen to die in the night. The doctor didn't consider his condition serious. Nevertheless his parents had planned to have him taught privately for the first year instead of sending him to school, but at the last moment they'd changed their minds.

Now he sat there on the edge of his bed, eyes full of sleep, yawning and scratching himself.

He'd known that this day would come sooner or later. But he hadn't believed that it would come so quickly.

He would have liked to defer it somehow.

Reluctantly he pulled up his long black socks, which hung loosely on his legs. He stood for a long time at the washstand, dipping his hands and taking them out again and again, watching the rings of light that shimmered on the surface of the water.

His mother washed him herself and put him in a clean shirt. She'd got his best clothes ready, a dark blue linen shirt trimmed with white which she'd made from an old blouse of hers, set off with feminine heart-shaped mother-of-pearl buttons. She pulled a wet brush through his hair.

She put some coffee in front of him, and an S-shaped kifli. He didn't want any coffee that day. Said he wasn't hungry.

At that his mother pressed into his hand his ABC book, his slate and slate-pencil, and took him to the school.

The autumn sun was by then shining in its full splendor over the Alföld town. Peasant carts were jolting along in clouds of yellow dust. A train whistled on the bridge. In the market square sacks of red paprika and white dried beans were on sale.

He trotted irritably along at his mother's side. He felt awkward, silly, and above all girlish in his "best" clothes—which he knew were the worst, both cheap and old. He'd have liked to tear them up and trample them into the ground. But he knew that his father was a poor teacher at the secondary school and couldn't really afford anything else. He took revenge by not saying a single word the whole way.

Very soon they reached the Red Ox.

The Red Ox was the elementary school. This two-story palace of public education took its quite lamentable name from the fact that at one time a rickety, tumbledown inn had stood on the site, with a red ox daubed on its sign. The building had burned down a generation ago, but the drunkards of that wine-swilling town still liked to recall the nights of dissipation spent there, and so the name of the inn had been unkindly transferred to the school and in that way was passed down from father to son.

When they reached the dim entrance hall of the school he turned pale and had an attack of "breathing difficulty." As was his custom, he leaned on a pillar and hugged it to him with all his strength. His mother bent over him and asked what was the matter. He didn't answer. Just held her hand tighter and tighter.

First grade was upstairs. His mother gave him a kiss outside a brown double door and made to leave. But he wouldn't let go of her hand.

"I'm frightened," he whispered.

"What're you frightened of?"

"I'm frightened," he repeated.

"Don't be frightened, darling. Look, the others are here as well. Everybody's here. Can't you hear how happy they are? Go and see your little friends."

"Stay," he pleaded, and clung to his mother's skirt.

Waving good-bye to her son with the hand that he had released, she slipped away from him and walked slowly down the corridor. At the corner she took out a handkerchief and wiped her eyes. She even looked back once to encourage him with her smile. But then she suddenly vanished.

The little boy stood for a while rooted to the spot and waited, waited, staring after his mother. He hoped that perhaps she'd come back and that the whole thing was a joke. But it was *not* a joke.

When he realized that, and also realized that he was alone, more alone than he'd ever been on this earth before, a spasm seized his entire body, something akin to colic. He tried to run away. He slunk along the wall as far as the stairs, where that skirt had just then mysteriously vanished into nothing. There a staircase yawned, completely unfamiliar and cheerless, with a cavernous, gray, echoing vault. To go down there would have called for death-defying courage. With the instinct of the damned, he thought it wiser to creep back instead to where he had lost her, back to the door of the classroom. At least he was a little bit used to that.

He peered in through the gap in the half-open door.

He could see children, more children than he'd ever before seen in one place. It was a crowd, a crowd of completely unknown little people like himself.

So he wasn't alone. But if it had previously plunged him into despair that he was so alone in the world, now an even more alarming despair seized him, that he was so very much not alone in the world, that all those other people were alive as well. That was perhaps even more terrifying.

Everyone was chattering at the same time. What they were saying he couldn't make out. The noise was a babble, fearsomely swelling, roaring like a thunderstorm.

While he was thus musing, someone—a grown-up whom he didn't know—picked him up and put him in the classroom. There he stood, his little cap crooked on his head.

He expected some miracle to happen. He expected all those children to jump up and shout his name. Expected them to greet him, waving their handkerchiefs. Only the miracle didn't happen. No one took any notice of him.

He took his cap off, greeting them politely. They didn't return the greeting.

It was a room, not like other rooms where there were sofas and curtains, but frigid, official, bare. Daylight poured in through three large curtainless windows. A table stood guard on the dais. Behind that a blackboard, yellow sponge, white chalk. In front of it the abacus stood erect and haughty, like a mad thing. All around on the whitewashed walls were colored pictures of animals, a lion, a fox, and sheets of cardboard on which things could be read: *man, animal, toy, work*. In his agitation he read them all. He had been able to read from the age of four.

His classmates were now all sitting down. He too would have liked to sit somewhere.

The front benches, almost inevitably, were occupied by the children of the "gentry"—the sons of landowners, town councillors. These good-humored, fair-haired, chubby-cheeked little boys were wearing sailor suits, starched collars, silk ties. Their faces were like roses dipped in milk. They surrounded the dais politely but self-consciously, as the government supporting a Party edict surrounds the prime minister's velvet chair. He likewise considered himself a "gentry" child. He therefore forced onto his lips a stupid smile and approached them to take his seat on the front row. Only almost every seat there was already taken. They didn't exactly hurry to make room for him. They muttered among themselves like close friends, and looked with cold civility and some surprise at this timid latecomer. Some even smiled, enjoying his discomfiture.

Ashamed and offended, he made his way toward the rear. If he couldn't be first on the front bench—he thought—at least he would be last on the last. There at the back of the class the peasant children had taken their places, muscular, powerful lads, some barefoot, some in boots. They had unpacked their food from their red handkerchiefs. They were eating black bread and fat bacon with jackknives, and watermelon. He looked here and there. The stale smell that rose from their boots and clothes turned his stomach. But he would gladly have sat among them. He begged with his eyes to be accepted by them at least. He watched for a word to be spoken, a sign given. But these boys were otherwise engaged. They were throwing paper pellets and balls of paper filled with rinds of bacon and melon, and one such paper ball hit him on the forehead. The shock was greater than the damage, but he staggered against the wall. At that everyone laughed out loud, lower and upper houses alike, without distinction of party.

With rage and irritation in his heart he withdrew from there too.

He didn't know where to go, where he belonged. And so he went and stood alone by the stove. He felt ashamed at being so cowardly and gauche. From the stove he assessed the whole illiterate company with infinite disdain. If they only knew what he knew! He knew, for example, that the average temperature of a human was 98 degrees, and that anyone that had a temperature of 104 degrees was all but past saving. He knew that there was ordinary writing and shorthand. He knew that quinine was bitter and ipecacuanha sweet. He also knew that just then it was evening in America. But they didn't know that he knew all that.

The little bell of the Red Ox tinkled melodiously in the little wooden tower on the roof, indicating that it was eight o'clock and lessons were about to start. While the bell was ringing, on and on, heartbreakingly, like the bell that mourns the dead, he took leave of everything that was dear, the rooms at home, the garden, and all his individual toys too, the soap bubbles and the balloons. Close to fainting, he clung to the cold tinplate stove.

Silence fell. The teacher had appeared in the doorway, a stout man with cropped dark gray hair and a very ample light gray suit. He took great strides, like an elephant. He rolled onto the dais.

The teacher asked the children one by one if they had slates and pencils, and then spoke of all the fine, noble, useful things that they were going to learn there. But then he suddenly stopped speaking. He had caught sight of the boy lurking beside the stove.

"Now then, what're you doing there?" he asked, turning his great face in his direction. "Who put you there? Come over here."

The little boy hurried, almost ran, to the dais. In terror, almost beside himself, he gabbled:

"Please let me go home."

"Why?" inquired the teacher.

"I don't want to come to school anymore."

The class roared with laughter.

"Silence!" said the teacher. "Why don't you want to come to school?"

"Because nobody likes me here."

"Has anybody hurt you?"

"No."

"Then why're you talking such nonsense? Aren't you ashamed of yourself, you little sissy? Just understand, you're the same as everyone else here. No exceptions here, everybody's equal. Understand?"

The class nodded in approval.

The teacher looked again at the frightened little boy. This time he saw that his face was quite green.

"Are you feeling ill?" he asked, in a kinder tone.

"No."

"Got a pain anywhere?"

"No."

"All right," he said, "go back to your place. Where is your place?"

"Nowhere."

"Nowhere?" The teacher was puzzled. "Well, sit down somewhere."

The little boy turned toward the class. Faces grinned at him, lots and lots of little faces, which blended into a single huge, frightening idol-face. He stumbled unsteadily this way and that. Once more he had to pass the first bench, where there was no room for him. He found a tiny place somewhere in the middle, on the very end of a bench. He could only get one leg onto the seat, the other dangled in space. Anyway, it was better to sit there away from the eyes, to vanish into the crowd.

"Children," said the teacher, "take your slates and pencils. We'll do some writing. We'll write the letter i."

Slates rattled. He too tried to place his slate on the desk but the surly, swarthy boy at his side pushed it off in an unfriendly fashion. The boy didn't let him write.

At that he burst loudly and bitterly into tears.

"What's going on?" asked the teacher.

"He's crying," reported the surly, swarthy boy.

"Who is?"

"This boy here."

All the children looked in his direction. Many stood up to get a better view.

"He's giving the mice a drink," they exclaimed.

"Be quiet!" the teacher exploded, striking the table with his cane.

He came down from the dais and went and stood by the little boy. He stroked his face with his warm, tobacco-scented hand.

"Don't cry," he calmed him. "Sit properly on the bench, square on. Why don't you move over for him? There's plenty of room. There you are, now. Put the slate in front of you, get hold of your pencil. Wipe your nose. Now, we're going to learn to write. Or don't you want to learn to write?"

"Yes, I do," sniveled the little boy.

"Right, then," said the teacher approvingly.

He went and wrote a letter i on the blackboard.

"Up," he showed them, "stop, back down and a little hook."

Slate pencils squealed like little pigs.

The teacher came down from the dais once more. He walked around the room, scrutinizing the squiggles on the slates. He looked at the little boy's i too. He had written a nice, fine letter. He praised him for it. Now the child wasn't crying.

"What's your name?" he asked.

The little boy stood up. He mumbled something very quietly.

"I don't understand," said the teacher. "Always speak up and answer so that I can hear what you say. What's your name?" he asked again.

"Kornél Esti," said the little boy, firmly and distinctly.

III

*In which, at night on a train, shortly after leaving school in 1903,
a girl kisses him on the lips for the first time*

WHEN, IN 1903, KORNÉL ESTI WAS DECLARED PRAECLARE
maturus in his school leaving examination, his father laid before him
a choice: either he would buy him that splendid bicycle for which
he had long yearned, or he would give him the money—a hundred
and twenty koronas—and with that he could travel wherever his
fancy took him.

He decided on the latter. Though not without a little hesitation
and soul-searching.

It was hard to be parted from his mother's skirts. He had grown
up in Sárszeg,* among books and bottles of medicine. In the evening,
before going to bed, he had always had to convince himself that his
mother, father, brother and sister were in bed, in the usual place, and
only then could he go to sleep to the tick-tock of the wall-clock. If,
however, any of them had gone to visit in the country and happened
not to be spending the night at home, he would rather stay awake and
wait for their return, which would once more tip everything back

---

* Sárszeg was, at the time of the story, a village to the northeast of Nagyvárad, in
Bihar county, eastern Hungary. The region was lost in 1920 under the treaty of Trianon, and Sárszeg is now in Romania. Here it is the pseudonym of Kosztolányi's native Szabadka (post-Trianon, Subotica in Serbia); it is also the setting of his novel *Pac-
sirta* (*Skylark*, 1924).

into the old, happy balance. The family was for him the refuge from everything that he feared. It surrounded him like a dovecote, stuffy, dimly lit, tacky with rubbish.

On the other hand, he also longed to get away. He had never yet left that Alföld nest where there was neither river nor hills, the streets and the people were all alike, and days and years brought little change. Here were stifling, dusty afternoons and long, dark evenings. Exercise books and calendars filled the windows of the bookshops. His mind was waking, his tastes developing, but second-rate plays were put on in the theater and for want of better entertainment he watched these from a student seat in the rafters. He would have liked to see the world. Most of all, he would have loved to see the sea. He had imagined it while still in primary school, when he had for the first time looked at that smooth, endless blueness on the wall map. So, with an heroic decision, he proposed that come what may he would go to Italy,* and alone.

One dull, hectic day in July he set off. The whole household was up and about at three in the morning. His worn and battered traveling basket had been brought down from the attic and a futile attempt made at mending its lock. He said good-bye with a smile, but his heart sank. He didn't believe that he would ever return. Everyone went with him to catch the slow train for Budapest. They waved their handkerchiefs, while his mother turned away in tears.

After five hours' rattling he reached Budapest without mishap. He immediately informed his parents of that fact by postcard. He took a room in a third-rate hotel near the station. There he spent only a single night.

That evening he used to get to know Budapest. Happy, electrified, he set out into the city, *this modern Babylon*, as he described it in another postcard to his parents. His self-esteem rose because he was going about all by himself. In the National Museum he looked at the antiquities, at the balcony from which Petőfi had spoken, at the stuffed animals. Later he got lost on Andrássy út. A policeman

---

* Kosztolányi himself left school and traveled to Italy in 1903.

kindly put him on the right road. Map of Budapest in hand, he found the Danube and Gellérthegy. The Danube was big, Gellérthegy high. Both were splendid. Budapest was altogether splendid.

What interested him most of all were the people of Budapest. Everybody going along the street, sitting in a coffeehouse or on a tram, shopping in the shops, was a "Budapest person." He could tell at a glance that they were very different from the people of Sárszeg, and as like one another in clothes, attitudes, and manners as members of a single family. In his eyes, therefore, a High Court judge, a horsetrader, the wife of a landowner, and a nursemaid were "Budapest people." This statement—from a higher point of view—is undeniable.

The "Budapest person" was in a hurry and took no notice of him. He found that out immediately upon arrival. The porter who carried his luggage up to the third floor of the hotel likewise belonged to the people of Budapest. He didn't say a single word to him, expect it though he might, but ill-humoredly deposited his basket on a trestle, muttered something, and simply left. Kornél found this behavior hard to bear, but it filled him with great admiration. He wrote to his parents—a third postcard—that *the people here aren't coarse, indeed, in a certain respect they're more refined, more attentive than people in Sárszeg*. Sometimes, however, they did seem cold, even heartless. No one asked him what at home everyone from the *főispán** down would certainly have done: "Well, Kornél, isn't Budapest splendid?" "Isn't the Danube big?" "Isn't Gellérthegy high?" And then, neither did they look him in the face, so open, so yearning for affection, which at first—for the first few hours—he raised to everyone with such boundless confidence that some involuntarily smiled and laughed together behind his back at the sight of such naïveté and youth until—hours later—he learned that one should keep one's face straight if one didn't want to seem ridiculous. At this point the broad, convivial world ceased to be—that sugary toy world, that doll's dinner party—which he had been so accustomed to in the provinces.

---

* The appointed representative of the crown in a Hungarian county, something like the English lord lieutenant.

Things were quite different from then on: both more and less.

Confused by these novelties, brought low in all situations and repeatedly cut to the quick, he sauntered hither and thither and, like someone flayed, things stuck to his flesh; he painfully tore off the healing scabs and became unhealthily receptive to every impression, his every sense became sharpened and refined, and a word that struck his ear, the smell of mash from a brewery, or a glass of unfamiliar shape—a "Budapest glass"—became, in the dingy back room of his hotel, a symbol, an unforgettable memory, and when at length, dazed from the comings and goings of the day, he took refuge in bed—the "Budapest bed," among the "Budapest pillows"—there welled up in his heart a nostalgia for the old things, the old people, and in despair he yearned for home. Nor did sleep come to his eyes. He propped himself up on the pillows in his dark room and pondered.

Next afternoon he boarded the express for Fiume.* He quickly found a seat. There were not many traveling. In the second-class compartment where he first opened the door there were only two: a woman and her daughter. He greeted them. The woman received that with a wordless nod, good-natured but reserved, as if to inform him that she occupied a position of friendly neutrality. He crammed his basket onto the luggage rack and settled down by the window. The lady sat across from him, her daughter beside her, obliquely opposite him.

Esti fanned himself. An African temperature prevailed. The sweltering carriages, which had been baking all day in the blazing sun, were now oozing their poison, fuming and dusty, and the seats exuded the stench of some animal hide. The dark patches in the clouds of steam swirled drunkenly before his eyes in that yellow waxwork light.

He spared his traveling companions scarcely a glance. He didn't even wish to know who they were. Schooled by bitter lessons, he feigned indifference. He could by then dissimulate better than those

* Now Rijeka in Croatia.

who had devoted their whole lives to it. He opened his book, Edmondo de Amicis' *Il Cuore*.* It amused him that even with his patchy knowledge of Italian he could understand it perfectly and read it almost fluently on the basis of his Latin.

The train ran out of the glass cage of the station. The woman made the sign of the cross. That surprised him. It wasn't customary in his family. But it made an impression on him. What beautiful, womanly humility. "We are all in the hand of God." Indeed, traveling impairs our life expectancy. It isn't a deadly danger, only about as bad as a quinsy from which can develop—perhaps—blood poisoning or heart failure. That journey, furthermore, was no trifling matter. It lasted twelve hours without a break: part of the afternoon, then the whole of the night until eight the next morning. When they arrived the sun would be shining again—who knew what might happen during that time?

He delighted in that uncertainty. He was also pleased that no other passenger had come into their compartment, so that he would probably have a comfortable journey all the way with only that woman and her daughter, who, if not actually friendly, were not hostile.

They rattled through the marshaling yards. Now they were out of Budapest, among the fields. The sticky heat had cooled, been diluted. There was even a slight breeze. He felt that he had become free, had left behind him all sorts of things, that all sorts of things no longer restricted him as they had previously, and that the young man who was sitting there with the Italian book in his hand was really him and not him, could be anyone he wished, because with the constant change of place he was entering an infinite variation of possible situations, a kind of spiritual masked ball.

The woman adjusted her ash-blonde hair, fiddled with the chignon at the back and her tortoiseshell hairpins. She had a calm face and an uncomplicated, clear forehead. Esti now discovered for the first time what intellectually fertile soil a railway compartment is. Here the

* De Amicis (1846–1908), Italian novelist allied to Manzoni in the "purification" of Italian. *Il Cuore* (1886) is his most popular work, much translated and titled in English *An Italian Schoolboy's Journal.*

lives of strangers appear before us in, as it were, cross section—suddenly and condensed—as in a novel opened haphazardly in the middle. Our curiosity, which otherwise we conceal by false modesty, can be satisfied under the constraint of our being enclosed together in a moving room, and we can peep into those lives and speculate on what the beginning of the novel must have been and how it will end. Esti had already, in his school literary circle, produced some decent work as both poet and novelist. Here too he could practice that craft. However gauche he was otherwise, he could cloak his intentions and give himself over completely to creative inquisitiveness, his eyes sliding more and more frequently from the guileless sentences of *Il Cuore* to the woman.

She must have been thirty-nine or forty, the same age as his mother. Straightaway, in the first moment, he felt an extraordinary warmth toward her. She had ivy-green eyes. She, however, looked at neither Esti nor her daughter, but stared into space—tired, sad, and perhaps even a little disinterested. She was looking into herself. She wouldn't allow anyone else to look there.

She evinced a languid gentleness and trustfulness, like a dove. She wasn't fat, not at all, but she was shapely, like a dove. The only jewelry on her hand was a gold wedding ring. That hand—the white hand of a mother—rested for the most part in her lap, in the pleasant, mystical softness of a mother's lap.

She had with her two pigskin cases covered in coffee-brown canvas, decorated all over with the hummingbird brilliance of stickers from foreign hotels. Leather-framed name cards hung from the handles, swinging with the motion of the train. Beside her on the seat lay an elegant shagreen handbag.

Poise and taste were evident in her every movement. For that matter, she scarcely did move. That great calm was a trifle odd. She mused and did nothing. Sometimes Esti thought that at some point—when she sneezed or blew her nose—he would suddenly lose interest in her. But he was mistaken. As time went by, every such little tiny surprise merely reinforced his swift feeling of warmth toward her. Even inactivity didn't make her boring. Everything that she did, or didn't do, was good, beautiful, pleasing, and it was good, beautiful, or pleasing the way she did it, or didn't do it.

As profound an affection for her awoke in him as if he were seeing his own mother. It did him good to look at that woman, to know that she was in the world and so close to him.

Meanwhile, time slipped by in such a way that he didn't notice it.

Naturally, he gathered these observations slowly, bit by bit, something every minute, because he couldn't be indiscreet, could only watch her for short periods, as if by chance, and then fly back with the precious, stolen pollen, to make it into honey in the buzzing beehive of his imagination.

Once, just as he was withdrawing again to hide behind the cover of *Il Cuore*, frowning and reading most intently, it struck him that the girl was whispering something to her mother.

In fact, he had been hearing this whispering—if such it may be called—this sotto voce murmuring ever since entering the compartment. He had, however, paid no attention to it. After a while he had become accustomed to it, as to the droning of a fly in a room on a summer afternoon.

The girl clung to her mother's arm and whispered into her ear. Sometimes she made her hand into a funnel and whispered like that. What she whispered couldn't be heard. Her mother sometimes paid attention to it, sometimes not. She would nod or shake her head in denial. When the whisper—or rather rustling sound—rose to a mutter or a buzz, she would quiet it, try mechanically, with half-words, to check it: "Hush, dear." "Yes, dear." "No, no, dear." But that was all.

Esti didn't understand the situation. This business made him a little anxious. The girl's disquiet unsettled him. As did—perhaps even more so—her mother's calm. Now, therefore, he stopped peeping from behind his book in search of further data on the dear unknown acquaintance, and didn't watch, but listened.

It was a feverish, hasty rustling, a confused flow of words, inarticulate, incomprehensible, and as gabbled as if it were being read from a book, badly.

Until then he had, so to speak, paid no attention to the girl, as her mother had fully absorbed his interest. On entering the compartment, he had seen that she was a teenager, at the most fifteen. He had also seen that she wasn't pretty. That was probably the reason why he had instinctively avoided looking at her.

Now he squinted at her round the edge of Edmondo de Amicis.

She was a slip of a girl, insignificant, quite insipid. Skinny legs, a thin, piping voice. She was wearing a white, spotted cambric dress, an expensive Swiss brooch, and new, showy, patent leather shoes. In her lusterless, pale blonde hair gleamed a huge bow of strawberry-colored satin ribbon, which made her pale face seem even paler. She wore a ribbon of the same material at her neck, very broad, to conceal her scrawniness.

She was dressed as if she were being taken not on this summer journey but to a ball, a glittering winter ball, a quite improbable children's ball, quite unsuitable for her.

Her small head, flat chest, lean shoulders, the two "saltcellars" that showed above the scooped neckline of her dress, her hands, her ears, her everything at first aroused pity, but then straightaway displeasure. This creature wasn't only graceless; she was repulsive, definitely loathsome.

Poor thing, thought Esti. He couldn't even bear to look at her for long. He looked out the window.

It was slowly getting dark. The girl was vanishing in the gloom, blending into her mother. All that could be heard was her whisper, her unending, irritating whisper, which in the darkness became more agitated, more rapid. She buried herself in her mother's ear and whispered. It was beyond understanding that she wasn't tired out after all those hours and that her mother wasn't tired of listening to her. Why did she lisp all the time? Why wasn't she hoarse by now, why didn't she have to stop? Esti shrugged. It was all quite beyond him.

The train had long ago left Gyékényes* and was heading at full speed into the starless summer night. Overhead on the ceiling the gas lamps were lit. Esti escaped into his book.

He made every effort to concentrate on the text. He had scarcely read four or five pages, however, when he noticed something that thoroughly annoyed him.

He noticed that the girl kept pointing at him. She was clinging to her mother's arm and whispering, as ever, and pointing at him. That was too much, really too much.

At this, now, he became indignant. But he was so overcome by anxiety that his indignation cooled. He tried to think calmly. So the pointing was directed at him. But in that case the one-sided dialogue had also been about him from the start, and he had become the focus of an interest of which he knew neither the origin nor the purpose.

What the devil did this girl want of him? He had to suppose that she was making fun of him for some reason. Perhaps because of his clothes? He had dressed in his best for the journey, his dark blue suit, new that spring. He was distinctively attired. He wore a high collar, reaching to his chin, and a narrow, white, piqué tie, which made him resemble both an international tenor and a provincial clerk, but he was perfectly satisfied with it and thought that nothing could express more appropriately his bohemian nature, his whimsical poetic soul that sighed for the infinite. So perhaps that chit of a girl now found him amusing, or did she think he was ugly? But he knew that wasn't it. He was a slight, slender boy. His brown hair, parted on the side, fell abundantly over his forehead. His gray eyes burned with a pained longing, a hesitant curiosity, at that time even much more clearly and fierily than later, when disappointment and doubt about everything had clouded the gleam of those eyes to as leaden and drunken-murky a hue as if he were in a state of permanent intoxication.

* Gyékényes is in Somogy county, southwest Hungary, near the present Croatian frontier.

He didn't beat about the bush for long. He waited for the girl to point at him again, and when her finger was next waving in front of her nose he dropped his book into his lap and turned toward her, requiring an explanation.

The girl, like one caught in the act, was taken aback. Her slender finger seemed frozen into ice. It hung in the air like that. Slowly she lowered it.

Yet even then her mother spoke not a word. She took the girl's hand—the erring little hand, the one that had been pointing—put it between her two hands, enclosed it, and began with gentle, infinite gentleness and patience to pat it, as if she were playing "bunnies" with it. "This man went rabbiting … this man caught it …"

Something like an armistice ensued. The whispering died away, or became so quiet as to be almost inaudible. Midnight approached. The woman opened her handbag. She took out a knife, a golden knife with a sharp, pointed, slender blade. Next she took out something wrapped in cotton wool. From the cotton-wool wrapping there emerged a lovely, butter-yellow Calville apple.* Dexterously and carefully she peeled it, cut it into segments, picked them up on the point of the knife, and raised them one by one to the girl's mouth.

She ate. Not nicely. She chomped.

As she caught the segments between her slightly swollen lips a white, sticky froth began to form as on the beaks of swallow chicks, like a scum or foam setting under internal warmth. She opened her beak clownishly for every morsel. In so doing she exposed her anemic gums and her few rotten little teeth, which shone black inside her mouth. "D'you want some more, dear?" her mother asked from time to time. The girl nodded.

In this way she ate almost the entire apple. Only the last segment remained.

Suddenly she leapt to her feet and rushed into the corridor. Her mother tore after her in alarm.

Now what was happening? What was wrong with the apple and

* A highly esteemed French variety, introduced to Hungary in the early 20th century.

the mother? What was the matter with this girl? Esti too jumped up. He looked around the empty compartment.

He was left alone. At last he was alone. He breathed deeply, like one released from a spell. It was only then that he dared really to admit that he had been afraid. He understood his traveling companions less and less. Who were they? What were they? Whoever was that ignorant girl who whispered and pointed all the time, then rushed out, with her mother after her like a gendarme? What scene was taking place out there, and what scene had ended in the compartment just now—when at last the apple was being peacefully eaten in the silence which had suddenly fallen—the dénouement of which couldn't be so much as guessed? Whoever was this mother who endured simply anything from her daughter, indulged her in everything, never ever called her to order, was indeed so soft—or so foolish—as to respond to her naughtiness with doting? It was now rather her that he blamed, not the girl. He began to be annoyed with that extraordinary, warm-hearted woman, whom he had become so fond of. She should be firmer, stricter. Or couldn't she handle her daughter? Of course, that was the trouble. She'd spoiled her, brought her up badly.

He could easily have found out their names. He would only have had to look up at the leather-held labels that dangled above his head. But that he regarded as improper. And in any case, what good would it have done him to read their names? His curiosity went deeper; he wanted to penetrate not names—for what does anyone's name matter?—but people, their lives, these two lives which were clearly highly enigmatic.

But enigmatic or not, he could stay there no longer. He couldn't spend a whole long night under the same roof. He had to decamp. Fate had opened an unexpected way of escape to him so that he could leave without making a fuss, take his things to another compartment, anywhere. They still hadn't come back. Now he thought with a sinking feeling that they might come back at any moment. He hurried to look around.

There wasn't a soul in the narrow, dimly lit corridor. The mother wasn't there, nor the girl. Where could they have disappeared to? The question made him anxious. He searched everywhere. He even looked in both toilets. They were empty. They were nowhere. Not a sign of them.

Had they gone into another carriage? Unlikely. The communicating doors to the next carriage were closed. So had they jumped from the speeding train, and were they now lying, expiring, their skulls smashed and slowly oozing, on the stones of the track bed, or were they continuing their journey entangled in the wheels and accompanying him as mutilated corpses? That would be dreadful.

He opened every compartment in the carriage like a secret policeman, partly to shed light on the whereabouts of mother and daughter, and partly to find himself another seat for the night.

In most of the compartments it was dark. The passengers were snoring behind lowered curtains and tightly shut doors. The familiar idyll of the bedroom greeted him: sleeping children and half-oranges, wagons circled and walled for defense with suitcases, morose men in their shirtsleeves, milk gurgling in green water bottles and women, breathing heavily, heads bent over their chubby infants—cheese rinds, flowers, and shoehorns scattered in nightmare disorder on the floor as if after a savage attack, smelly feet in sweaty stockings on the seats, emitting storm clouds of fumes—and meanwhile simply dozing on the bombast of the patriotic leading articles in yesterday's paper, spread out as a covering. Everywhere there had formed that hastily contrived, disgustingly family-like traveling companionship, that fortuitously forged train-fellowship, recruited of necessity from total strangers who greet another total stranger, arriving late and unexpectedly, not much more warmly than they would a masked robber equipped with chloroform.

Esti didn't impose on anyone. Once he was convinced that mother and daughter really were not in a particular compartment and that there was no room for him, he apologized to everyone and discreetly withdrew.

He remained standing in the corridor. He enjoyed watching the sparks from the engine. At every moment it flung a shower into the sky. Myriads and myriads of sparks soared in great arcs, then were extinguished in a ditch like swiftly fading falling stars. One smut, however, went into his eye. He went back into his compartment.

This was still deserted, though with the memories of two lives in the air. He sat down in his old place. Now he himself took it for certain that he was trapped there. This bothered him, and yet it didn't.

Even if he found a seat elsewhere—which he might, the train wasn't full, he'd only have to speak to the guard—it was very doubtful that he'd move into another compartment and that his curiously prickly conscience would be able to stand the thought that by his furtive, panicky escape he might offend his traveling companions, those two people whom he had seen for the first and perhaps the last time in his life. It was probable, highly probable, that even then he would change his mind and turn back at the last moment and decide to stay there all the same, as he had now done.

The affair interested him, that was for sure. However much he dreaded the situation, he was curious about how it would develop. He wanted to see more clearly whom he'd been traveling with until then, he would have liked to clear up a thing or two.

His conduct couldn't be explained by just that. Nor by the fact that he was a "well-brought-up boy." Nor because timidity or a lively imagination made him indecisive—often when he avoided danger those were the qualities that urged him into it. Nor that he was, as it were, an excessively kindly soul, in the everyday sense of the word. There was a lot of cruelty in him, many bloodthirsty, evil instincts. He alone knew what he had done, as a small boy, to hapless flies and frogs in the secret torture chamber that he had set up in the laundry room. There he and his younger brother had dissected frogs and their grandmother's cats with a kitchen knife, cracked their skulls, extracted their eyes, conducted real vivisection on a purely "scientific, experimental basis," and their grandmother—that loud-voiced, addlepated, shortsighted woman—had been very cross that whatever she did, her cats kept disappearing, ten or twenty a year. If need be he could certainly have committed murder, like anyone else. But he was more afraid of hurting someone than of killing them.

He was always horrified that he might be harsh, merciless, and tactless toward anyone—a human being like himself, that is: frail, craving happiness, and finally in any case doomed to perish wretchedly—horrified of humiliating them in their own eyes, of upsetting them with even one innuendo, a single thought, and often—at least, so he imagined—he would rather have died than entertain the belief that he was someone superior in this world and that the person in question might blushingly repeat as he slunk away, "It seems I've been a burden to him … it seems he's tired … it seems he looks down on me …"

This moral position, which Esti developed in greater detail in his later work, even then was germinating in his youthful heart. He knew that there is little that we can do for each other, that for the sake of being happy ourselves we are forced to injure others, sometimes even fatally, and that in great affairs pitilessness is almost inevitable, but for that very reason he held the conviction that our humanity, our apostleship can only be revealed—honestly and sincerely—in little things, that attentiveness, tact, and mutual consideration based on forgiveness are the greatest things on this earth.

Following this train of thought he had come to the conclusion, bleak, even pagan though it seemed, that since we can't be really good we should at least be polite. This politeness of his, however, was no mere ceremoniousness, not a thing of compliments and idle chatter. It often consisted of nothing more than subtly slipping in at a crucial moment a word which might seem noncommittal, but which someone was desperately awaiting from him as an acknowledgment of their existence. He considered that tact his most particular virtue. Better than so-called goodness, in any case. Goodness preaches constantly, wants to change humanity, to work miracles from one day to the next, makes a show of its substance, wants to question essentials, but in fact is most often just hollow, lacking in substance and merely a matter of appearance. Whereas even if politeness does look entirely formal, in its inward nature it is substance, essence itself. A good word which has not yet been put into practice holds within itself every virgin possibility and is more than a good deed, the outcome of which is dubious, its effect arguable. In general, words are always more than deeds.

He waited anxiously for his traveling companions to return. They didn't come, didn't come. He looked at his pocket watch. It was a quarter to one. It had been exactly three-quarters of an hour since they'd disappeared.

At one o'clock footsteps were heard in the corridor. The guard was passing his compartment with a lamp in his hand, the new Croat guard, a friendly man with a mustache, and looked in on him and asked in faultless German and with Austrian cordiality where he was going and why he wasn't asleep. He couldn't, however, enlighten him on the whereabouts of the woman and the girl. Then, in his perfect German and with Austrian cordiality, he said "*Ich wünsch' Ihnen eine scheene, gute Nacht,*" saluted, and as he left, closed the door of the compartment after him.

A couple of minutes later the door creaked open. Esti thought that the guard had come back to chatter on, to fraternize, Slav fashion, in the hope of a tip, because life was hard, the children many, and so on. There wasn't a word spoken in the corridor. It was as if the door had opened itself with the motion of the train. From where he was sitting he could see no one. This must have lasted ten or fifteen—very long—seconds.

Then a voice could be heard breathing, "Go in, dear. In you go." It was the woman. They were back.

Minutes went by. Not another sound, no movement. Then the girl stepped in.

After her—on her heels—her mother. She shut the door, sat down by the window. Opposite Esti.

The girl didn't sit down. She just stood there, moodily, obstinately, tensely. But those are just words, tentative words, an attempt somehow to appreciate her resolute petulance. She looked a little flushed, too, as if she'd taken a hot bath or had rouged her face a little—it was still very pale. Esti looked questioningly at the mother, as if to ask where they could have been. The mother's face was unchanging and negative.

The girl—like lightning, like the snapping of a spring—knelt on the seat in the opposite corner, by the corridor window, face to the wall, turning her back on the other two. She knelt and didn't move. Knelt rigidly. Rigidly and wilfully. Her neck muscles were tensed. Her back was as flat as an ironing board. Her long arms, her long rachitic arms, dangled. She was showing her long, rachitic legs—left uncovered by the short white stockings—her skinny legs and the almost unworn soles of her patent leather shoes. There was something comical about it all. It was like when someone's made to "be a statue" in a game of forfeits and the company can do what they like by way of teasing the person concerned. Only there was something very serious and frightening in her immobility and her pose.

So what was all this about? Esti again gave the mother a questioning look. This time a couple of words were on his lips, he meant to implore her, to say that the time had come for her at last to explain things to him, because it was becoming a little unbearable. She, however, avoided his eye. Esti choked back his words.

He was no longer surprised at the girl. What surprised him was that the woman wasn't surprised at her. She just sat there, staring at nothing. Clearly, she was used to her. Had she seen such things before, and stranger too? Clearly, she could have acted no differently. She made nothing of it. And that was the most natural thing.

The train clattered on. Esti took out his pocket watch every five minutes. Half past one. Two o'clock. The girl still didn't tire. They were approaching Zagreb.

Now the mother got up and, like one acting against her principles and better judgment, went to the girl. Once more she was warm-hearted, as she had been at the start of the journey. She knelt down beside her, put her face to hers, and began to speak. She spoke quietly, nicely, sensibly, cheek to cheek, spoke into her face, her ears, her eyes, her forehead, her whole body, talked and talked without tiring, with a constant flow and impetus, and it was all incomprehensible, as incomprehensible as the girl's whispering had been before, and incomprehensible too that one could find so much to say: what old words, pieces of advice, exhortations, what banalities she must have been repeating—previously painful but now no longer felt, known by heart, deadly dull—banalities which she had obviously used thousands and thousands of times before in vain, and which had long since been gathering dust in a lumber room, unused.

The part of the heroine in a five-act tragedy can't be so long, nor can a single prayer, not even the whole rosary, that a believer mumbles to his unknown, unseen god. The girl took no notice whatever. She wasn't disposed to budge from the spot.

Thereupon the mother grasped the girl's neck, pulled her hard to her, with great force lifted her into the air, and sat her at her side.

She stroked her hair. She dabbed her forehead with a cologne-scented handkerchief. She smiled at her too, once, just once, with a smile, a wooden, impersonal smile which must have been the remains, the wreckage of that smile with which long ago she must have smiled down at that girl when she was still in swaddling clothes, gurgling in the cradle, shaking her rattle. It was a wan smile, almost an unseeing smile. But like a mirror that has lost its silvering, it still reflected what that girl must have meant to her back then.

She was holding a silver spoon in her hand. She filled it with an almost colorless liquid which Esti—who was the son of a pharmacist—recognized from its heavy, volatile scent as paraldehyde. She meant to administer this to her daughter, and that was why she had smiled. "Now, dear, you have a nice, quiet sleep," she said, and put the spoon to the girl's lips. The girl gulped the medication. "Go to sleep, dear, have a nice sleep."

They arrived in Zagreb.

The sleepy life of the train came to. There was shunting, whistling. The heated wheels were tapped with hammers, and the sound wafted musically through the nighttime station. The engine took on water, and a second engine was attached so that two could pull the carriages to the great height of the Karszt mountains. The friendly Croat guard appeared again with his lamp. Just a few passengers got on. They were not disturbed.

The woman gave the girl a sweater, pulled her skirt down to her knees, and retied—more neatly—her strawberry-colored bow. She dressed her for the night rather than undressing her. She spread a soft, warm, yellow blanket over her legs. The girl closed her eyes. She breathed deeply, evenly.

The woman too now prepared to rest. She tied a light black veil over her ash-blonde hair.

When they left Zagreb she looked at the lamp. Esti took the hint. He got up and closed the shade round the glass globe.

Eyes open, hands in her lap, the woman waited for sleep. The scenes that she had gone through couldn't have excited her excessively because she soon fell asleep. She gave one sigh and was asleep. Her eyelids closed heavily. She must have been tired, deathly tired. Her face was motionless. She slept without breathing. The girl's deep, even breathing became quieter too. It could no longer be heard.

There was silence in the compartment, complete silence. The gas lamp gave out a green misty light, the sort of opal-milky twilight that one sees in an aquarium or in underwater pictures.

Esti began once more to experience that sense of relief that he'd had when the two were away. This too was real solitude. His traveling companions—heads pressed against the back of the seat—sat there torpid and unconscious. While the train hurtled in one direction their spirits wandered elsewhere, who could say on what journeys, who could say on what rails. His soul wandered around those two souls, glancing now at the mother, now at the girl. What sufferings, what passions must tear at them. Poor things, he thought.

Coughing, panting heavily, with ever-increasing effort, the two engines set about the ascent into the barren rocks. Now they were in the mountains. This was an alien world. Dark forests murmured up and up, on the heights, with their impenetrable mysteries. Waterfalls splashed here and there, mountain streams and torrents, sometimes startlingly close to his window. Lights burned on hilltops. The single Cyclops eye of a forge glowed blood-red. Then came the mirror gleam of a river. Dark gray, ice-cold water swirled this way and that, stumbling from rock to rock. It followed the train a long way. It trotted after the train, racing it, until it tired. The air was suddenly cooler.

Esti was cold. He turned up the collar of his jacket and stared into the romance of the night.

Now strange little stations appeared from the darkness, bathed in yellow lamplight, with the deserted seats and table of a closed waiting room, a kitchen garden with lettuces and cabbages, grassy banks, the stationmaster's wife's cherished petunias and geraniums. Glass globes bulged on sticks in the garden. A black cat sprang across the path in a sudden ray of light. Even at that late hour the stationmaster saluted, raising a gloved hand to his hat. At his feet his knowing dog pricked up its ears faithfully. A summerhouse sped toward them out of the gloom, the chatter of sunlit family tea parties long silenced, and, quite out of place, a convolvulus quivered among the branches of wild vine, frightened to death, blackened by night, dark blue with terror. These things, those people and animals, however, at which Esti was now looking—like a person who throws off the blankets and talks in his sleep—exposed themselves to him almost immodestly; they allowed a good-for-nothing young poet like him to steal their lives, until then so jealously guarded, so carefully concealed, and to take them with him forever.

Since setting out on that "first Italian journey" of his, he hadn't slept a wink in more than two days. The many experiences had taken their toll. His ears were burning, his spine aching. He shut his eyes to rest a little.

As he dozed, drifting between sleep and waking, he heard a quiet rustle of clothes. Someone was standing beside him, so close that a hand was poised above his. It was the girl. Esti moved. At that she crept back to her place.

That girl wasn't asleep. She hadn't woken just now, but long before. After Zagreb, she hadn't gone to sleep under the drug but had deceived both him and her mother. She was waiting for something, meaning to do something. At the moment she was lying there, head back and breathing deeply, evenly. Pretending to be asleep, as before. Esti watched her through half-closed eyes. Her eyes weren't completely shut. She was likewise watching him through half-closed eyes. Esti opened his eyes. The girl did the same.

She giggled at him. She giggled in so strange a way that Esti all but shivered. She was sitting cross-legged. Her lace-edged under-skirt dangled, showing her knees and thighs, a bare part of her spindly thighs. Again she giggled. Giggled with a foolish, unmistakable flirtatiousness.

Oh, this was frightful. This girl had fallen for him. This ghastly, hideous chit of a girl had fallen for him. Those legs, those eyes, that mouth too had fallen for him, that dreadful mouth. She wanted to dance with him, *with him*, at that obscene children's ball, with her hair ribbon, the strawberry-colored bow, that little dress, that little specter at the ball. Oh, this was frightful.

What could be done about it? He didn't want to make a scene. That was what he dreaded most of all. He could have woken the woman sleeping opposite. But he felt sorry for her.

Perspiration broke out on his forehead.

His tactics were partly intended to restrain the girl, partly to trick her into action and discover her intentions. Therefore he showed at regular intervals that he wasn't asleep by coughing or scratching his ear, but he also simulated sleep for equally regular periods because he wanted to find out what the girl's intentions actually were. These two ploys he alternated, always being very careful that the one went on no longer than the other.

The contest went on for a long time. Meanwhile the train raced on toward its destination. Sometimes it seemed that it was held up at a station but then rattled on, sometimes it seemed to rumble on and on but then would loiter in a station, and the strangely watchful voices of linesmen would be heard and machinery would crunch over the track bed toward the coal store. Were they going backwards or forwards? Had half an hour gone by? Or only half a minute? The strands of time and space were becoming tangled in his head.

This pretense was extremely tiring. Esti would have liked to escape from the trap, reach Fiume, be at home in Sárszeg, in the bedroom where his siblings were sleeping to the ticking of the wallclock, in his old bed. But he dared not sleep, nor did he mean to. He clenched his teeth and struggled on. If he became a little more sleepy she would resort to all sorts of tricks. He frightened himself most of all with the idea that while he was asleep, that creature would crawl toward him and kiss him with her cold mouth—nothing could be more revolting and terrible.

And so at about three o'clock, Esti, constantly dwelling on these nightmarish thoughts and on his guard as to what to do—whether he should show that he was awake or pretend to be asleep—tried to open his eyes, tried to wake up, but couldn't. He couldn't breathe. There was something on his mouth. Some cold foulness, some heavy, soggy bath mat, lying on his mouth, sucking at him, expanding into him, growing fat on him, becoming rigid, like a leech, wouldn't let go of him. Wouldn't let him breathe.

He moaned in pain, writhed this way and that, waved his arms about for a long time. Then there burst from his throat a cry. "No," he croaked, "oh."

The woman leapt to her feet. Didn't know where she was. Didn't know what had happened. Couldn't see a thing. It was completely dark in the compartment. Someone had put out the gas lamp. Thick smoke was billowing in through the window. Again, a cry for help. She thought that there'd been an accident.

When she had quickly lit the lamp, there stood her daughter facing Esti. She was holding her index finger mischievously to her lips, begging him to hush, he must keep quiet about it. Esti was standing facing the girl, in a fury, trembling from head to foot, deathly pale. He was wiping his mouth and spitting into his handkerchief.

"Oh," said the woman dully, "I'm so sorry. But surely you can see …" That was all that she said. And she said it as if apologizing for her dog, which had licked a traveling companion's hand. She was infinitely humiliated.

Then without looking at Esti she turned to her daughter.

"Edit!" she exclaimed, "Edit, Edit," several times, one after another, perhaps just so as to hear her name. She pulled the girl this way and that. It seemed that her amazing poise had deserted her for a moment. That troubled her at once. She embraced her daughter, began to kiss her. Kissed her frantically, anywhere she could, even on her lips.

Esti, who had not yet recovered from the horror of the first kiss and was so disgusted by it that he could have vomited, watched this scene and tried to get his breath.

He could sense the enigma of the kiss. When people are helpless with despair and desire, and speech is no longer of use, the only means of making contact is by the mingling of their breath. They try in this way to enter into one another, into the depths where perhaps they will find the meaning and the explanation of everything.

The kiss is a great enigma. He had not been aware of it before. He had only known affection. Only adventure. He was still pure at heart, like most boys of eighteen. That had been his first kiss. He had received his first real kiss from that girl.

Edit was crouching at her mother's side. Now she shrugged her shoulders. Every ten seconds—every ten seconds precisely—she raised her left shoulder almost imperceptibly. She wasn't being defiant. She didn't speak either to her mother or to Esti. She was making signs. To whom or to what she was making those signs no one knew, not even she herself. Only perhaps He knew, who created the world to His glory and set man therein.

The woman, who must have been overcome with remorse at forgetting herself, was clinging to both her daughter's hands. By that she was showing that she was with her, now and always.

They were silent. All three were silent. Silent for a long time.

Suddenly the woman spoke. "Dawn's coming," she said to no one in particular. "It'll soon be light." Why was that so dizzily solemn? Because it meant, "Dawn isn't coming, it never will."

Esti ran out into the corridor. He had to go quickly. Scarcely was he out than he burst into tears. Tears streamed down his face.

But dawn was coming, it really was. A pale strip of light had appeared in the east.

He thought over what had happened. What had happened was tragic and interesting. It even flattered his pride a tiny bit that he had gone from the school bench—by some unforeseen process—straight into the darkest center of life. He'd learned more from this than he had from any book.

The year before he'd had other struggles. He'd maintained in the literary circle that one of his poems was a ballad. The teacher in charge had opened the matter to debate, and after the opinions of the members had been heard had decided that the poem in question wasn't a ballad but a romance. As a result Esti "immediately drew a conclusion." He'd resigned as secretary, with which responsibility his fellow members had clothed him.

How that had hurt him at the time! Now he could see that it wasn't so important. What mattered wasn't ballads and romances. Life was what mattered, only that. That kiss too had come from the richness of life and had enriched him. He wouldn't be able to tell anyone about it, not even his brother, because everyone would laugh at him. But in his own eyes he wasn't ashamed.

"*Homo sum,*"—he quoted Terence—"*humani nihil a me alienum puto,*" and thought back with a shudder to that shivering kiss. Perhaps his pleasure in it could have been full if he were a little more daring and could surrender himself completely, because sensual pleasure—he guessed—cannot be far from disgust. Nor should that be a cause for shame. *Epicurus non erubescens omnes voluptates nominatim persequitur.* Now who had said that? It had been somewhere in the middle of the grammar, on a certain page, at the top, a little to the left, an example of the use of the *participium praesens* with a negative particle. One must not be ashamed of anything. Our fate is stars and rubbish.

Now other people were standing around him, early risers, with mustache trimmers and traveling soap. Watching the sunrise. They pulled down the windows and drew into themselves the dawn air. Esti followed their example.

The lamps were extinguished. The train rumbled on, fleeing night and nightmares, toward the daylight. The first ray gilded a hilltop with magical speed. On it stood a little church with a wooden tower, awaiting the faithful. It stood so high that his imagination, by the time he reached it, was exhausted, collapsing and giving up the ghost right at the door of the church, but down below was a green valley at the bottom of a fearsome ravine so deep that his imagination fell headlong into it and was killed outright on a rock. It was a barren, picturesque landscape. Stone walls stretched along the hillsides, ramparts with which the local people defended their produce, their potatoes and oats, against the wrath of the elements. Here one had to fight a bitter battle against nature. Howling gales tore up trees, roots and all, flattened out furrows and flung seed into the air. In those parts even eagles were afraid. In those parts even cows looked interesting, they were so thin and melancholy. In winter, snow fell and covered everything. Packs of wolves plodded slowly through the whiteness, their tails shaggy. *Guzlica* and wailing songs were heard in huts. This was where he would have liked to live. He imagined getting off the train at once, settling down in this stony hell, becoming a forester, or rather a quarryman, marrying an apple-faced Croat girl with a black headscarf, white skirt, and black apron, then growing old without ever sending word of himself and being buried anonymously in the valley. But he also imagined himself owner of those hills and forests, rich, powerful, known and admired by all, greater perhaps than a king. He imagined all sorts of things. He played with life, for it was still before him.

At six o'clock an army doctor came on board—or as Esti later boasted to his brother, "a high-ranking regimental doctor." He came without luggage, fresh, having slept. The gold stars sparkled cheerfully on his velvet collar. He lived in the region and was making for Fiume to bathe.

He was a very cultured man and widely traveled. He took honey-sweet snuff from a slender, colored snuffbox. He grew his manicured nails long and shaped to the pads of his fingers. He had often seen the sea, too.

Esti beset him with the most foolish questions, mostly to do with the sea. The doctor dealt with these as best he could. Sometimes at length, sometimes only briefly, with a yes or a no.

At half past six, at Plase, he pointed out that the gulf of Buccari would soon be in sight. The quivering of branches indicated that the sea wasn't far away. There was a tang of salt in the air.

The sea could be there at any moment. But it still wasn't. Esti believed by that time that the doctor was either mistaken or joking, it would never come, didn't want to show itself to him. He walked up and down as if to speed up the racing train. In his agitation he composed a dithyramb, celebratory lines with which to greet the sea. His words slowly froze on his tongue. The sea was late in arriving.

Finally they were standing in line in the carriage. Old civil servants, a honeymoon couple, women and children, even nursemaids with infants in their arms, even sick people, consumptives, incurables, traveling in search of treatment, all were standing side by side and behind one another, craning their necks so as to welcome the sea when the time came with uplifted hearts and a outburst of happy sighs. The sea had a full house. But nevertheless it didn't appear. Like a prima donna it made itself wanted, aroused curiosity. It needed a crescendo, intensification, scenery even more impressive.

The two engines, coupled one before the other, climbed higher and higher up the steep mountain track. Now they too were becoming impatient, thirsty for the liberating, redeeming water. They increased their speed and hurled themselves toward it. So ardent was their desire that perhaps they didn't care that they might slip and crash headlong down onto the limestone and be smashed to bits. Their wheels turned with such eye-baffling rapidity that they almost looked stationary. They rushed into tunnel after tunnel. First they gave terrifying whistles, then plunged between the streaming, black cliffs, rattled and snorted, and when they emerged gave shrieks of inquiry. They were looking for the sea, but still hadn't found it. Their pistons gleamed, pumping on the oily bearings. Inexhaustibly they raced on. Again they thundered into a tunnel. Esti had by now abandoned all hope. As the train curved out of the tunnel, however, the army doctor stretched his index finger with its carnelian ring to the sunlight and said:

"There it is."

Where was it? There below him, there it really was, the sea, the sea itself, smooth and blue as he had seen it on that wall map in primary school. Just one more point, the bay of Buccari, the Quarnero strip. He gaped at it, mouth wide open. But before he could admire it properly it had vanished. The sea was playing hide and seek with him.

Then it spread out before him, for a long time, in its calm majesty.

He had not imagined it any lovelier or bigger. It was lovelier and bigger than he had ever imagined. A smooth, blue infinity, and sailing ships on it leaning sideways, like the wings of butterflies, parched butterflies that had alighted on the mirror of the water and were drinking from it. From a distance it was a pure panorama, a picture in a book, silent, almost motionless. Not even the hiss of the waves reached him. Nor could their ripples be seen. The ships themselves moved no more quickly than that toy boat of years gone by which he had pushed around in the bath as a child. And yet it was festive, it was a giant, alone in the ancestral glory of vasty ages.

Then there burst forth within him that poem on which he had been working earlier, that dithyramb which he had conceived in the anguished hours of the night, and the shouts of Xenophon's men, the scattered army of the Anabasis, that starving, homesick ten thousand, could have been no louder for all their ten thousand throats, than he himself: *Thalatta, thalatta, immutable, eternal one, thou art whole in the cathedral of mountain ranges, among the church pillars of peaks, thou the holy water of earth in the stoop carved out of the rocks, baptismal font of all greatness that has ever lived in this world, thou milk of mother earth. Suckle me, redeem me, keep evil spirits far from me. Make me what I was born to be.* He immersed himself in the smell of the sea, washed himself first in its breath. He held out his arms to be nearer to it.

Later the Scoglio di San Marco loomed into view, the ancient, ruined pirate stronghold. After the crescendo, a decrescendo followed. The train was descending the stepped slope among the crags. The first Italian house came into view. It wasn't as neat as a house in Hungary, nor as comfortable and clean. It was slim and airily graceful. Pieces of colored cloth and shirts hung from windows with the honest grime of life which here wasn't concealed. Red, white, and green flags flapped in the wind on tall poles, triumphantly announcing the Hungarian seaport. He had to fetch his luggage.

Mother and daughter were still there together. He was almost horrified—he'd forgotten about them in the meantime. Hadn't given them a thought for hours. This forgetfulness brought home to him how much together those two had been, and would forever be. Now he realized the meaning of fate.

They too were getting ready. The mother had put a broad-brimmed hat on the girl's head, and slipped the elastic band under her bony chin. She herself was now wearing a hat. A nest-shaped straw hat. There were two white roses on it. Esti helped her get her cases down.

It was almost time to say good-bye. He'd decided, word for word, what he meant to say to her: "Madam, I have an inexpressible respect and deep sympathy for you. Right at the very first moment I felt a remarkable warmth toward you. I noticed on your forehead a sign, such pain as I had never before seen. Near Zagreb you tied up your hair, your ash-blonde hair, in a light black veil. At dawn, when I ran hastily—and ill-manneredly—out of the compartment, I suddenly saw the whole world blackened by that veil. You are a martyr-mother, a sainted martyr-mother, with seven daggers in your heart. I'm very sorry for you. I'm very sorry for your daughter too. She's a strange girl. Perhaps you should dose her with potassium bromide solution, a teaspoon every evening, and bathe her in cold water. That helped me. As for the—what shall I say—the affair, I'm not offended. I was a little afraid. But now I'm not. I've forgotten it. The only thing that worries me is where you vanished to after midnight. I looked for you everywhere and couldn't find you. Even now I can't think where you could have been all that time. The idea crossed my mind, madam, that for the sake of your daughter, whom you love so, for the sake of your daughter, who doesn't live in this world, you'd gone away with her into the realm of fantasy and with her become invisible. That's not a satisfactory explanation, I know. But it's a profound poetic thought. And so I'll take the liberty of telling you. I'm going to be a writer. If once I master that difficult craft—because please believe me, one has to learn to be constantly watchful, to suffer, to understand others and oneself, to be merciless to oneself and others—well, then perhaps I'll write about this. It's a very difficult subject. But things like this interest me. I want to become the sort of writer who knocks at the gates of existence and attempts the impossible. Anything less than that I despise—please forgive my immodesty, because I'm nothing and nobody yet—but I do despise it, and profoundly. I'm never going to forget what happened to me here. I'll keep it among my memories and by it express my ceaseless grief. I no longer believe in anything. But in that I do believe. Permit me now, madam, before I finally take my leave, to kiss your hand as a mark of sympathy and filial homage." That was what he meant to say, but he didn't. Eighteen-year-old boys can, as yet, only feel. They can't compose speeches like that and deliver them. So he only bowed. More deeply than he'd intended. Almost to the ground.

The woman was surprised. She looked at the ground, still all the time hiding her eyes, in which there must once have been life but now were only fear and everlasting anxiety. She thought, "Poor boy, poor boy. What a dreadful night you must have had. When you came into our compartment, my first thought was to send you away somehow. I could see that you were trembling. Sometimes you were a little ridiculous too. I wanted to enlighten you. Only I can't do such a thing. Then I'd have to talk on and on, tell everyone, here on the train, the neighbors at home, people abroad and everywhere what's happened to us. It can't be done. So I prefer to say nothing. And then, I've truly become a little unfeeling toward people. At midnight, when my daughter and I left this compartment and— somewhere else—a scene was played out such as you've never witnessed—you can be eternally thankful—I hoped that you'd change your mind and move somewhere else in the meantime. You didn't do that. Out of politeness you didn't. You didn't want to let me know that you knew more or less what you did. You behaved beautifully. You behaved as a well-brought-up young gentleman should. Thank you. You're still a child. In fact, you could be my son. You could be my son-in-law. Yes you could, you could be my son-in-law. You see the sort of things that a mother thinks of. But you can't be my son-in-law. Nobody can. You don't know life yet. You don't know what the doctors have diagnosed. The experts in Switzerland and Germany aren't very encouraging. We've come away against their advice. There's a little island near here. It's called Sansego. Fishermen live there, simple people. They grow olives and catch sardines. They won't notice anything. I'm taking her there to hide her away. I want to keep her with me this summer. It may be our last. Then, it seems, I'm going to have to 'put her away' after all. The specialists have been recommending that for years, in Hungary and abroad. There are some reliable 'establishments.' She'll get a private room there, her bodily needs will be taken care of. I'll be able to visit her as often as I like. You don't know about this sort of thing yet. Don't ever find out. God bless you. I believe in God. I have to believe in Him, because otherwise I wouldn't be able to do my duty. Off you go, my boy. Forget the whole thing. Be happy, my boy." So she thought. But she didn't speak either. People who suffer don't talk much. She merely tossed back her head, raised her ravaged face and now, for the first time, looked at Kornél Esti, and as a reward granted him a long look into her ivy-green eyes.

By this time the train had crossed a Fiume street between lowered barriers. Porters stormed the carriages. Esti picked up his own basket and deposited it in the left luggage office, as he didn't intend, for the sake of economy, to take a room in Fiume; he would only be there until eight that evening when his ship, the *Ernő Dániel*, left for Venice. *O navis referent in mare te novis fluctus ...*

Among the cabs in the square outside the station building a private carriage was waiting. Mother and daughter got into it. Esti stared after them. He watched them until they disappeared in the dreaming lines of plane trees on Viale Francesco Deák.

He too set off along that shady, sun-dappled avenue, light of heart, with his raincoat over his shoulder. Shopkeepers called out *"latte, vino, frutti,"* as he passed, passersby said *"buon giorno"* to one another. *"Annibale,"* shouted a mother after her son, and a market woman selling figs at a street corner scolded her little daughter, *"Francesca, vergognati."* Everyone was chattering in that language, that language which is too beautiful for everyday use, that language of which he wasn't ignorant, which he had taken to his heart in the cramming torments of schoolboy nerves. There was in the air a ceaseless din, a happy racket, a great and unrestrained street merriment. While people were alive they made a noise, for they wouldn't be able to later.

A barrow loaded with fish was pushed along, big sea fish and crabs. Cake shops exhaled a scent of vanilla. He saw bay-trees and oysters. In front of the dangling glass bead curtain of a hairdresser's shop stood the coiffeur, splendidly accoutred like a divine actor, setting an example to his customers with a white comb stuck in his high-piled, pomaded black hair. Toilet soap: *italianissimo*. All was exaggeration, superlative, ecstasy.

Esti sat down on the terrace of a café. He hadn't eaten or drunk since the previous afternoon. But more than food or drink, he was yearning at last to speak Italian to a real Italian for the first time in his life. He prepared for this with a certain amount of stage fright. Very slowly the waiter approached him, an elderly Italian with a pointed white beard.

He knew that the Budapest express had arrived, and so he addressed his guest in Hungarian, with an almost spicy accent: "Breakfast, sir?" Esti didn't reply, waited a moment, then said, "*Si, una tazza di caffè.*" The waiter happily reverted to his native language: "*Benissimo, signore,*" and was about to go. In his delight at having passed that test with flying colors, Esti called after him: "*Camariere, portatemi anche pane, acqua fresca e giornali. Giornali italiani,*" he added nonchalantly and unnecessarily. "*Sissignore, subito,*" replied the waiter, and hurried away with his indescribably pleasant *s*-es.

Esti was happy. Happy that he had been taken for something other than what he was, perhaps even for an Italian, but in any case a foreigner, a person, and that he was able to continue to play his role, escaping from the prison in which he had been confined since birth. He sipped his espresso, which the waiter poured into his glass from a large aluminum jug, devoured six croissants and four rolls, then, as if he'd been doing it all his life, buried himself in the *Corriere della Sera*.

While he was thus reading a voice rang out: "*Pane.*" A ragged, filthy street urchin was standing by his table, a four-year-old child, barefoot, and pointing most determinedly at the basket of bread. Esti gave him a roll. But the little boy didn't go away. "*Un altro,*" he exclaimed again. "*Che cosa?*" inquired Esti. "*Un altro pane,*" said the child, "*due*," and held up two fingers as is customary in those parts to show that he was asking for not one but two, "*per la mamma*," and her too he indicated, standing a few yards away on the road as if on stage, to be seen and exert influence as in a tear-jerking farce, but even so, dignified. She was a youthful, weather-beaten mother, also barefoot, wearing a chemise but no blouse. A wretched skirt hung from her, and her hair was unkempt, but the skin of her face was that olive shade that one sees in Abruzzo. Her eyes gleamed darkly. She and her child watched, standing erect, not bending, watched what the *straniero* would do. Esti held out another roll to the little boy. He and his mother, his *mamma*, whom he must have loved so much, strolled slowly on. Neither of them thanked him for his kindness.

This, however, pleased Esti beyond words and made him feel good. "See," he thought, "these people don't beg, they demand. They're an ancient free people, glorious even in penury." He sat on at the table of life. He knew that life was his, as the bread was. "I ought to live here. This sensitivity, this sincerity, this sunlight that permeates everything, this easy-going exterior which must conceal all sorts of things, all excite me. No blood relationship can be as strong as the attraction that I feel to them. They alone will be able to cure me of my muddled sentimentality."

When the time came to pay, a few problems cropped up, as Esti failed to understand a couple of Italian words, and the waiter, who had immediately realized from Esti's accent that he wasn't an Italian, began to ask, with the frankness that is permissible with the young, what his nationality was. He listed numerous possibilities—*Austriaco? Tedesco? Croato? Inglese?*—and Esti just shook his head. Then the waiter inquired where he lived, from what town he came, where he was from. With a stern gesture Esti dismissed the old man, who withdrew behind a pillar not far from the table and from there continued to assess this inscrutable boy.

"Where am I from?" recited Esti to himself, intoxicated by the espresso and lack of sleep. "Where everybody's from. The purple cavern of a mother's womb. I too started out from there on an uncertain journey, and neither destiny nor destination are stated in the passport. A pleasure trip? I hope it will be, because I very much want to enjoy everything. Or a study trip? If only I could know all that has been known until now. Or just an *affaire familale*? I wouldn't mind that either, because I adore children. So, I'm an earthworm, a man like you, my dear old Italian, good and bad alike. Above all, however, sensitive and inquisitive. Everything and everybody interests me. I love everything and everybody, every nation and every region. I'm everybody and nobody. A migrating bird, a quick-change artist, a magician, an eel that always slips through your fingers. Unfathomable and unattainable."

He saw the sea close to from the Adamich jetty. Fruit peels, old shoes, and fishbones floated on its oil-stained surface. He was incensed at the idea of the majestic ocean being used this way, not just constantly adored. A steamship was leaving for Brazil, for Rio de Janeiro. Gulls screamed in the air, seagulls, kings of the storm.

He ought to send another card home to his anxious mother. But he put off doing that. There wouldn't have been room on a card for all the adventures that he'd had. All the people that he'd met, all the new people and two more mothers as well. His family had grown.

He went for a swim to wash away the aching head and throbbing heart of the night, the dust of school and everything.

He undressed and sat for a long time on a rock in his bathing costume. He listened to the sound of the water: a different hiss and crackle at every moment. Then he went down to it, befriended it, caressed it. When he saw that he didn't hurt it he slapped it in the face with both hands, with the treasonable insolence of youth, as recklessly as an infant would a Bengal tiger. He sank into it. He sprang back up spluttering and laughing aloud. He rocked to and fro on its fragile, glassy surface. He rinsed his throat with that salty mouthwash, spat it out, for the sea is a spittoon too, the spittoon of gods and recalcitrant youth.

Then he flung his body, arms outstretched, into the pearly blueness, at last to be united with it. He no longer feared anything. He knew that after this no great harm could come to him. That kiss and that journey had consecrated him for something.

He swam a long way out, beyond the rope that marked the limit, where he thought that there were dangers—sharks, corpses, rusty anchors and wrecked ships—so that everything that was lovely and ugly, everything that was visible and invisible, should be his.

On he swam with the waves and the morning wind, toward where he guessed golden Venice lay in a golden mist, the land which he didn't yet know but loved even unknown, and as his shoulders rose and rose again from the water he lifted his face passionately toward the distant Latin shore: toward Italy, the holy, the adored.

IV

*In which he makes an excursion
in the "honest town" with his old friend*

"SO YOU'LL COME WITH ME?" ASKED KORNÉL ESTI.

"With pleasure," I exclaimed. "I'm sick and tired of all this dishonesty."

I jumped into the aircraft. We roared, we circled.

We swung around with such whirling rapidity that golden eagles became giddy alongside us and swallows felt blood rushing to their heads.

Soon we landed.

"This is it," said Esti.

"This? It's just like where we came from."

"Only on the outside. It's different inside."

We strolled into the town on foot to take a close look at everything.

The first thing that struck me was that the passersby scarcely spoke to one another.

"Here people only greet each other," explained Esti, "if they really like and respect the other person."

A beggar in dark glasses was crouching on the sidewalk. On his lap a tin plate. On his chest a card: *I am not blind. I only wear dark glasses in summer.*

"Now, why is the beggar wearing that?"

"So as not to mislead people that give alms."

On the avenue were shops as bright as could be. In a gleaming window I read:

Crippling shoes. Corns and abscesses guaranteed. Several customers' feet amputated.

A colorful, eye-catching picture was displayed of two surgeons with big steel saws cutting off the feet of a screaming victim, his blood running down in red streaks.

"Is this a joke?"

"Not a bit."

"Aha. Does some legal requirement force traders to brand themselves like this?"

"Not at all," Esti made a gesture of denial. "It's the truth. Just understand that: it's the truth. Here nobody hides the truth under a bushel. Self-criticism has reached such a high level in this city that there's no longer need of anything like that."

As we went on, one thing after another astounded me.

At the clothes shop this sign shrieked:

Expensive poor-quality clothes. Kindly bargain, because we will swindle you.

At the restaurant:

Inedible food, undrinkable drinks. Worse than at home.

At the patisserie:

Stale cakes. Made with margarine and egg substitute.

"Have these people gone mad?" I stammered. "Or are they suicidal? Or saints?"

"They're wise," replied Esti firmly. "They never lie."

"And doesn't this wisdom ruin them?"

"Look in the shops. They're all crowded. All flourishing."

"How is that possible?"

"Look. Everybody here knows that they themselves, and their fellow men, are honest, sincere and modest, and they'd rather put themselves down than boast, rather reduce a price than raise it. And so people here don't quite take at face value what they hear and read, any more than you do at home. The difference amounts to this—at home you always have to subtract something from what people tell you, in fact a great deal, while here you always have to add something to it, a little. Your goods and people aren't as excellent as they say. Here goods and people aren't as inferior as they say. Actually, the two come to the same thing. In my view, though, the latter way is more honest, more sincere, more modest."

In the window of a bookshop the proprietors drew attention to a book, framed in colored paper ribbon:

Unreadable rubbish ... latest work of an old writer who has gone senile, not a single copy sold up to now ... Ervin Hörgő's most nauseating, most pretentious verse.

"Incredible," I was amazed. "And will people buy it?"

"Why on earth not?"

"And read it?"

"Don't they read things like that back at home?"

"You're right. But there, at least they find out about them differently."

"I repeat: this is the city of conscience. If somebody knows perfectly well that he has bad taste, and likes thunderous phrases—the sort of thing that's cheap, inane and overdone—then he'll buy Ervin Hörgő's verse, and he won't be disappointed in it, in fact, it'll meet his requirements. The whole thing's just a matter of tactics."

Reeling, I looked for a café where I could restore myself.

Esti took me to a tasteless, gilded café which a sign described as *the favorite haunt of con-men and spongers,* and enticed customers in with *unaffordable prices, rude waiters.*

At first I didn't want to go in. My friend pushed me.

"Good morning," I said.

"Why are you lying?" asked Esti. "You don't want a good morning here, but you'd like a nice coffee, but you can't get that because here they lace the coffee with chicory, and it tastes like second-rate shoe-polish. I just want to show you the papers."

There were a lot of newspapers there. Now I can only recall the *Lie,* the *Self-Interest,* the *Cowardly Bandit,* and the *Stooge.*

In place of a masthead, on the front page the *Stooge* carried in large type the message:

Every single letter in this paper is corrupt. It depends on all governments in the same way, and never prints their views except when the desire for filthy lucre calls for it. For that reason we advise our readers, each and all of whom we deeply disdain and despise, not to take our articles seriously and to execrate and look down on us too as much as we deserve, if that is humanly possible.

"Wonderful," I enthused. "See that, I really like it."

"Here speaking the truth is so general," my friend went on, "that everybody does it. Listen to the small ads, for example," and he started to read from various papers. *Cashier seeks employment, criminal record, several convictions, former prisoner ... Mentally ill nursemaid will look after children ... Language teacher speaks French with Göcsej* accent and wishes to acquire local accents from pupils, has a few vacancies.*

"And these people will find jobs?" I asked numbly.

"Naturally," replied Esti.

"Why?"

"Because," he drawled, "life's like that."

He pointed to a fat booklet with something printed in dark gray letters on a dark gray cover.

"This here's the leading literary periodical. Lots of people read it."

"I can't even make out the title."

"*Boredom*," said Esti. "That's the title."

"What's interesting in it?"

"That the title is *Boredom*."

"And is it really boring?"

"I don't want to influence you. Look it over."

I read a few items.

"Well," I said, pursing my lips, "it's not all that dull."

"You're a stern critic," Esti raised a warning finger. "It's no good, no expectation can ever be fully satisfied. The title's lowered your expectations too much. I can assure you, if you read it at home you'd find it quite boring enough. It all depends on the angle from which you look at things."

Someone was making a speech to a crowd of several thousand in the square outside the Parliament building:

"One look at my low forehead and my face, deformed by bestial

---

* A region of Hungary to the south of Lake Balaton, noted for its local dialect.

cupidity, is enough—you can see at once whom you are dealing with. I have no trade, no skill, there's nothing on earth that I'm fit for, least of all to explain to you the meaning of life, so let me lead you toward the goal. What that goal is I will reveal. In brief, I want to be rich, to extort money, so that I shall have as much as possible and you as little as possible. And so I shall have to go on making fools of you. Or do you think, perhaps, that you're fools enough already?"

"No, no," the crowd roared indignantly.

"So act in accordance with your conscience. You all know my opponent. He's a noble, selfless man, a great brain, a brilliant mind. Is there anyone in this town to compare with him?"

"No!" shouted the crowd in unison. "Nobody at all!" and clenched fists rose into the air.

Darkness fell.

I went out for a walk and suddenly the black sky was lit up as if day had broken, several days, the whole calendar.

Letters of flame sparkled:

We steal, we swindle, we rob.

"What's that?" I asked Esti.

"An advertisement for a bank," he said nonchalantly.

Late at night we returned to Esti's house. The extraordinary experiences had evidently worn me out. I was running a temperature. I was sneezing and coughing. I called a doctor.

"Doctor," I complained, "I've got a bit of a chill, caught a cold."

"A cold?" the doctor was taken aback and retreated to the far corner of the room, covering his mouth with his handkerchief. "In that case be so good as to turn your head aside, because even here, five yards away, I can catch it. I've got children."

"Aren't you going to examine me?"

"Waste of time. There's no cure for a cold. It's incurable, like cancer."

"Should I sweat?"

"You can. But it won't do any good. Broadly speaking, our scientific experience is that if we treat a cold it can last a month. If we don't treat it, it can be gone the next day."

"What if I develop pneumonia?"

"Then you'll die," he informed me.

He thought for a moment, then said:

"Frederick the Great was once walking on the field after a battle. A dying soldier, moaning in pain, stretched out his arm to him. The emperor flicked his riding crop at the soldier and shouted at him 'You swine, d'you want to live forever?' I always quote this little story to my patients. There's profound wisdom in it."

"Indeed," I replied. "But I've got a headache. A splitting headache."

"That's your affair," said the doctor. "That doesn't matter. You know what does? What does matter is that I haven't got a headache. Even more important is that I charge double for visits at night. Let me have my fee quickly, I'm in a hurry."

He was right. Next day I was better. Fresh and cheerful, I hurried to the Town Hall to obtain the documents necessary for taking up residence in that honest town.

"Delighted," I muttered when I appeared before the mayor.

"Well, I can't say as much," said the mayor coldly.

"I don't understand," I stammered. "I've called in to swear to be a loyal citizen."

"The fact that you don't understand shows that you're a stupid blockhead. I'll explain why I'm not delighted. In the first place, you're disturbing me, and I don't even know who or what you are. Secondly, you're involving me in public affairs, whereas I only deal with my personal rackets. Thirdly, you're lying about being delighted, from which I deduce that you're a hypocritical scoundrel and not fit to join us. I'm having you deported at once."

Within the hour I was deported by express aircraft to the town from which I had escaped.

Since then I've lived here. Lots of things were more to my taste there. I have to admit, though, that all the same it's better here. Because even if people here are more or less the same as there, there's a lot to be said for the people here. Inter alia, that at least they sometimes tell each other imaginative, amusing lies.

V

In which he is concerned with the animated and edifying description
of a weekday, September 10, 1909,
and the time is evoked when Franz Josef was still on the throne
and modern poets who favored various trends and schools
took their ease in the coffeehouses of Budapest

AT ELEVEN IN THE MORNING ESTI WAS STILL FAST ASLEEP ON the couch which those who gave him accommodation let him use as a bed.

Someone came to call. Esti opened his eyes.

The first thing that he noticed of the world which he had lost in his sleep was the grave figure sitting on the edge of the couch.

"Have I woken you?"

"Not at all."

"I've written a poem," said Sárkány, like an excited emissary from another planet. "Will you listen to it?"

Without waiting for an answer, he straightaway read out, rapidly:

> *The moon, that pale lady of the sky,*
> *Kisses the wild, sable night.*
> *He has drunk champagne ...*

"Lovely," murmured Esti.

The remark disturbed Sárkány. He acted like one interrupted in mid-kiss. He gave him a cross look. Once he realized, however, what Esti had said, a smile of gratitude spread across his face.

Esti asked his friend:

"Start again."

Sárkány started again:

> The moon, that pale lady of the sky,
> Kisses the wild, sable night.
> He has drunk champagne and his somber, tousled hair
> Enfolds her ...

He was holding in his left hand a page of squared paper torn from a notebook and pressed his right hand to his face as if a tooth were aching slightly. Thus he read.

This boy looked like an unhappy first violinist in a Gypsy band, dark and passionate. His pale face was crowned by a shock of jet-black hair. His mouth was red, almost as red as blood. A brass ring shone on his hairy index finger. He wore a narrow tie. A cutaway, purple waistcoat. A worn but pressed black suit. Brand new patent-leather shoes. He used an orchid perfume. The whole room was permeated with it.

Esti listened to the poem all through, eyes closed.

The day before they had been for a walk together and had admired the moon above the tenements and railway warehouses of Ferencváros.* Now that moon reappeared behind Esti's closed eyelids, in his darkened eyeballs, as in the sky the previous night. There floated the moon, the moon in the poem, somewhat crudely painted, as was the fashion of the 1930s, a little flirtatious and overdressed, but much more beautiful than the real thing.

"Magnificent!" exclaimed Esti when the poem came to an end. He jumped up from the couch.

"Really?"

"Really."

"Better than *Crazy Swing?*"

"No comparison."

"Swear?"

---

* A suburb of Pest.

"I swear."

Sárkány was still throbbing to the pulse of his poem. He felt that a tremendously important event had occurred.

Esti too felt that. He rummaged round in the disorder of his rented room. As he searched the floor for his socks he asked:

"When did you write it?"

"In the night. As I was going home."

They were silent for a while.

Sárkány turned to him:

"Didn't you write anything?"

"No," said Esti gloomily. "Not yesterday. Where are you going to send it?"

"To *Független Magyarország*."*

He sat down at Esti's desk to make a clean copy in ink.

Meanwhile Esti slowly dressed. As he pulled on his trousers he read the literary section and poetry in the morning paper. He moistened his face slightly. That passed for a wash with him. He was so attached to his individuality that he was loath to wash off the layers that accumulated on him in the daytime. He considered people who bowed to the fetish of excessive cleanliness devoid of talent.

He used neither brush nor comb. He ran his fingers through his hair so that it should be disheveled in a way different from that of the night—feathers from the pillow were sticking to it—and arranged his curls in front of the mirror until he could see in it the head which he imagined as himself and was happiest to consider his own.

Sárkány, busy at his copying, was humming a popular song.

"Hush," said Esti, nodding toward the door, which was obstructed by a cupboard.

Behind it lived the people of the house, two elderly ladies, the principal tenants—enemies of subtenants and of literature.

They both became solemn. They looked at the cupboard and in it saw reality, which always made them feel helpless.

"What shall we do?" they asked in a whisper.

* *"Independent Hungary,"* a fictitious paper.

Before them was a day, a new day, with its boundless freedom and opportunity.

For a start, they went downstairs and sat in the nearby restaurant, the dining room of a hotel.

There they were still themselves.

The dining room gleamed white. The mauve light of arc lamps rustled on the freshly laundered linen tablecloths, the untouched, undefiled altars at which no sacrifice had yet been made. Waiters bustled about, shirtfronts gleaming, fresh before work, like escorts at a ball. An elevator rattled between the walls of the hotel. The half-open door gave a glimpse of the foyer, leather armchairs, palms. A chambermaid yawning with the divine promise of a chance love affair. They reveled in the morning still life. They imagined that when there was no one there but them, all that was theirs, and as they imagined it, in fact it was all theirs.

Neither of them was hungry, but they decided to have lunch just to be done with it. On the strength of his new poem, which he could take to the office at three that afternoon, but without fail between six and seven, Sárkány asked for a loan of two koronas on his word of honor. They had rolled fillets of anchovy, mopping up the oil with bread, haunch of roe with cranberries, and vanilla creams. They drank spritzers and each smoked a green-speckled, light Média.

Noon was striking by the time they reached the Ring Road. Budapest, the youthful city, was glittering. The early September sun enveloped the facades of the houses in sheets of gold. Their heads baked in the hot sun. The sky was blue, a pristine blue, like the ceilings of newly painted flats, still tacky and smelling of paint. Everything around them was so new. This was the time when the new school term was starting. Primary school pupils were going around with satchels on their backs, clutching transfers they had been given at stationery shops.

Suddenly Esti and Sárkány stopped.

A young man was approaching them, his back to them, going backwards, crabwise, but with great skill, at a very swift pace.

On top of his head danced a cheap straw hat. He wore white trousers and a gray coat of thick material with flesh-colored rubber bands at the cuffs. He twirled an iron-tipped stick.

A moment later they too had turned round and were making for him in the same fashion, at a smart pace.

When they drew level with him they burst out laughing.

"Hello, you idiot!" they called to him, and embraced one another.

At last they were all three together, Kanicky, Sárkány and Esti, no one was missing, the circle was closed, the world was complete; the club was in session, the Balkan club, the prime objects of which included the free, courageous, and open practice of such eccentiricites.

The passersby looked ill-humoredly, with a certain contempt but also an undisguised interest, at these three cheerful young men, these three frivolous, immature boys. They didn't understand them, so they hated them.

Kanicky spat on the asphalt. His saliva was black. As black as ink.

He was chewing liquorice.

The liquorice was in his left pocket, and in the right was a medlar, in a paper bag.

They made for their favorite resort, the New York coffeehouse.

On the way Sárkány read his new poem to Kanicky. There was a bedroom in the window of a furniture shop, two wide poplar wood beds, made up, silk eiderdowns, pillows and night tables. In their thoughts they got into the beds wearing their shoes. They imagined at their sides putative spouses, as big as titanic china dolls, with bouffant hairstyles and eyebrows drawn in India ink. All that was so farfetched and improbable that they were ashamed of the fantastic idea and dismissed it as a subject for a poem. They went into a pet shop. They bargained for a monkey and inquired how much a lion would cost. The shopkeeper saw what kind of customers he had to deal with and showed them out.

"What about greeting people?" Kanicky proposed.

At that they greeted everyone who came along. The three hats swung low in unison as if by magic. Their eyes looked frankly into the eyes of the persons they saluted. These were sometimes pleased to be publicly acknowledged in that way, but sometimes were surprised, realized that it was a silly trick, looked them up and down, and went on their way. Out of fifteen, eleven returned the salute.

That too they gave up.

On the corner of Rákóczi út,* Esti bought two balloons. He fastened the strings in his buttonhole and hurried after his friends.

Not far from the coffeehouse a crowd had formed. It was said that two gentlemen were fighting, the one had bumped into the other and they had immediately begun to box each other's ears.

A heated exchange could be heard.

"Do you mind!"

"Impudent devil!"

"You're the impudent devil!"

Kanicky and Sárkány, pale of face, glared at each other. Kanicky raised his fist. A level-headed gentleman came between them.

"Really, gentlemen, for goodness' sake!"

Kanicky looked at the level-headed gentleman, and as usual on such occasions asked Sárkány:

"I say, who's this?"

"I don't know."

"Well, come on, then."

He linked arms with Sárkány as if nothing had happened, and to the astonishment of the onlookers went off with him. Esti joined them.

"Did anyone fall for it?" he asked.

"Yes," they said with a grin.

They let one of the balloons go.

And so they came to the coffeehouse.

The coffeehouse—at lunchtime—was quiet, deserted. Cleaning ladies were going about with brooms and buckets, wiping the marble tabletops. Morning coffee drinkers who had lingered were paying. A slender acrobat passed through the ladies' room.

The afternoon coffee beans were being roasted. The aroma tickled their nostrils. Upstairs the balcony, with its twisting, gilded columns, like a Buddhist temple, seemed to be expecting something.

Here they settled down at their tribal table. First they tried to or-

* A principal Pest street.

70

ganize their material affairs. Kaniczky had sixteen fillér, Sárkány thirty. Esti had one korona and four fillér.* Not much on which to fight the battles of the day.

Sárkány, who had the best prospects that day since he had written a poem, beckoned to the morning headwaiter, got him to count out twenty Princeszász, ordered coffee, then showed him the manuscript which he would be able to sell to the *Fületlen†* at three that afternoon, but at the latest between six and seven, and asked him for a loan of ten koronas. The waiter resignedly advanced the sum. Esti ordered a double espresso. Kanicky called for bicarbonate of soda, water, and a "dog's tongue."‡

The bicarbonate came. Slowly, absentmindedly, Kanicky sipped the three glasses of water that stood before him, even though Esti tapped the ash from his cigarette into one of them. He began to write a sketch, so as to have some money. Suddenly he jumped up, clutched his head: he had to make an urgent telephone call. Nervous anxieties swarmed around his glistening brow. He asked his friends to go with him down to the telephone. He didn't like to be alone.

On the way to the ground floor they pushed, joked, met friends, and forgot what they actually wanted. Loathsome figures were hanging like leeches on the telephones, speaking German, old fellows, forty or fifty, who couldn't really last much longer. It took Kanicky half an hour to get through. He emerged from the booth triumphant. She was coming at three that afternoon. He borrowed five koronas from Sárkány on his word of honor, and then Esti got one of the two that he had lent him.

After organizing their material affairs, they lightheartedly went back to their places at the table. Kanicky wrote a couple of lines of

---

* Strictly speaking, 1 korona = 100 krajcár. 100 fillér = 1 pengô or forint, but the terms were often interchanged in popular speech as the name of the unit of currency changed.

† "Having no ears," but here a pun on *Független*, "independent."

‡ The New York, in the Erzsébet Ring Road, was a principal haunt of writers and artists. Not only did it cater specially for the impecunious tastes of many, it also provided paper, pens and ink. A "dog's tongue" (*kutyanyelv*) was a slip of paper.

his sketch. Again he left off writing. He called a messenger and sent a letter to the girl whom he had telephoned. They smoked and sighed, laughed and were sad in quick succession, and waved through the plateglass window to women passing in the street. When the waiter placed some fruit before them they gave each one a name: the apple was Károly, the grapes were Ilona, the plum had to be Ödön, the pear, because of its softness and voluptuousness, Jolán, etc. A sort of restlessness stirred in them. They played party games with letters, colors, voices, mixing up, exaggerating, and patching together everything. They asked the oddest questions: what would happen if something were not as it was? No, they were not satisfied with Creation.

At three o'clock Sárkány hurried off for the money order. The coffeehouse was buzzing, the noise on the balcony was becoming louder and louder. In that raucous din they felt the pulse of their lives, felt that they were getting somewhere, making progress. Every table, every booth was occupied. Storm clouds of smoke towered in the air. It was good to relax in that vapor, in that warm pond, to think about nothing, to watch it seethe and bubble, and to know that those who were splashing in it were being slowly softened by it, steamed, cooked through, reduced into one single simmering *korhelyleves*.* They could see the usual crowd strewn about at various tables, on velvet settees and chairs. Every single one had arrived.

There was Bogár the young novelist, Pataki, and Dániel Ürögi. There was Arácsy the painter, who had had himself photographed dressed as a Florentine knight, rapier at his side, as he played the piano. There was Beleznay the famous art collector, personal acquaintance of Wilde and Rodin. There was Szilvás the "marquis," with his bone-handled walking stick, the incomparable conversationalist, who mischievously and masterfully blended the very latest Hungarian slang with the esoteric expressions of up-to-date dictionaries, antiquarians, and academic lectures. There was Elián the psychiatrist,

---

* Sometimes known as "Souse's Soup." A cabbage soup served in the small hours to reinvigorate the jaded reveller. There are various recipes, according to George Lang's *The Cuisine of Hungary*, all slightly greasy and very piquant.

Gólya the industrial artist, Sóti the scholar, who had studied in Berlin, and Kopunovits the youthful tragic actor. There was Dayka, blond son of a big landowner, who read the Neo-Kantians avidly and talked about epistemology. There was Kovács, who never spoke, collected stamps, and smiled sardonically. There was Mokosay, who had been to Paris and quoted Verlaine and Baudelaire in the original French with great enthusiasm and a terrible accent. There was Belényes the "chartered chemist," who had lost his job on account of some irregularity and now hung about newspaper offices, obtaining information for investigative articles. There was Kotra the playwright, who demanded pure literature on the stage, and wanted to put on the as yet unfinished drama *Waiting for Death* by his friend Géza, Géza who was sitting beside him, in which no people performed, only objects, and the key held a long and profound metaphysical discussion with the keyhole. There was Rex the art dealer, who flouted public opinion, praised Rippl-Rónai and criticized Benczúr. There were Ikrinszky the astronomer, Christian the conference organizer, Magass the composer. There was Pirnik the international social democrat. There was Scartabelli the aesthetic polyhistorian, explaining in his warm bass now Wundt and his experimental psychology, now the back streets of Buda, very sentimentally, while insisting that he wasn't sentimental. There was Exner, who everyone knew had syphilis. There was Bolta, who didn't regard Petőfi as a poet, because Jenő Komjáthy was the poet. There was Spitzer, who maintained that Max Nordau was the greatest brain in the world. There was Wesselényi, a highbrow chemist's assistant. There was Sebes, two of whose stories had appeared in the dailies and one had been accepted for publication. There was Moldvai the lyric poet. There was Czakó, another. There was Erdődy-Erlauer, a third. There was Valér V. Vándor the literary translator, who translated from every language but didn't know any, including his native one. There was Specht, the son of wealthy parents, a modest, laconic young man, who hadn't written anything but had been treated for two years in a mental institution and always had in his pocket the certificate, signed and sealed by three doctors, to the effect that he was compos mentis. Absolutely everyone was there.

They were all talking at once. About whether man had free will, what was the shape of the plague bacterium, how much wages were in England, how far away Sirius was, what Nietzsche had meant by "eternal reversion," whether homosexuality was lawful, and whether Anatole France was Jewish. Everyone wanted to have their say, quickly and profoundly, because although they were all very young, scarcely more than twenty, they felt that they had little time left.

Esti knew this company vaguely. He wasn't always certain who was who, but that didn't really matter, they themselves weren't sure who they were because their individuality, their characters, were taking shape right there and right then. On one occasion he confused a photographer with a poet, and was mistaken for a photographer himself. This caused no mutual embarrassment. They talked about their lives, their memories, their previous loves, their plans, and then, if it seemed right, they introduced themselves for the sake of politeness and sometimes made a note of one another's names.

He sat there among them, listened to the buzz of their conversation. He was captivated by them. In that racket every voice touched a key in his soul. He didn't understand life. He had no conception of why he had been born into the world. As he saw it, anyone to whose lot fell this adventure, the purpose of which was unknown but the end of which was annihilation, that person was absolved from all responsibility and had the right to do as he pleased—for example, to lie full length in the street and begin to moan without any reason—without deserving the slightest censure. But precisely because he considered his life as a whole an incomprehensible thing, he understood its little details individually—every person without exception, every elevated and lowly point of view, every concept—and those he assimilated at once. If anyone spoke to him sensibly for five minutes about converting to the Muslim faith, he would convert, on condition that he would be spared the bother of action, would be taken at his word, and would not be given time later, nevertheless, to retract.

In his opinion, living like that, in great folly among lesser degrees of folly, was not so foolish, but was indeed perhaps the most correct, most natural way of life. Furthermore, he needed that wild disorder, that piquant sauce! He wanted to write. He was waiting for the moment when he would reach such a pitch of despair and loathing that he would have to lash out, and then everything important and essential would pour out of him, not just the superfluous and incidental. That moment, however, hadn't yet arrived. He didn't yet feel badly enough about things to be able to write. He sucked in the nicotine and ordered another double espresso to flog his heart, further to torture his ever inquisitive, clownish, and playful mind, and he feverishly felt the internal throbbing within him; he took his pulse, which was a hundred and thirty, and took it happily, as a usurer does his money.

Women surrounded him. The "woman from Csongrád,"* who every fortnight took a trip away from her husband and spent her free time among writers, literary girls, semi-demons, a pale lady acrobat who must have been ill, and a yellow-faced, bloated woman, as large and terrible as Clytamnestra. They would sit there in white, blue, and black, blossoming in the hot swamp like water lilies at Hévíz.† He longed for every one of them. His eye hesitantly, uneasily, darted from one to another. He enjoyed his sudden ambushes and deathly caprices, which at any moment could change his life or become his doom. He noted the Csongrád woman's hands, the nails at the ends of the soft fingers, which she polished pink and trimmed to points, he imagined that perhaps that woman could be his fate, but was repelled by her alien talons, which scratched gently like rose-thorns, and dismissed the thought in alarm. The Csongrád woman asked him what he was thinking at that moment. Esti gave a superior smile and told some lie so that she could make what she liked of what he was thinking.

Kanicky was resting his head on his friend's chest. He was not waiting for just any woman, only the one who, through some misunderstanding, had not appeared, though it was well past three

* A small town on the Alföld, southeast of Kecskemét.
† A spa at the west end of Lake Balaton in western Hungary.

75

o'clock. The messenger whom he had sent at noon with the important message had not returned. He charged another with looking for the first. He had looked across into the coffeehouse opposite and the small restaurant named Rabló. Returning to the telephone, he had spent a whole hour calling various places, without result. He ordered a *kis-irodalmi*,* which he dispatched with a hearty appetite, then had another bicarbonate of soda.

Toward seven Sárkány arrived, having been off somewhere since three. He was radiant with pleasure. He told them that a new period in his life had begun. He had met that supposed kindergarten teacher, about whom he had said so much to his friends that they perhaps knew her better than he did, he had made it up with her, and now everything was at long last coming together, once and for all. Esti and Kanicky heard every day that a new period was beginning in Sárkány's life, and that he had met *the* woman. They were more interested in the money order. Sárkány's face fell. Firstly, he informed them that he'd spent all his money. As for the money order, what had happened was that he'd called on the publisher at three, as was correct, but he'd been in a bad mood and had called over his shoulder at him to come back between six and seven. So he'd done that, modestly and quietly handed over his poem, and requested payment, at which the publisher, that wretched and sour-tempered villain who rather resembled Herod, took it with unspeakable vulgarities, spat on the manuscript, stamped on it, and in the full sense of the word, kicked him out. His friends couldn't really imagine, on the basis of his personal description, quite how this scene had transpired, but they were indignant at the publisher's lack of delicacy.

So there they were, the three of them, penniless, with all those espressos, cigarettes, and messengers to pay for, not to mention the *kis-irodalmi*, and ahead of them the empty night with no prospects. Something had to be done. Things were not going well. Scartabelli talked to them about the Bhagavad Gita and Nirvana without

---

* "Small-literary." The *irótál*, "writer's plate," was a speciality of the New York, an inexpensive plate of cold meats, salami, cheese, etc. served only to writers. The *kis-irodalmi* was a reduced version for the even less well off.

getting their full attention. Valér V. Vándory was translating a French novel. In that connection he inquired of those present the meaning of *derechef*. Mokosay took exception to his pronunciation. Asked him for the book. It was his opinion that it was the name of a flower that didn't grow in Hungary. Others suspected an obscenity. Most advised him to leave it out, at which Valér V. Vándory cut the whole paragraph and worked on. Then up came Hannibal, the night hawker, with his poker face, a frozen grin on his lips, offering dirty picture postcards and immediately after that contraceptives, as if the mere sight of those postcards would damage their health.

Esti got up and went to speak to the night headwaiter. He got ten koronas out of him. One gold coin. He should have shared it with his friends, to whom he had been indebted for some time, and after complex calculations thought that the deal was more or less good, hoping that he would at least soon get back the korona which Sárkány had still not given back from that morning. But he decided differently. He simply ran away. Ran and ran down the street. He planned to go to the Writers' Circle, win at least sixty koronas, and share them out three ways in brotherly fashion, twenty koronas each. At the baccarat table Homona, the famous gambler, a noted journalist who lived by blackmailing the banks, was sitting at the shoe. That he took for a bad sign. Nevertheless he tossed the round, alluring gold coin onto the green baize, all in one. His stake was swept up without a flicker of emotion.

That he could register at once. He stood rigid for about ten minutes, however, as if expecting world revolution to change the incontestable decision of fate and the banker to give back his gold coin.

In the coffeehouse they were waiting for him as a savior. Two messengers, who had come back and wanted their money, were dunning Kanicky. He tried for a while to explain by rational arguments that they weren't entitled to any, then took an aspirin, dashed off his sketch under the watchful eye of the messengers, and sold it, also under the watchful eye of the messengers. He even brought money back and tossed some to his friends.

They went off to Sárkány's, in Mária utca, as he was expecting a letter from the kindergarten teacher. They went to the Kanickys', where they drank tea. The family lived in one enormous room. One of Kanicky's sisters was painting, the second was playing the piano, while the third, all the time the visitors were there, sat facing the wall, goodness knows why. The father, a likable, kindly old man, was sitting writing in the middle of the room with the sobriety of age, dipping his pen in the inkwell, carefully tapping off the excess ink, and taking no notice of the roaring din about him. They went downstairs after the gate was shut. Kanicky was reciting loudly from *The Tragedy of Man*.* In a dark square, a peasant who was a coachman or something, whip in hand, came straight up to him, put a hand on his shoulder and said:

"Tell you what? I'll give you back your fifty fillérs, but give me the halter."

"No!" replied Kanicky. "I need the halter."

Esti didn't know what the fifty fillérs and the halter were all about, didn't know whether this was actually something planned or something unexpected, and felt nervous. The black rags of night lay about him. He would rather have been back at home, lying by himself on his couch. He despised himself, despised his friends too, but couldn't bring himself to leave them. The sense of foreboding came over him which he had known in childhood when he'd felt that he was asking for something forbidden. Beneath the gas lamps, people, stupefied by the day's work, stared into his face as if paying attention to him, came after him with noisy footsteps as if following him. He was glad when they went into the Rabló.

The pianola was playing the overture to *Tannhäuser*. József Gách, his cousin, the medical student, put both his hands to Esti's nose and made him smell them. He'd done his first dissection that day. Faltay, the leather-sandaled Tolstoyan, was eating semolina pudding. Bisszám, the bearded young theosophist, with a face as red as an apple and teeth as white as porcelain, looked warmly into their eyes and

* The verse drama by Imre Madách—the most translated item in Hungarian literature.

urged them to love Nature and live in harmony with the Universe.

For that, they thought, they had plenty of time, and called into the coffeehouse again.

There the elevated, intellectual drinking was now becoming a carousal. The second team had taken its place on the gallery, youngsters of eighteen or nineteen. Over espressos with rum and Egyptian cigarettes, Putterl, little Hajnal, and young Wallig were setting up a polemic periodical, of the highest possible quality, against ossified traditions, the Academy, and the old guard. Next to them Abmentis was writing words to music and singing his first line: *Oh, lágy madárkám.* Instead of *lágy* he could have gone with a two-syllable, iambic word, and so tried the line *Oh, kemény madárkám.** That he couldn't use either. As he sang he tried to find a new adjective which would do both for the text and for the little bird. The older generation was represented by Erdôdy-Erlauer. He was sitting hunched in the first cubicle, staring at his writing paper, on which all that he'd written all afternoon was *Such is my life …* And then he'd been unable to go on. He didn't know what his life was like, couldn't find anything to compare it to, which wasn't surprising: Erdôdy-Erlauer's life wasn't like anything; that was exactly how his life was.

They left them there to their manuscripts, their grief-filled lives. They strolled along the Danube embankment, round the Keleti station. In all parts of the city they picked up would-be writers who were wandering in the dark as if performing an all-night service: Exner, Szilvás, Dayka the Neo-Kantian, Moldvai, Czakó, and a few more besides, who likewise had something to do with the arts and the intellectual sciences: Orbán the music teacher, Csiszér, and Valentini too, who must have been a cabinetmaker or something. This storm-swept little group drifted around the houses of Ferencváros at about three in the morning.

On the corner stood a girl of the streets. Exner spoke to her and the rest surrounded her. They allowed no opportunity to pass of studying the depths of life and, in the meantime, of showing off

---

* "Oh, my soft little bird" and "Oh, my hard little bird."

their well-informed state. They addressed these women with a superior, amiable informality, though they were usually much older than themselves, at least of an age with their mothers' women friends, whose hands they would politely kiss at home with a deep bow. This disrespectful libertinism increased their self-esteem.

They talked about something. A dialogue took place between the men and the girl, interrupted every few moments by the laughter of the group. In the middle Exner flourished his jaunty walking stick. The girl replied quietly.

Esti stood apart from them. He didn't want to become involved in that game. He thought it both tasteless and immodest. But he knew that part of the world better than any of them. He knew those streets at all times of day and night because some kindred horror drove him there, often in such a way that at home he jumped out of bed and ran there. He had known that quarter early in the morning, when there was no one about, on Saturday evenings between nine and eleven, when activity was at its peak, and on sweltering days at the height of summer between one and two in the afternoon, when the girls in their finery gleamed from the clinging heat like cheap sugar cakes. He knew the houses one by one, the doors and windows in which lamps burned and were extinguished. He knew the men too, who hung about here abstractedly, as if looking for something else, and scuttled in looking at the ground so as at least not to see anything else, and then the unfeeling and stupid, who openly inspected the goods on sale, the fat, lonely old gentlemen who puffed at their cigars in holders as they speculatively eyed the prostitutes walking the other sidewalk, and then with sudden decisiveness, as if something were pulling them on a string, made for a chocolate-colored gate. He knew the special expressions of the region, which constantly met his ear, concerning the objective details of the profession. Above all he knew the women, personally or by sight, the pleasant ones and the brutish-dulled, the ladylike and the uncouth, the tall and the short, those that had pink scars or bites like caterpillars on their chins, or who had dogs on leashes, or wore glasses, or the nightmares that sometimes appeared toward dawn, double black veils covering their faces because they had no noses. He knew this girl too, whom his friends were now entertaining: he had often seen her going this way, had watched her, kept an eye on her.

The girl took Exner's walking stick and set off slowly down the side street. The group followed her. Esti too trailed after them to see what else would happen. They rang at the gate. In they went, all eleven.

Inside, in the low, ground-floor room, the din was like that in a house on fire when the brigade arrives. They shrieked and cried out because of the strangeness of the situation. The woman was afraid that the police would charge her with disturbance of the peace and scandalous conduct. She hushed them, but to no effect. Five of them sat on the bed, so that it creaked and all but collapsed under their weight. The "marquis" spread out his arms and in rounded periodic sentences preached to the woman that she should flee from pollution, return to a better way, then blessed her as his daughter and called her "a violet." Exner looked at her glue-backed photographs. Sárkány rummaged among her belongings. Czakó lifted the lid on the red glazed pot that stood on the iron stove, in which he found the remains of her dinner, cold beef stew with cold tarhonya,* which was being kept for next day.

The woman stamped her foot demanding quiet. She kept an eye on the men in case they made off with anything. Her eyes flickered this way and that.

Kanicky whispered something to Sárkány. He passed it on, and the word went round, and as it reached all eleven eardrums a general, stormy guffaw broke out. Everyone looked at the woman.

In the lamplight one could see that in fact she was much older that they had thought outside in the street. She wore a round, black beauty spot above her chin and a heavy, red-blonde wig. According to Kanicky her head under the wig was as bald as a billiard ball, and she had not a single tooth. That was what they were laughing at.

The mood had turned sour. No one spoke. Now they regretted

* A kind of pasta.

having come in and were considering how they could get out. The woman looked at them uncertainly. In her eyes flickered an anxiety that she dared not express.

Kanicky slunk to the door and sidled out without taking his leave. After him went Sárkány, then Szilvás, then Exner, then Moldvai, then Czakó, then Dayka, then Valentini, Csiszér, and Orbán.

The whole lot fled headlong.

"Are you going as well?" asked the woman in surprise, looking at Esti, who was the last to make for the door.

"Yes," and he put his hand on the door handle. "Good night."

"Good night."

Esti opened the door, which his friends had slammed in his face as a joke. He listened.

In the stairwell the friends were conferring as they waited for the concierge. A dreadful shouting was heard, Sárkány's voice, then Kanicky's, bawling horrible things toward the room.

"What's that?" said the woman.

"Nothing," said Esti, and shut the door so as not to hear it.

The woman looked at him.

"Have you changed your mind, then? Are you staying?"

"Yes," Esti replied, "I might sit down for a minute," and he continued to stand.

At that moment the gate banged shut as the concierge let them out. There was silence.

"They're mad," said the woman in the sudden silence.

She shrugged, uncomprehendingly.

That movement made Esti feel sorry for her. His heart, his sick heart, filled with tears like a sponge.

A couple of moments later the din broke out again outside the window. The company were standing out there. Exner rattled his stick over the slats in the shutter, and familiar voices called good night to Esti, wishing him much good fortune and a good time.

He looked at the window like one who has fallen into a trap and would like to climb out.

They had abandoned him. He had been made the victim of a piece of fun, the ultimate ugly piece of fun. The noise had stopped. There was silence again, a decisive, great silence.

"They've gone," said the woman, and locked the door.

Esti wanted to make amends for their bad manners. In his view, all "bad manners" were a fundamental flaw—there was no worse flaw than bad manners. He couldn't abide anyone being insulted to their face. Such a thing was so painful to him that he would stay with boring people for hours because he couldn't devise a decent way of tactfully shaking them off.

The woman pulled up a wicker chair toward him. She too sat down, facing him on the settee.

They'd been right: this girl was no longer young, she was worn out, and there was something idiotic in her smile. But she could be seen another way too. He began to work on his imagination, and then reality vanished. No, they hadn't been entirely right, they'd been exaggerating: her skin was faded, but it was white, lily white. And she *did* have teeth, nearly all of them. He liked her misty, green feline eyes, her round, hunger-pallid face, her narrow forehead.

"What's your name?"

"Paula," answered the woman, in a soft, husky voice.

Words had an illogical effect on Esti. That name made him think of a wilting tea rose. He closed his eyes.

"What did you do before?"

"Hairdresser."

Now Esti grasped desperately at her hands and her skirt.

•

Reveille had sounded in the barracks. A column prepared to move out of a courtyard. At the head was the captain, on a high-stepping horse, sword drawn, rapping out German words of command,*

* German was the language of the army.

at which that fearsome machine of human flesh and steel moved, wheeling out into Üllôi út.* Young subalterns, redolent of eau de cologne, were at their posts. The morning sun gleamed on their swords, their black and yellow sword knots. King and Emperor Franz Josef I ruled, up there on his high throne in Vienna.

Esti strolled home along Üllői út. The gate was open now, he didn't have to pay gate money. He rushed up to the fourth floor, to his room, where Sárkány had woken him at eleven o'clock the day before.

On his desk he found a postcard from the country, from his parents. That pleased him greatly.

They had sent him news of his uncle's splendid birthday celebration, at which every year the three related families gathered, the Csendeses, the Estis, and the Gáches. There had been *ludaskasa, cigánypecsenye*, vanilla and almond *kifli*.† Many, many greetings came from everyone, relations, friends, his sister's girlfriend too. His brother wrote that he had a strict schoolmaster, his sister, that she was going to dancing lessons, his mother, that she'd love to see him—he must come without fail at the end of the month for the grape harvest. His father just put his name in his severe, upright hand.

Esti read the messages several times one after the other, and was overcome. He was at home, in the vineyard, in the copse where the wild vines grew, among the green velvet chairs in the sitting room. He embraced his dear ones fondly, because after all he was still a good son and a loving brother. He thought, mother's got an amethyst bracelet just the color of her eyes. He thought, father's up there now, he's been working since four o'clock. He thought, I'm going to come to nothing, I'm wasting my time. He thought, I'm going to make good. He thought, I shall die next year, at the age of twenty-one. He thought, I'm never going to die. He thought of everything all at once.

* Presumably from the Ludovika barracks.
† *Ludaskasa*, "goose porridge," is goose giblets boiled with millet, a Martinmas dish. *Cigánypecsenye*, "gipsy roast," is pork cutlets, spit-roasted or fried, with fat bacon and red cabbage. *Kifli* is a pastry, similar in shape to a croissant.

The day which he had just lived through had been crowded and animated, but not much different from his other days. His agitation now froze into solid grief. He trembled and clutched the card to him for reassurance; he took refuge behind the peace of the countryside, where his roots were and his strength.

Remorse gnawed at him. He ran quickly over his Spanish irregular verbs. Then he undressed.

But he got up again. He wrote an answer to the card, so as to be able to post his letter as soon as he went down in the morning.

He wrote:

Dear parents, brother and sister, Thank you for your kind messages. I am always with you in my thoughts.

He also had to say something in reply to the invitation. Then he thought of Sárkány and Kanicky, whom he loved no less than his siblings. He went on:

I'm afraid I won't be able to get away just yet. New literature is in a ferment, I've got to stay here, watch for my opportunity.

He tried to think of a better excuse, but just added:

I'm working.

VI

*In which he comes into a huge inheritance
and learns that it's hard to get rid of money
when a person wants to do only that.*

AS DAWN APPROACHED WE WERE SITTING IN A NIGHTCLUB.
The Negro band was taking a break. We were yawning.

Kornél Esti whispered in my ear:

"Quick, let me have a fiver."

He paid, then said:

"Strange."

"What is?"

"That expression 'money trouble.' You'd think it means that money
causes trouble. Whereas it's not money that causes trouble but the
opposite, lack of money, impecuniosity. Tell me," he turned toward
me with keen interest, "you're a bit of a linguist in your spare time:
is there any expression that denotes that money can be a burden?"

"Yes, it's French. *Embarras de richesse.*"

"Isn't there a Hungarian one?"

"No."

"Typical," he muttered.*

On the way home he continued to ponder in the street.

"No doubt about it, money trouble's a nasty business. But the

---

* Actually, there is such an expression in Hungarian: *a bőség zavara,* "the quandary
of plenty."

other's just as nasty. When it really is money that causes the trouble. When there's far too much of it. I know all about that."

"You do?"

"Uh huh. At one time I had a huge amount of money. Once upon a time," he said dreamily, "heretofore, in days of yore."

"In Singapore?"

"No, here in Budapest. When I came into money."

"Who left you money?"

"An obscure aunt on my mother's side. Teresa Maria Anselm. Lived in Hamburg. Wife of some German baron."

"That's interesting. You've never mentioned her."

"No. I must have been thirty-five. One morning I got an official letter telling me that my aunt had left everything to me. The news wasn't completely unexpected. But it did come as a surprise. That is, I'd heard that my aunt had another nephew and that she was dividing the inheritance between us. In the meantime he'd died. Somewhere in Brazil. Haven't got a cigarette, have you?"

"Help yourself."

"So off I went to Germany. To tell the truth, I scarcely remembered my dear departed aunt. I'd been taken to see her a few times when I was little. She lived in a luxurious mansion on her estate, on her model farm. She was stinking rich and as dull as ditchwater. There were white and black swans on the fishpond. That was all I knew about her. Apart from the fact that she had a lot of land, several big houses in Berlin and Dresden, and a huge amount in Swiss banks. Considering that I hadn't answered her letters for ten years, I'd no idea what she was worth. When the inventory was compiled it turned out to be more than I'd thought. By the time I'd sold everything, realized it all—and after paying taxes, fees, lawyer's expenses—a Hamburg bank paid me out almost two million marks."

"Two million marks? You're pulling my leg."

"I'm not. Let's talk about something more serious, then. How's your blood pressure?"

"I beg your pardon. Go on, then."

"That's all there was to it, I changed the money into Hungarian currency, stuffed it into my suitcase, and came home. Here I went on living as before, scribbling poetry. I was careful not to say a word about the business, because I knew that it would be the end of me."

"Why?"

"Look here—a poet that's wealthy, in Hungary? That's a total absurdity. In Budapest people think that anybody who's got a bit of money's an idiot. If he's got money, why should he have a brain, feelings, imagination? That's how they punish him. This town's far too clever. It doesn't want to understand that nature's a savage, doesn't share out its favors in a predictable fashion or on any kind of compassionate basis. Nobody here would have recognized that Byron— a lord and a multimillionaire—had the slightest ability. Here the rank of genius is doled out as compensation—as charity—to those who've got nothing else, who are starving, sick, persecuted, more dead than alive. Or actually dead. Mainly the latter. I've never been disposed to stand up to people's titanic stupidity. I've bowed humbly before it as a mighty natural phenomenon. On that occasion too I didn't break with the compulsory Bohemian tradition. Kept going to dirty little restaurants. Owed for my coffee. Inked my collars every morning. Made holes in my shoes with a fretsaw. Wasn't going to damage my reputation as a poet, was I? Anyway, things were more comfortable and more interesting that way. If I'd let my good fortune be known, people would've been round at once, pestering me all day long, stopping me from getting on with my work."

"So what did you do with all that money?"

"That was no trouble. Of course, I didn't put it in a bank. That would have given the game away at once. I locked it in my desk drawer with my manuscripts. It's surprising how little room two million koronas takes, two thousand thousand-korona notes. It was a pile only so big. It's just bits, just leaves, like any other paper. When I looked at it in the evening I had mixed feelings. I'd be telling a lie if I said that I wasn't happy about it. I've got a lot of respect for money. It means calm, respectability, power, all sorts of things. But so much money was a burden to me, not a relief. By that time I was too sensible to start a new life, buy a car, move into a nice three-room apartment with a sitting room, get out of the old ruts, take on new responsibilities and anxieties. I've never wanted to swill champagne. I've despised luxury, you know. All my life I've had bread and butter for dinner, and water to go with it. I've just been keen on rotten cigarettes and rotten women. So I started to think hard, logically. What was my purpose, my calling, my passion? Writing. By that time my pen was earning me five hundred koronas a month, easily. I added another thousand to that, so as to guarantee my independence for good. How long could I live? My parents and grandparents died before they were fifty. We aren't a long-lived family. I gave myself sixty years. That generous allowance only came to 360,000 koronas in thirty years, my entire life expectancy, ignoring interest. The rest, I felt, was superfluous. So I decided to pass it round."

"To whom?"

"Ay, there's the rub! I've got no brothers or sisters. I've only got one relative, a wealthy manufacturer. I always see him in my dreams as a beggar in rags, and my greatest desire is that one night, when wolves are howling and I'm warming myself at the fireside after a good dinner, he'll be outside gnawing at my doorstep, asking me for a crust, and I'll be able to call to him that I'm not at home. Was I going to give him my money, or his well-educated, repulsive brats, whom I disliked even more than him? No, no."

"Didn't you think of your friends?"

"Didn't have any at the time. I hadn't met you then."

"Thank you."

"I really didn't have a single acquaintance—close or distant— whom, from a certain elevated standpoint, I'd have considered more congenial than the complete stranger in the street that I'd never seen before. I didn't collect people. I just looked on them with a kind of sad resignation, I was conscious of the futility of life and the uncertain nature of everything. That was why I didn't want to leave any money for the authorities to deal with, either. I knew—knew from my own example—how ungrateful people are that receive bequests. Tell me, what would you have done in my position?"

"What anyone would do in such a situation. I'd have offered it to some noble cause, some charitable institution."

"Quite. I too turned that over in my mind. First I thought of orphanages, homes for the aged, the blind, the deaf-mute, abandoned girls, hospitals, and so on. But at once there rose before my eyes a fat swindler buying diamonds for his wife and mistress with the money left for orphans, old people, deaf-mutes, abandoned girls, and the sick. I dropped the idea. My dear boy, I wasn't born to save that branch of humanity that, when not afflicted by fire, flood, and pestilence, organizes wars and artificially causes fire, flood, and pestilence. I finished with so-called society a long time ago. I've nothing to do with it. My kith and kin is nature—mindless, unbridled, and alive. Then I thought about a literary prize, a large-scale foundation. I confess, that attracted me for a while. But I soon saw clearly how, as the years went by, the various committees would misrepresent my original intentions: they'd reward fools and half-wits who ought to be put firmly in their places, use my money to encourage intellectual pygmies, noxious freaks, rather than people who might amount to something. And then I could hear the winning entries as well, talking about 'the varieties of drama' or 'the influence of French literature,' and I despaired at the idea that this stupidity would run on from generation to generation, to the end of time, like some perpetual curse. I gave up that as well."

"What did you decide to do in the end?"

"Throw the money away a bit at a time, to individuals, just as unexpectedly as I'd come into it. I suddenly thought of that crazy old Roman emperor, the one who rode about pressing handfuls of gold coins on the fortunate and unfortunate alike, without distinction, so that it should be everybody's and nobody's."

"You mean, you gave some to everybody you met?"

"Ah no, my dear fellow. It wasn't that simple. Then I'd have been recognized and it would all have come out. Of course, that way people would have smirked at me, been grateful to me, come around flattering me, the papers could have made a fuss about a 'noble-hearted giver.' I simply can't stand that sort of thing. I had to remain incognito."

"And did you manage to?"

"Wait a bit, please. I worked out on paper that apart from the 360,000 koronas for myself, I had another 1,640,000 koronas to give away over the rest of my life—foreseeably thirty years at the most. I had to dispose of roughly 54,000 a year to individuals, about 4,500 a month, 150 a day. How did I begin? At first it went smoothly. In the evening, when I'd finished work, I'd write out a money order—on the typewriter, of course—without the sender's name and send 150 koronas by post, always to a stranger whose name and address I copied out at random from the electoral roll, without inquiring whether the person was rich or poor. I just acted on the spur of the moment. Once I sent money to one of our biggest banks. Blessings showered all over the place. I could feel this wretched city fizzing, effervescing around me. People who received my money orders were certainly amazed in the first moment. Who could it be from? But then everybody could think of somebody, a relative, a generous friend, somebody that owed them money and was finally paying up. Obviously, they'd think, 'How nice of him,' 'Well, well, so he's honest after all....' The way I did it, it was as if some blind force, some mischievous fairy, was all over the place, shaking blessings from an invisible horn of plenty. But after a year—unfortunately—I was caught."

"Through the post office?"

"I was too careful for that. I worked with errand boys, messengers, servants in various parts of the city, often from the provinces, even from abroad, through my agents. But I was stupid enough on one occasion—on the spur of the moment—to send the usual sum to a newspaper reporter, the crime correspondent of a big Budapest daily. This fellow had heard a vague rumor about mysterious gifts—you know, out of 365 people at least 300 will be chatterboxes, even if it's against their own interest and that of their pocket—and the next day he put his information together and printed in his paper the accounts of various eyewitnesses and those who'd heard something, he even published my typewritten money order, concocted some stupid, lurid tale, wrote an account of some Indian maharajah in exile here under the headline *Rain of Gold*. Yes, I was discovered but not unmasked. In any case, I took fright. I had to stop sending money orders at once. Which was bad enough. I had to think out a new, more devious scheme."

"I don't understand. Why didn't you stake it all on a single card?"

"Because in that way I would have revealed myself."

"Then why didn't you give it to the women you loved?"

"Because that would have meant lowering myself. As long as possible I shall cherish the delusion that women love me for myself. It looks as if you don't understand. The decision had stuck in my head to share out this money, not on a basis of human justice or careful thought, but randomly, that is, according to the greatest, most mysterious truth of nature. I don't consider life to be rational. But all the same that irrationality was painful to me, and it upset me that such an enormous fortune should simply rot in my desk drawer, and that not only should I be unable to make use of it but that others too should get nothing from it. If I failed to dispose of the prescribed daily amount my conscience pricked me. My task became harder, more complicated. It happened that several days' amounts would sometimes pile up. Now and then I even committed acts of reckless stupidity. I risked being discovered and caught. One night, as I was walking over the bridge—quite without thinking—I tossed six hundred koronas into the lap of a beggar who was squatting there, and then ran for it. But I didn't do that sort of thing often."

"Anyway, how did you manage to give it all away?"

"One way and another. For example, when I was traveling I'd get off at the bigger stations, have a virsli, an apple, and get into conversation with the wine vendor, who would have his goods on a tray held on a strap round his neck. I'd delay paying till the last moment, then as the engine whistled I'd toss him a hundred koronas, jump into my compartment, duck down, and let him look for me and wave the change at my carriage window. I'd leave a fifty korona coin under the tablecloth in a coffeehouse, then avoid the entire area. I'd join a lending library and put bank notes between the pages of the books. I'd go for walks and keep dropping various amounts.

At such times I'd hurry along holding my breath, like somebody up to no good. The trick often worked. But a couple of times people ran after me—once a schoolboy, once a lady in mourning—and brought my money back. I blushed, stammered something, and crammed the note into my pocket. They, poor things, took it amiss that I didn't even thank them for their kindness or give them a reward for being honest."

"Amazing."

"You can't imagine how little use money is if you really want to squander it. Then you simply don't need it. Nobody wants it. I struggled bitterly on for a year like that. I handled it so badly that—as they say—'after going over the books,' I had 1,574 koronas left which had no owners anywhere. At the start of the third year my luck turned. I came across a nice little dentist who'd set up in Buda. He polished the plaque off my teeth and gave me that lovely gold tooth which has been part of my poetic persona ever since. There were four or five coats hanging in the waiting room, and in a moment when no one was watching I stuffed a couple of notes in the pocket of each. Next day I did the same. On the third day as well. In a week I'd succeeded in getting through all my backlog of money. The patients sat in the waiting room, eyes shining. They'd creep out one by one into the anteroom and come back happy and electrified with the money in their pockets which they had taken from their coats and put in a safer place. They usually hid their faces with their handkerchiefs, as if they had a toothache, so as not to show their pleasure and so the others wouldn't know they'd been looking for money. Some of them strolled out into the anteroom more than once in the hope that this inexplicable natural marvel would be repeated several times in an afternoon, or perhaps they were afraid that somebody else would collect the present. I lay low in the middle of them. I was enjoying the situation. But I soon dropped that too."

"Perhaps the journalist discovered that as well?"

"No. But the word went round that there was no dentist in Budapest as clever and gentle as mine, and his practice flourished so much that they had to draw lots for appointments. I drew number

628, so I wasn't going to get an appointment for the foreseeable future. The receptionist wouldn't even let me in. So I went elsewhere. I operated where my fertilizing golden rain hadn't fallen before. By that time there was hardly anywhere left. Especially as I had to be more and more careful all the time. That's right, my dear boy. The noose was tightening round my neck."

"Poor fellow."

"At the start of the fourth year I had a brilliant idea. I have a very good friend who's served five years for picking pockets. I got him to teach me. The lessons were really hard. First he lengthened my index finger, stretched it, loosened the knuckles, to make it the same length as my middle finger, because pickpockets only 'dip' with those two fingers. When I'd finished the training I could work quite confidently, even daringly at times. On one state occasion I succeeded in smuggling my daily 150 koronas into the court dress of an elderly, widely respected Hungarian nobleman of European distinction, and another fifty into the fur of his egret-plumed hat. In fact, while I was in the corridor of Parliament, chatting with the finance minister about the economic crisis, I slipped a hundred into his pocket. For the most part I hung about in the crowds at soccer matches and amusement parks, where people are jammed together, lining up to get on the rides. One Sunday—I mention this as a particular piece of luck—750 koronas were taken from my pocket at the Hüvösvölgy tram terminus.* That day I had nothing to do. At the time I only risked placing smallish amounts. It seemed that the detectives were keeping their eyes open. Just imagine, I was putting koronas into my fellow men's pockets and bags. Gradually I became careless. I used to sit on trams from morning to night to achieve my self-imposed task. One day in May—I remember it clearly—an old man with blue eyes and a neat silver beard sat down beside me and rested both hands absentmindedly on the crook of his walking stick. He was wearing a threadbare coat. He looked like a tax-office clerk or something. I'd just got a silver five-korona piece out of my pocket

---

* On the northwest edge of Budapest.

and was about to slip it into his coat pocket with my two long, agile fingers, when the old man trapped my hand under his arm and shouted 'thief.' The conductor immediately rang the bell, stopped the tram, and called a policeman. It was no good my protesting. I'd been caught in the act. That was the end of my career ..."

Kornél Esti was silent. He said no more. He walked pensively down the street, now flooded by bright sunlight, and stopped outside the big, dark red house where he lives on the sixth floor, in the attic. He rang to be let in.

"You're mad," I said, and embraced him.

"So it's not dull?" he asked. "Interesting enough? Absurd, improbable, incredible enough? Will it be annoying enough to people who look for psychological motivation, understanding, even moral lessons in literature? Good. Then I'll write it up. If I get paid for it I'll let you have your fiver back tomorrow. Well then, good-bye."

VII

In which Küçük appears, the Turkish girl,
whom he compares to a honey cake.

"IT WAS THE HEIGHT OF SUMMER, AND I WAS RACING HOME-ward," said Kornél, "on the electrified line from the East.

"In the curtained first-class compartment where I was sitting, there were also three Turkish women, three thoroughly modern Turkish women without veils or prejudices: a grandmother, a mother, and a fifteen-year-old girl whom they called Küçük, that is, Little One, Tiny.

"I admired this delightful family for a long time. Grandmother, mother, and daughter formed a unity, were as close to one another as Winter, Summer, and Spring on certain mountains in the Alps.

"The grandmother, a gaunt matron in her eighties, dressed in black and with enormous black pearls round her neck, was sleeping on the seat. She spoke in Turkish in her sleep. From time to time she raised her hand, her wrinkled, blue-veined hand, to her face to cover it, because for the greater part of her life she had worn a veil, and even in her sleep she must have felt that her face was improperly exposed.

"The mother was more modern. She almost flaunted her progressiveness. She had dyed her hair straw yellow—it must have been raven black at one time. Her manner was free and easy. She smoked one cigarette after another. When the guard came in, she—democratically—shook his hand. Furthermore, she was reading Paul Valéry's latest novel.

"Küçük was like a pink and white honey cake. She wore a pink silk dress, and her little face was as white as whipped cream. Her hair too was dyed straw yellow. In every respect she looked the disciple of her mother. She was almost ashamed of being Turkish. All that gave her away were the red leather slippers that she wore on the train and the huge bunch of roses that she had brought with her, all those fiery red, blood-red Constantinople roses, and then her Angora cat, for which she spread a Turkish mat to sit on, the blue-eyed, deaf Angora cat over whose slumber she tenderly watched.

"Mohammed came to my mind, their stirring, kindly prophet, who on one occasion when his cat had gone to sleep on his cloak, preferred to cut off its corner rather than wake his favorite kitty.

"They were making for Vienna, and from there for Berlin, Paris, and London. They were astoundingly cultured. The girl talked about vitamins B and C, and her mother about Jung and Adler and the latest heretical schools of psychoanalysis.

"They spoke all languages perfectly. They began in French, the purest literary language, then slipped into argot, followed shortly by German—alternating between the speech of Berlin and Lerchenfeld patois—passing meanwhile through English and Italian. This was not at all showing off. They were just content, like children making themselves understood in adult western European society, comfortable, finding themselves a niche everywhere. It seemed that their ambition was to be taken seriously and regarded as western Europeans.

"I felt inclined to tell them that they were possibly overesteeming western Europe a trifle, and that I was by no means as entranced by its culture. But I decided against doing so. Why spoil their fun?

"Instead I showed them my eight fountain pens, which I always keep in my pocket, my two gold fillings, which I likewise always have in my mouth, and I boasted that I had high blood pressure, a five-valve radio, and an incipient kidney stone, and that several of my relatives had had appendectomies. I tell everyone what they need to know.

"This had an extraordinary effect.

"Küçük smiled and stared at me with her dark, bewitching eyes with such honest, frank sincerity that she quite perturbed me. I didn't know what she wanted of me. At first I thought that she was making fun of me. Then, however, she took both my hands and pressed them to her heart. A dove can thus attack a sparrowhawk.

"In all this there was no coquetry or immorality. She just thought that was how cultured, advanced, western European girls behaved toward men whom they met for the first time on trains. Therefore I too tried to behave as cultured, advanced, western European men do in such circumstances.

"Her mother saw this, but paid us little attention. She—as I've said—was immersed in Paul Valéry.

"We went out into the corridor. There we walked about, laughing, holding hands. Then we leaned out the window. And so I courted her.

"'You're the first Turkish girl,' I told her—we were on *te* terms by then—'the first Turkish girl I've met, Küçük, Little One, and I love you. Years ago, in school, I learned about the battle of Mohács. I know that your ancestors spilled the blood of mine and kept us in shameful slavery for a century and a half. But I'd be your slave for another hundred and fifty years, serve you, pay you tribute, my dear little enemy, my dear oriental relative. Do you know what? Let's make peace. I've never been angry with your people—they have given us our most lovely words, words without which I'd be unhappy. I'm a poet, a lover of words, crazy about them. You gave us words like *gyöngy*, *tükör*, and *koporsó*. You're a *pearl*, you'll shine in the *mirror* of my soul until they close my *coffin*. Do you understand when I say *gűrű*, *gyűszű*, *búza*, *bor*? Of course you do, they're your words as well, and *betű*, the *letters* by which I make my living. You're my *ring*, my *thimble*, the *wheat* that feeds me, the *wine* that intoxicates me. I have your people to thank for our three hundred and thirty finest words.* I've been looking for ages for someone, a Turk, to whom I could express my unfailing gratitude for them and pay back at least

* There are indeed quite a lot of Turkic loanwords in Hungarian, but most of them, including all eight that Kornél lists here, are of ancient origin, and far fewer date from the years of the Ottoman occupation (1526–1699).

in part that loan of words, discharge that linguistic debt which has accumulated so very, very much interest for me.'

"I was burning thus in rapture when suddenly the train ran into a dark tunnel. Küçük sank warmly into my arms. And I, quickly and passionately, began to kiss her lips.

"If I remember correctly, I gave her exactly three hundred and thirty kisses."

VIII

In which the journalist Pál Mogyoróssy suddenly goes mad in the coffeehouse and is then confined to the lunatic asylum.

"PÁL, PÁL," THEY TRIED TO CALM HIM.

"Pál, be careful. Everybody's looking at you."

"Waiter!" Gergely, the long-established outstanding journalist, who knew of every secret scandal, clapped his hands, "Waiter! A large espresso! Pál, sit down and have an espresso."

"Pál, sit by me," urged Zima, who was on a German paper.

"Pál, take your hat off."

"Pál, Pál."

So said the journalists, all crime reporters, who, at about eleven on that delightful August evening, had dropped into the coffeehouse which was their favorite nocturnal haunt.

In the middle of the group was someone who was not immediately visible. He was wearing a transparent raincoat and a brand new straw hat, and was likewise a crime reporter—Pál Mogyoróssy.

They'd settled down at the table that had been theirs for a decade. All five journalists were watching Pál with ill-concealed curiosity.

Pál took off his new straw hat. They looked at the silky blond hair, parted on one side, which covered his tiny, girlishly delicate head. When he'd hung up his splendid raincoat on the iron hook, a slim, very pleasant, gentlemanly fellow stood before them, who despite his forty years seemed almost a boy; he wouldn't have looked out of place in short trousers. He was elegantly dressed: pea-green Burberry suit, zephyr shirt, and white silk bow tie on which gleamed a scarcely perceptible yellow stripe. It all looked brand new.

He tossed onto the marble tabletop a paper parcel, which contained another zephyr shirt and two pairs of buckskin gloves. That was all that he had with him.

He had arrived at the South station at half past one that afternoon on the express from the Balaton, and since then hadn't even been home.

He had been taking his regular month's summer holiday at Hévíz, where he rested, and combining the pleasant and the useful, attended to his health. He bathed in the warm, radioactive lake, on the dark mirror of which floated luxuriant, huge Indian lotuses, sprawled in the mud bath, slapping the greasy stuff on himself and especially on his left upper arm, in which he had recently had stabbing pains.

In a week his rheumatism had disappeared. With it went the headaches and the lassitude caused by keeping late hours. In his leisure he woke up. He wrote five "graphic" reports, which he sent by first-class registered mail to his editor. The weeks flew by with electric speed. But he could only hold out for three. At the start of the fourth he packed his bags, his patience exhausted, and abruptly went home.

As he got off the train and, at half past one, glimpsed the Vérmező and the Gellérthegy, an inexpressibly sweet joy filled his heart.* A true son of the capital, he adored Budapest. The afternoon sun was shining, all was promise and happiness. Carrying his little light suitcase he went up into the Castle district, looked down from the promenade on the bastion, had his photograph taken—he had thirty prints made, so that he could hand them round to his friends and possibly get one into a picture paper—had a bite to eat in a

---

* Vérmezô, "Field of Blood," is an open space of grass and trees adjoining the South station, to the west of Buda castle; it takes its name from its former use as a place of public executions. Gellérthegy is a hill on the Buda side of the Danube, commemorating the archbishop who led the conversion of the ancient Magyars to Christianity.

coffeehouse, and then just strolled; the pleasant, refreshing hours slipped by until suddenly it was twilight, the beery sunlight turned rusty brown, and he wandered down from the hill beneath the cool branches, crossed into Pest, and looked up his friends at police headquarters.

"Six more espressos!" called Gergely to the waiter, who was approaching their table. "Make that seven," he indicated with his fingers, "seven," because at that moment Esti came into the coffeehouse.

They had phoned Esti half an hour before, asking him to come at once. And had told him why.

The articles that he wrote were not about aggravated robbery, bank swindles, or arrests, but stories about himself and his fellow men, things which perhaps had not actually happened, only might—poems, novels—in short, he was a practitioner of the stricter profession of writing.

He'd never before even set foot in that coffeehouse where the crime reporters smoked little, nervous cigarettes, hanging on the phone at about two in the morning, shouting into the mouthpiece to the duty stenographers accounts of rapists, murderous servants, and monsters who had exterminated their families, spelling out their names and those of their victims, or where they dozed until first light on the worn plush sofa, yawning, cursing, and keeping watch on the endless series of the nation's dying, so that when an aging politician or an old and distinguished writer finally had the goodness to die, they could call the night editor to have the lead columns, set weeks beforehand, framed in black and oozing with fresh consternation and tears, inserted in the paper.

He looked around with unfamiliar eye.

Esti was a tall man of powerful physique, strong in appearance but inwardly soft and gentle. His watchful blue eyes constantly reflected alarm. His gestures were limp, hesitant. In his lack of confidence he was always inclined to let his opponent have his way. His skeptical spirit was ill at ease. His sensitivity used to be of such a degree that formerly he could have burst into tears at any moment over anything, at the sight of a battered matchbox or a tired face, but over the years he had schooled this inherent shakiness of nerve, hardening it to the point of harshness and consciously harnessing it to his art like a driving force. All he wanted was to see and feel. This was the one thing that kept him alive and to some extent bound him to the fellowship of men, together with the fact that he was afraid of the ultimate requirement of death. In his home, therefore, he barricaded himself behind medical books, washed his hands in disinfectant before meals, was appalled by and attracted to the sick and the sickly, the ruined and the special, and sought the opportunity of seeing deadly diseases, perhaps in the knowledge that if he could not overcome death, at least he could look into its entrance hall, and he was in general morbidly aroused by dreadful things, dramas small and great of annihilation, of destruction slow or swift, because he hoped that nonetheless he would be able to descry something of the moment when the unknown foot tramples us and being imperceptibly drifts into non-being.

Now too this was what had brought him there.

When he heard the news on the telephone at home he slammed the earpiece onto its hook, put out the light, left the manuscripts on which he'd been working in disorderly heaps on his desk, and rushed to the journalists' coffeehouse.

His friends were installed beneath a chandelier: its half-burnt-out bulbs drizzled onto the company an inhospitable reddish light. In the thick, pungent smoke he could scarcely make them out. Gergely extended his right hand, in which a light Media glowed in a cigar holder.

Esti shook hands with his colleagues—Gergely, who had phoned for him, Skultéty of the long, sallow face, Vitényi, whom he was meeting for the first time, Zima, the German journalist, and dear, bald Bolza, who as a joke greeted everyone with "Lo."

He left Pál Mogyoróssy for last.

Pál, it seemed, was pleased that Esti had come. He immediately stood up and waited while he shook hands with the others, and then would not release his hand for a long time, warming it in the velvety, glycerine-softened palm which was hotter than Esti's own. He leaned toward him slightly too, as if intending to embrace him, to lay his head on his chest.

"Esti," said he, in a quiet, hoarse voice, "it's really good that you're here as well. I need you tonight," he said with a look of gratitude. "I was waiting for you."

That took Esti by surprise.

The two of them had never been close friends, though they had known each other since childhood. Their work and spheres of interest had called them to different areas. In all their lives, therefore, they had scarcely exchanged more than thirty or forty sentences, and those too of disjointed words such as "Hello, what're you up to?" "Nothing much." "Good to see you, bye." Esti, however—only now was he aware of it—had a secret sympathy for him. It suddenly came to him that in the course of the twenty years that had gone by while their youth was fading, he had, despite himself, been observing him and had paid more attention to him than he'd thought.

Above all he had been intrigued by Pál's boyish ways, which had preserved his exterior from apparent aging. He also liked the fact that he was an inexorable listener, who sometimes went weeks without speaking to anybody and never talked about himself. His financial problems, which were almost considered a glory in that set, he never mentioned. His suit, his shirt, his brilliantly polished fingernails were always immaculate. He said nothing about his ancient noble family. In addition, he cultivated his shrewd professionalism to a high degree but with a certain diffidence, and though he treated people with fastidious politeness, he knew how to remain aloof. Consequently, Esti had involuntarily felt himself honored if Pál, with a barely perceptible lordly gesture, invited him to his table in a wine bar; he would sit down beside him and look at him for a couple of minutes but would soon go away, because Pál would not, on his account, forsake his obdurate, apparently enduring, silence. He would drink like a fish—wine, pálinka, whatever came his way. He used to "put away" a huge amount, and was almost constantly drunk. This, however, did not show on him. He merely became somewhat paler:

a waxen mask would spread over his face which served rather to intensify his grave appearance.

All this Esti recalled so quickly and suddenly that at that moment he could scarcely have analyzed it into its component parts. Then he saw two further images, two scenes clipped long ago from films, which had not faded in his excellent memory. Once—it must have been twenty years previously—Pál had been drinking champagne in the Orfeum, in the small hours, and in the light of the arc lamps had his hand on the cellulite-flabby thigh of a yellow-skirted danseuse on whose face was a beauty spot, larger than normal, which was obviously covering some infection or wound. The other image was less significant, but still germane. A couple of years before, at a quarter to five one November afternoon, Pál had been sitting idly in the plateglass window of the big coffeehouse in the Ring Road, alone, lost in thought, holding a bamboo-framed newspaper in his hand but not reading it, while Esti, passing on the sidewalk right before him, tapped on the window student-fashion. Pál did not hear this and kept staring into space, but all the way home Esti wondered what Pál could have been thinking of.

Now Pál gestured him to his table with that grand, scarcely perceptible movement. Esti sat down. He asked what was new. But no one replied.

From then on the five reporters paid attention only to Esti. Pál was no longer the focus of their interest, as he had been the moment before, because they knew what they knew. Now they would have liked to see the surprise, which they themselves had painfully and with creepy pleasure drunk to the dregs, the horror, and the laughter spring up again on Esti's face, as well-worn anecdotes acquire new charm if they are told to others.

Esti's face gave nothing away. He lowered his head toward the floor, whether in embarrassment or arrogance. He picked up a newspaper from the marble table to hide behind.

From behind this he took just one glance at Pál. He was more restless than usual, and his face was a bright pink. It looked as if he had had more to drink, and stronger stuff too, than was good for him.

The espressos were brought, all seven together.

They were hot, undrinkably so. At least a hundred and forty degrees. The vapor condensed on the inner rims of the glasses in fat drops.

The reporters pushed them aside. Zima complained to the waiter for serving such things to "the press."

Pál picked up his steaming glass, which must have burned the skin of his hand, and tossed it back to the dregs.

Esti dropped the paper. He leaned back in his seat, horrified, and stared at him. He was thinking—and the very thought was terrible—of that red-hot liquid scalding his esophagus and stomach wall.

Gergely observed the effect and glanced at Esti. Zima clasped his hands together. Vitényi and Bolza shook their heads. Skultéty, however, who had seen some strange things in his time and was almost immune to the stimulus to laugh, released a gale of laughter into his handkerchief.

Pál noticed the laughter and as a defense against it, joined in. He too laughed, abstractedly.

"Give me a cigarette," he said.

Five cigarettes flew toward him from the five reporters. Pál lit one. He inhaled the smoke and blew it out. The others lit up too, with the exception of Gergely, who only smoked cigars. Otherwise they all lit cigarettes. Esti too.

Pál didn't really want to perform to order. He merely said to Zima, sitting beside him:

"I'm going to have my teeth seen to as well."

"Why?"

"Why?" He shrugged. "Well, so that they'll be in order. You know, so that I can chew. I've just got to have two at the back here out. I've got a first-class dentist."

He opened his mouth wide in an unsightly gape, and showed Zima, whom he scarcely knew, the back of his mouth. The gold of bridges gleamed darkly among the various saliva-bright stumps. He cautiously poked a finger toward the two which the first-class dentist would painlessly extract.

This was still not amusing. Gergely tried to provoke him into doing one or other of his better numbers.

"Fortunately Pál's got a hearty appetite."

"Yes," said Pál, "I eat thirty apricots a day."

"How many?" asked Skultéty.

"Thirty."

"Couldn't you manage, say, forty?"

"Not that many. Thirty."

He launched into a wide-ranging account, for the benefit of Zima, of the importance of food, clothing, and health. And he mentioned that he had ordered four new suits.

"Let me have a cigarette," he said.

Again the five journalists tossed cigarettes, but they paid scarcely any attention to him. In the course of the evening they had heard on numerous occasions about the teeth, the thirty apricots, the four suits, and were beginning to find it all boring. Their quick nervous systems, attuned to immediately accepting and dismissing every horror, then registering "boredom," could find nothing to sustain them, and furthermore they were embarrassed in front of Esti for having dragged him out to no purpose and drawn a blank over Pál. And so Skultéty fished out of an inside pocket a galley proof, Pál Mogyoróssy's last article, sent from Hévíz a week before, and which the editor had naturally not used. Pál had signed it with his full noble style: *Pál Mogyoróssy of Upper and Lower Mogyoród.*

While Pál was giving an account of his love affairs and conquests, as if holding a rapid, cut-price clearance sale of his life, Esti took the opportunity to read the article at leisure under the table.

It was a report, a straightforward, beautifully written piece of reportage. It told of how that summer by the Balaton, an unpickable lock had been invented, all the villas fitted with it, and in consequence *within twenty-four hours the burglars of the region had moved to the northeastern part of the country.* At the last sentence Esti could not prevent a smile.

Gergely saw that smile and, together with Skultéty, went for Pál with inquisitorial ferocity.

"Now, Pál, what's this about the widows and orphans of journalists?"

"Oh yes," said Pál, turning his flushed but flaccid face. "Shall we tell him as well?" And he winked at his friends who had already heard it.

"Of course, that's what he's come for," and they gestured at Esti.

"Esti, you won't breathe a word to anybody, will you?" requested Pál in a confidential tone.

"No," replied Esti, "not a word."

"Well," said Pál, and looked round. "We're all millionaires. You are, and I am. How much do you want for one of your stories? Go on," he said, encouraging Esti with the sort of forgiving kindliness that would overlook any greed. "Five hundred? A thousand? You'll get it."

"Where from?" mumbled Esti, so as to get a word in edgeways.

"Where from?" repeated Pál scornfully. "Give your word of honor not to tell anyone. Otherwise the jig's up. Other people will be doing it."

"Go on, then," the journalists urged him.

"Give me a cigarette first. Look," he said, as he struck a match, "the whole thing's simple. Not to mention, noble in purpose. Journalists' widows ... journalists' orphans ..."

"We know, we know. Just get on with it."

"Anyway, tomorrow you and I and somebody—we'll decide who—will go into town by car and call on all the shopkeepers in Budapest and tell them my idea, which I'll let them have for nothing. For the widows of journalists ..."

"Never mind the widows," said the reporters.

"So we'll tell the shopkeepers to put in their windows signs saying, *Starting today, everything 25% off.* That's all. But you haven't got the point yet."

"No," replied Esti decisively.

"Wait a bit. What will be the result? The public will storm the shops like madmen, the shopkeepers will sell out and take millions, and we, from the vast profit, will contract for only 5 percent, say;

just five percent. That's not a lot. It's reasonable. They're sure to agree. Do you still not get it?"

"No."

"The point is," and now he was whispering, "the shopkeepers will go on selling their goods at the prices they did before. That's the clever bit. At the old prices. Now do you get it?"

"I see."

Esti was upset. He was amazed that "it" was nothing more, so routine and mechanical. The reporters too were disappointed in Pál: he'd flopped. It had been a silly business. Hats in hand, they proposed moving on.

Pál was happy to go with them because he too didn't think this coffeehouse was suitable, and he wanted another where there were fewer people and they could talk more confidentially. He took Esti's arm, and—forgetting his earlier plan—suddenly promised that he'd send a Lancia for him in the morning.

Outside the summer night had cooled somewhat. It was sweet and wonderful, perhaps even more enchanting than the afternoon, which had faded so quickly. Quiet and undulating, it moved this way and that, slowly, rhythmically, in its deep peace, throbbed with its great waves which, governed by the laws of the tides, rose and fell, driving each other away by turns, adumbrating beneath them vast plains and chasms. Sparks gleamed on the bridges, wreaths of fire on the Danube and Svábhegy,* which with its points of light resembled an ocean liner setting sail. Lights flared up. Street lamps blazed as at other times, but more sharply. The roadside acacias filtered the rays of the gas lamps and cast on the asphalt a black tracery of shadows, which seemed to quiver, expanding and contracting flexibly like the mirror of the water. Budapest had become a city submerged. Wagons floated along, rocking heavily in the swell of the night, trucks turned into motorboats, sweeping noisily through the splashing foam of darkness, and the many watercraft gave wings to Pál, who swam enraptured with arms outstretched, swept along at magical speed toward his goal. He delighted in that order, that sense

* A hill in Buda, to the north of Gellérthegy.

of purpose, that speed. And wherever the waves tossed him it was good, ecstatically exquisite, and blissful.

Esti spoke to Pál about going home, going to bed, and having a good rest. Pál seemed not even to hear him.

When they arrived outside police headquarters Esti took his leave. Pál seized his hand.

"Not going, are you?" he asked sorrowfully. "Are you leaving us?" and his eyes suddenly filled with tears. "Now? But you ought to have seen everything," and he would not release his hand.

So Pál pulled him inside.

Esti was touched. He lived so solitary a life in Budapest that he might well have been in Madagascar or Fiji, and had never experienced such warmth of friendship. He went with him.

The company burst into the building with a great to-do. Detectives, clerks, and officials all greeted Pál, whom they had known for twenty years. Many others came and joined the shifting group, in the middle of which stood Pál clinging to Esti's arm. Inquisitive strangers smiled sympathetically as they addressed questions to him and followed him beneath the echoing vaults. Pál was not surprised at this. He found it natural that everyone "was together" on that night, which was not like the rest, and that others too were aware of the pleasing change thanks to which epoch-making new plans flashed with unimpeded lightness in his brain. While Gergely and Skultéty were discussing with the office on separate telephones at the same time what ought to be done with the poor fellow, Esti turned his attention to something else. He observed the idyll of the night, the policemen's rooms bathed in green light, the hard plank beds on which policemen slept, swords at their sides, on rough mattresses, men stabbed in brawls awaiting medical reports, the healthy, smart, mustached constables who, untainted among so much corruption, watched at an iron rail over vagrants picked up by police patrols, the occasional headscarved nursemaid, street girls of almost aristocratic appearance, and youthful pimps, and he thought of how Pál's finest years had slipped by in this treasury of pain, this house of power and grief.

They were walking on the Ring Road again. Pál and Esti were in front. Pál no longer needed to take Esti's hand or arm. He felt safe in releasing it. Esti went without it being held. He was drawn by pity. Behind their backs the five journalists were arguing loudly. Bolza, kindly and bald, was of the opinion that Pál should be put into a cab straightaway and taken home to his family. Gergely objected, saying that he could injure someone—he was a public menace. Skultéty agreed. Pál, on the other hand, obstinately insisted that he had to meet a woman at the West station at half past one, and that at half past two he had to address at least five hundred colleagues in the Erdélyi wine bar concerning his plan for the widows and orphans of journalists and the 25 percent and 5 percent with the Budapest shopkeepers. In any case, the opinion that he should be "put away" that very night brooked no contradiction.

Meanwhile they went into another coffeehouse. There they drank sweet white wine. Ten minutes later they were in another, drinking *császárkörte** liqueurs. Another ten minutes and they were in a third, drinking red wine. Everywhere they smoked cigarettes. Everywhere they were known to the waiters, those faithful proletarian friends of the press, who migrate from one coffeehouse to another as journalists do from paper to paper. Everywhere they were objects of uncommon attention. Pál was still not content anywhere, none of these places was any good, he had to keep going on and on, driven by some religious passion from the fourth coffeehouse to the fifth. The coffeehouse is the journalist's place of worship.

At this point Gergely and Skultéty, after a lengthy professional consultation, decided to telephone the psychiatric department of St Miklós hospital. A Dr. Wirth replied that they should bring the patient in, he was on duty and at their disposal. At the cashier stand in the coffeehouse they discussed for some time the means of doing this, because as crime reporters they wanted everything to go smoothly and tastefully.

They were in that big coffeehouse where Esti had once caught sight of Pál, deeply immersed in himself, at a quarter to five on a No-

---

* A type of pear, "emperor pear."

vember afternoon. He and Pál now went and sat at that same table. On this occasion, however, the plateglass window had been lowered, and the night was flooding into the quiet, deserted coffeehouse as if melting into one with it. The two of them leaned their elbows on the brass rail. For a while the proprietor stood by their table, listening with furrowed brow to the poor *szerkesztô úr*,* and when he was called away bowed to them more deeply than usual, in a clear expression of sympathy. Kindly, bald Bolza prepared to leave. He had three daughters and so worked day and night and was always up early. He raised his bowler hat to Pál without a word. On this occasion he did not say "see you soon."

Vitényi and Zima went with him.

Pál dismissed them scornfully. As Gergely and Skultéty were still plotting at the cashier stand, he and Esti were left alone.

"I'm going to write," said Pál.

"Good."

"Novels, short stories," he went on, and with a sort of desperate movement leaned toward Esti's face. "I'm leaving the paper. I'm through with being a reporter. It's beneath me."

He looked out into the night. A cab was rumbling along the wooden roadway.

"The wheels of the cab are 'roaring,'" said Pál. "Roaring." He emphasized the word. "What a fine language our Hungarian is. That's the way to write. They're not 'going,' they're 'roaring.'"

"Roaring," repeated Esti, and he, who weighed every word so many times, became bored with it, and brought it up again, could not deny that he too liked the word.

"But what am I to write?" Pál burst out in a faltering, plaintive voice.

"Simply anything. Whatever interests you. Whatever comes into your head."

"Tell me, for example, is this all right? The woman comes up to my apartment. Are you listening?"

* "Mr. Editor," an honorific for a "gentleman of the press."

"Yes," said Esti, who had by that time a splitting headache.

"You know, she's got brown hair, but not black, or chestnut," Pál pondered, "her hair's a sort of chocolate color. Her eyes are like those little blue flowers, what are they called?"

"Violets?"

"No, no," Pál shook his head.

"Forget-me-nots?"

"That's right. Forget-me-nots. And she's like fire," he went on so wildly that he was alarming. "Her body's warm, but I don't like it. I sprinkle her thighs, her back, with ice-cold eau de cologne until she's quite cool. And I put a garland of those little blue flowers on her head. She's like a dead bride in her coffin. Then she goes away." He thought for a moment. "How am I to put it? What shall I say when she goes?"

"What people usually say: 'Good-bye.'"

"No," Pál did not like that, and an idea crossed his mind, "I'll say to her: 'Sincere tenderness of heart.' You can seduce any woman with that. She'll have a feeling that she can't resist. Do you hear? Like this: 'Sincere tenderness of heart,'" he enunciated with a peculiar, crafty smile, staring at Esti, and his eyes were like fire. "Nod if you feel it as well. Do you feel it now?"

Esti could not feel what that woman was supposed to, but he could imagine what Pál must be feeling, and he nodded.

It was a relief for him when Gergely and Skultéty linked arms with Pál and took him into the street. Pál would not hear of a cab. He protested to his journalist friends and let go of their arms time and again. He looked for Esti, speaking across to him as Gergely and Skultéty led him along.

"Esti, I'm going to learn Italian. This very night I'm going to learn Italian, Esti."

At the West station he had fortunately forgotten about the chocolate-haired woman. Not, however, about the Erdélyi wine bar.

There disappointment awaited him. He was expecting a seething crowd, such as he had seen at extraordinary general meetings of journalists, when a chairman was dismissed in an explosive atmosphere, but during that lull in the evening's entertainment, between two and three in the morning, when the diners had gone and the dawn revelers had not yet appeared, the place was deserted, and just a couple of waiters were sauntering about putting knives and forks on the freshly laid tables. The colleagues had not come. No one had come. Pál looked around in dismay. He blinked. Such wretched people didn't deserve to have anything done for them.

"Hungary," he sighed. "Journalists' widows, their poor little orphans," and he ushered his friends to a table.

He ordered *korhelyleves*. The others wanted nothing more to eat or drink.

Pál looked at his soup, did not taste it, but stirred it for a long time before tipping into it the entire contents of the salt cellar, the paprika pot, and the jar of toothpicks. He began to eat. The toothpicks crunched between his teeth.

All three of his companions jumped up.

"This is terrible," Skultéty was appalled, "terrible." He looked at himself in a mirror; he had gone green, and a twitching, bitter grin trickled from his face like vinegar.

"Terrible."

"Let's do something," said Esti. "This is awful."

Pál spat the toothpicks back out into his bowl. He could not chew them.

Gergely, who was fitting a fresh light Media into his cigar holder, and Skultéty made for the telephone booth which was by the table. They did not telephone, merely lamented: Poor fellow, poor fellow.

A couple of moments later Gergely burst out of the telephone booth, his hair in disorder. He rushed straight over to Pál.

"The swine!" he shouted, beside himself with rage. "The swine!"

Pál went on sitting there, oafishly unmoved.

"Hey, Pál," said Gergely, shaking his arm as if to wake him, "mental patients are being beaten up."

"Where?" said Pál from the depths of his torpor, and the muscles of his face twitched.

"At St. Miklós, of course. They've just been on the phone. Two mental patients have been beaten up in the night."

"It's a scandal!" exclaimed Skultéty. "A national scandal!"

"It's a scoop," said Pál. "Pay the bill," and as a soldier who hears a word of command in his sleep springs to his feet, he remembered his journalistic duty, his role as a guardian of enlightenment, at the command of humanity. "Don't put the paper to bed yet," he ordered. "I'll want ten columns. And give me another cigarette."

Esti felt that the time was ripe for him to be off. He couldn't stand any more. He hated tricks. He was even disgusted at himself. He made his way carefully to the far side of the sidewalk and from there watched to see what would happen.

First Gergely emerged from the Erdélyi wine bar, and like the experienced, born organizer of every dreadful deed, whistled for a cab. He promised the cabby a good tip and whispered something in his ear. Next came Skultéty and behind him Pál, bareheaded. He was putting his brand-new straw hat on his silky blond hair; the vegetable fibers in it, once alive, were now just as faded, just as dead, as the skull that it covered. He got into the cab first, followed by Gergely and Skultéty. Off they went.

Esti strolled homewards along Andrássy út. He had smoked thirty cigarettes that night and drunk nine espressos, and he was suffering from nicotine and caffeine poisoning. He was panting. He stopped again and again to lean on the walls of houses, felt his pulse at the radial bone in his right arm and at his neck. His weak heart was throbbing. He felt sick. He didn't even care how he had come to this. Together with the nasty experience he had brought away a kind of warmth, an animal warmth and affection, of which it was pleasant to think—a man's last love. He felt richer for having been selflessly loved by mistake for a couple of hours.

He was no gloomier than at other times. There were still stars in the sky. A light breeze blew on the bridge, and in its deep bed the Danube rolled on irrevocably to the beat of continuity and passing. When he opened the door of his study, where through years of practice he could always be in readiness, he sat down mechanically at his desk, fished out a couple of sheets from the untidy heap of paper, and read them, so as to find the voice necessary to go on and put on paper the chapter of the novel which he had already drafted in his head. What he had seen and heard that night he put aside to mature, to be forgotten somewhat and then retrieved from his soul one day, when the time was right.

The cab screeched through the night.

The driver drove well in excess of the permitted speed, flat out, in hopes of a tip. At the rear of the car the little mauve lamp burned with an unnatural chemical light. In front the headlights cast a carpet of glittering rays on the dark surface of the road—the rubber tires were never to catch up with it. This carpet of rays appeared to change, sometimes seeming new at every moment, but sometimes it stood still, and it seemed that it was the old one and the same that the cab was carrying along and, as it never wore out, spreading it again and again before itself with lightning speed in its immaculate brightness.

Pál sat on the back seat, watching this play of light and entertained by it. The sensation that he was gently rising and falling at sea came again, but this time much more strongly. He kept leaning out to look at his face in the mirror of the water, but the waves were now too high and he could see nothing.

Gergely sat beside him. Skultéty was facing them on the little folding seat. They were thinking of how the two of them would deal with him. Pál, however, was quiet. He gave no more thought to the assurances by which he had been turned against the cruel psychiatrists. He licked his thin lips, fragrant with alcohol, and did not speak.

Thus he quite faded into the background on that journey. In the gloom from time to time three heads moved: his own, Gergely's, and Skultéty's.

They did not speak either. Gergely yawned.

The car lurched on the uneven ground, gave a mighty blast on the horn, and stopped outside the gate of St. Miklós Hospital.

There was no need to ring, the porter opened the gate at the sound of the horn.

Gergely got out, Skultéty next. Finally Pál.

He went over to the porter.

"Who's on duty?" he asked officiously.

"Dr. Wirth."

Pál stood erect. The wind blew at the unfastened wings of his splendid raincoat.

When the others had joined him he said:

"Give me a cigarette."

The flame of the lighter lit up his face. Now it was as calm and serious as ever in the past.

"What's the time?" he asked.

"Quarter to three."

"Right, let's go," said he, and set off with resolute steps, with that air of being at home that journalists have in unfamiliar places.

Gergely and Skultéty followed a yard behind him.

On the first floor a lock creaked. A gray door opened on a long, narrow corridor lit by two dim electric lamps. At the door Pál stubbed out his cigarette and glanced back at his friends, but they were hanging back. Gergely was bending down as if tying a shoelace that had come undone. So he went inside by himself.

The iron door clanged to behind him and the attendant turned the key.

Gergely and Skultéty paused reflectively outside the door for a few seconds. Then they went back down the stairs and got into the cab, which had waited for them.

They both had a sense of death, the common fate of us all, which, in whatever form it comes, is equally final and sooner or later gets the better of us. Gergely, who had witnessed many a shooting and hanging, coughed and muttered something that sounded like a curse. Skultéty had been laughing out loud and braying so much all evening that his ribs ached. They did not speak. Gergely sat on the padded seat, Skultéty on the folding seat. The place where Pál had sat remained vacant. There was an air of mourning in the car.

Pál Mogyoróssy, staff reporter on the *Közlöny*, strode forth down the corridor, which was so long, so very long, that it seemed scarcely to end. A long way off, some hundred yards away, beneath the second electric light, a quite wretched little figure was waiting for him, puny, anemic, much smaller and weaker than Pál. Its ears were slightly projecting. A stethoscope peeped from its white coat. This was Dr. Wirth.

When Pál reached the doctor he introduced himself, as usual on such occasions, both personally and on behalf of his paper, modestly, with dignity, as the representative of the public at large.

"I've come for information," said Pál. "We've been told, my dear doctor ..." and he dried up.

Wirth came to his aid:

"What?"

"That," said Pál, "two mental patients have been beaten up here tonight."

"Here?" said Wirth, glancing at the floor. "No, indeed. Patients aren't beaten up here. And in any case, we have no mental patients, only sufferers from nervous disorders, who are rather tired and are resting."

"But we have definite information, doctor."

"No, *szerkestő úr*,* it'll be a mistake," and he patted Pál on the shoulder with an almost impudent smile.

The doctor took Pál by the arm, and they walked for a long time up and down the long, long corridor. On both sides were the wards, large open rooms lit by blue electric lamps like the taillight of the car. The patients, those who could, were sleeping, toying in their dreams with the trivia of their lives, putting them together and taking them apart, like other people. Many, however, could not sleep. One fat, unshaven man, who was in the third phase of encephalomalacia, was sitting up in bed, his head hanging before him, pressing his blue striped hospital gown to his face.

Pál inquired about their diagnoses and prospects of treatment, and Wirth chatted about politics and the police, about certain journalists of their mutual acquaintance too, and spoke with almost paternal good humor of syphilis. It was a friendly exchange of views, uninhibited and relaxed. Then without any transition the doctor

---

* As before. Pál addresses the doctor as *főorvos*, "principal doctor," in similar style.

asked for his pocket knife, which Pál actually handed over, and the doctor, without so much as thanking him for it, slipped it into the pocket of his white coat beside his stethoscope. He had by that time made a preliminary diagnosis. Detailed examination he postponed to the morning; it was getting late.

Pál was still talking, chattering of this and that. Suddenly he stopped. It seemed to him that something was not quite right. A vague and superficial sense of uncertainty had come over him. It was just the sort of misgiving that comes to us all when we have been in the street for hours and feel uncomfortable because one strap of our suspenders, which normally press evenly on our collarbones, has slipped down. He had remembered Gergely and Skultéty.

By then, however, Wirth had led Pál into a separate little room, the quietness and elegance of which he could not praise, as it was disagreeable, repugnant, and shabby, furnished with only a table covered by waxed cloth, a chair, a bed, a nightstand, and a radiator.

The doctor sat down on the bed. He appealed to Pál to undress and get some sleep, and next day he would be able to go for a walk in the lovely garden.

Pál wanted to protest in the name of the press against this infringement of his personal liberty, but couldn't hear his own voice. He could only hear his fury. His press cards. He, who had always been inside the cordon, at every suicide, every demonstration, every burial, inside the cordon. It was he, he.

Wirth disappeared. Pál ran after him into the corridor, but he was not there either. He could only see an attendant, not the one who had opened the door but another, whom he did not recognize.

He went back into the room. He looked through the barred window into the garden; on the weed-ridden lawn, surrounded by sumac trees, flowers of hemlock swayed, white, like scraps of writing paper. The electric light was still on, but even without it he could see. The sun, precise timepiece of the universe, in its relentless course was making its presence known below the horizon and whitening the sky. Dawn was breaking.

Pál leaned on his elbows on the shoddy waxed cloth of the table.

And he thought of Esti, Esti, who after correcting his dawn work, had pressed the switch on his electric lamp and was now standing in his bedroom in just his shirt, undressing, but could not sleep because he too was thinking of Pál.

Pál pondered what he was to do. For the present, however, nothing came to mind.

He just sat and wept.

IX

*In which he chats in Bulgarian with the Bulgarian train guard
and experiences the sweet dismay of the linguistic chaos of Babel.*

"THERE'S SOMETHING I MUST TELL YOU ALL," SAID KORNÉL
Esti. "A little while ago someone said at a party that he would never
travel to a country where he couldn't speak the language. I said I saw
his point. The main thing that interests me when I travel is people.
Much more than objects in museums. If I can only hear what they
say but not understand it, I feel as if I'm deaf or watching a silent film
without music or subtitles. It's irritating and boring.

"After I'd said all that, it occurred to me that the opposite was just
as valid, as is so often the case. It's marvelous fun going around in
a foreign country if voices are merely sounds which leave us cold
and we stare blankly at everyone that speaks to us. What splendid
isolation, my friends, what independence, what lack of responsibility. All of a sudden we feel like infants that need to be looked after.
We start to display an inexplicable trust in adults wiser than ourselves. We let them speak and act on our behalf. Then we accept everything, unseen and unheard.

'I've seldom had such an experience—as you know, I speak ten
languages—in fact, it's only come my way once, when I was en route
for Turkey. I was passing through Bulgaria. I spent a total of twenty-
four hours in the country, and that was all on the train. Something
happened to me there that it would be a shame to keep quiet about.

After all, I can die at any time, as I shall one day—a tiny vein in my heart or my brain will burst—and no one else, I'm sure, will ever have a similar experience.

"So, it was at night. After midnight. The train was racing along through hills and villages that I didn't know. It must have been nearly half past one. I couldn't sleep. I went out into the corridor for a breath of air. I was soon bored. Black shapes were all that could be seen of the beauties of the countryside. It was quite an event if a point of light appeared. All the passengers around me were sleeping the sleep of the just. Not a soul was stirring in the carriages.

"I was on the point of going back to my compartment when the guard appeared, lamp in hand. He was a Bulgarian, a stocky man with a black mustache, and he'd evidently finished his rounds. He'd seen my ticket some time previously, so he didn't want anything from me. But by way of greeting, in friendly fashion, he shone his lamp and his eyes on me. Then he stopped beside me. Clearly, he was bored too.

"I've no idea why or how, but I decided there and then, come what may, to have a conversation with him, and at length, meaningfully. I asked him in Bulgarian whether he smoked. That was all the Bulgarian I knew—and I'd picked that up on the train, from a sign. Apart from that I knew five or six words, the sort that stick to you when you're traveling whether you like it or not, such as *yes, no,* and the like. But I swear to you, I didn't know any more.

"The guard raised his hand to the peak of his hat. I flicked open my cigarette case and offered it to him. He took a gold-tipped cigarette with profound respect. He produced matches, lit one, and mumbled something to the effect of 'here you are' in his totally unfamiliar language. At that I held out to him the blue flame of my lighter and mouthed in imitation that word which I had heard for the first time in my life.

"The two of us smoked, letting the smoke out through our nostrils. It was a definitely reassuring start. Even today I swell with pride to think of it, because it still flatters my self-esteem that I set that scene up with such understanding of people, that I showed such psychological insight in planting that tiny seed—which, as it transpired, branched out into a tree so great that beneath it I threw off the fatigue of my travels and at dawn was able to retire all the richer for some rare experiences.

"You must recognize that from the very first moment my performance was confident and faultless. I had to convince the guard that I was a native Bulgarian, and that I knew Bulgarian at least as well as a lecturer in literature at Sofia University. Therefore I behaved a little stiffly and pompously. Principally, I didn't chatter. Actually, that wasn't entirely my fault, but that makes no difference. It's characteristic of foreigners always to try and speak the language of the country in which they're traveling, they're too enthusiastic about it, and in no time at all it emerges that they're foreigners. Natives, on the other hand, those born there, will just nod and make themselves understood by signs. Words have to be dragged out of them. Even then, lethargically, they toss out weary words from the treasures of their mother tongue that lie dormant within them, words that have lost their shine with use. Generally they shy away from elegant turns of phrase and succinct literary constructions. As far as possible they don't speak, which is wise, because if they had to give several hour-long lectures from a rostrum or write a hefty tome, both their students and their critics would be quick to point out—and not entirely without foundation—that they hadn't even the first idea of their own native language.

"And so the guard and I smoked on in that intimate silence from which great friendships, true understandings, and lifelong soul mates can arise. I was grave and courteous. From time to time I would crease my forehead, then—for variety—adopt a lighter appearance and glance at him quite attentively. Conversation, however, the entrancing possibility of which was now wafting in the air just above our heads, required me to start off somehow. I yawned and sighed, and then I put a hand on his shoulder and raised my eyebrows so that they formed huge question marks, tilted my head back and murmured 'Well?' The guard smiled; he must have discovered in this amicable form of interest some memory of childhood, or the behavior of a friend who inquired of him in this way, 'How are things?' He began to speak. He uttered four or five sentences. Then he fell silent and waited.

"I too waited. I had good reason to. I was wondering what answer I should make. After a brief uncertainty I decided. I said 'Yes.'

"Experience has taught me that much. Whenever I'm not paying attention to the conversation or don't understand something, I always say 'Yes.' This has never yet brought me any trouble. Not even when I've appeared to be approving something that I should have deplored. On occasion I can make people think that I'm speaking ironically. A *Yes* is very frequently a *No*.

"That my reasoning was not unfounded was demonstrated brilliantly by the consequences. The guard became much more communicative. Unfortunately, he then fell silent once more and waited. This time I showed interest with a 'Yes?' in an interrogative tone, somewhat redolent of incomprehension and uncertainty. That—if I may so express myself—opened the floodgates. The guard opened up and spoke, spoke for about a quarter of an hour, pleasantly and clearly, on a variety of topics, during which time I didn't have to consider what reply to make.

"This was when I scored my first decisive success. From the way the words poured from his mouth, the way he chattered and jabbered on, it became clear that even in his dreams he would never imagine I was a foreigner. This belief, firm though it seemed, I had to support. If, for the time being, I evaded the obligation to respond, extremely painful for me as it was, and if I could constantly stuff gold-tipped cigarettes between my lips as if to indicate that my mouth was 'occupied' and not really capable of speaking, I nevertheless could not entirely neglect my self-sacrificing entertainer and from time to time had to give thought to fueling the conversation.

"How did I manage that? Not with words. I put on an act, like an actor—a first-class actor—with all my might. My face, my hands, my ears, even my toes moved as required. But I had to beware of exaggeration. I mimed attentiveness, not that forced attentiveness which is suspect in advance, but that sort which is now lax and abstracted, now catches fire and flares up. I thought of something else as well. Sometimes I indicated by a gesture that I hadn't understood what he'd said. You will naturally think that would be the easiest of things. Well, you're wrong. That, my friends, was the hardest part. Just as I had not understood a single word of his ceaseless flow, I had to take care not to let my admission be too sincere and convincing. Nor did I miss my mark. The guard simply repeated his last sentence, and I nodded as if to say 'Ah yes, that's quite different.'

"After that there was no need for me to feed the blazing fire of the conversation with such kindling-wood of suggestion. Even without that it flared up like a bonfire. The guard talked and talked. What about? I would have liked to know myself. Perhaps about transport regulations, perhaps about his family and children, perhaps about growing beets. God alone knows what he was talking about. From the rhythm of his sentences I became aware that, in any case, he was telling a good-humored, cheerful, long-winded, and coherent tale which rolled slowly and with dignity on its broad, epic course down to the denouement. He wasn't in the slightest hurry. Nor was I. I let it deviate, wander off the point, and like a stream, burble, twist and turn, and divide itself into the eroded, comfortable bed of narrative. He smiled a lot. This tale must have been humorous, no doubt about it, and there were elements that were plainly risqué, perhaps even daring and spicy. He winked at me craftily, as at an accomplice, and laughed. And I laughed with him. But not every time. I was often not quite of the same opinion. I didn't want to overindulge him. I displayed only moderate appreciation of the truly heartfelt, tasteful, delightful humor with which he embellished his performance.

"It was almost three in the morning—we'd been chatting for an hour and a half—and the train began to slow down. We were approaching a station. The guard took his lamp and excused himself for having to get off, but he assured me that he'd be right back and would tell me the end, the punch line of that ridiculous piece of stupidity, because that was the best bit.

"I leaned out the window. I bathed my buzzing head in the fresh air. The peonies of daybreak were opening on the ashen sky. Before me lay a cream-scented little village. At the station a peasant and a couple of women in headscarves were waiting. The guard spoke to them in Bulgarian, as he had done to me, but with more effect, because the travelers understood him at once and made for the third-class coaches at the end.

"A few minutes later the guard was back at my side—the smile had not yet cooled on his lips—and was chuckling as he continued. Shortly, out came the punch line that he had promised. He roared with laughter. He laughed so much that his belly shook. Goodness, what a man, he was a terrific character. He was still shaking with laughter as he reached into his coat pocket and took out a thin notebook, held together by an elastic band, and from that a creased, soiled letter which probably played a vital role in the story—it might have been the decisive element—and put it into my hand for me to read and comment on. Good Lord, what was I to say? I could see penciled, smudged Cyrillic letters, which—alas—I couldn't read. I devoted myself to attentive perusal of the letter. Meanwhile he stood a little apart and watched to see the effect. 'Yes,' I murmured, 'yes, yes,' now statement, now denial, now question. From time to time I shook my head as if to say 'typical' or 'never heard the like' or 'such is life.' That can be used for anything. No situation has yet occurred in life for which 'such is life' isn't appropriate. If somebody dies, even then we just say 'such is life.' I tapped the letter, I sniffed it—it had a slight odor of mold—and as there was nothing else that I could do, I gave it back to him.

"There were all sorts of other things in his notebook. He took out a photograph which—to my considerable surprise—was of a dog. I pursed my lips as I looked at it, like a keen dog fancier. I noticed, however, that the guard didn't approve of that. I got the feeling that he was simply angry with that dog, so I too became serious and tut-tutted at it. My astonishment reached its peak, however, when he took from the canvas holder of the notebook a mysterious object wrapped in tissue paper and asked me to unwrap it myself. I did so. All there was inside were two large green buttons, two bone buttons like those from a man's coat. I shook them together playfully, as if I were altogether a particular lover of buttons, but the guard then snatched them out of my hand and quickly, so that I should never so much as see them again, crammed them into his notebook. Then he took a couple of paces and leaned against the side of the carriage.

"I didn't understand what was happening. I moved quickly to his side. I saw something that made my blood run cold. His eyes were filled with tears. That big, fat man was weeping. At first he wept in manly fashion, concealing his tears, but then he wept so much that his mouth twitched and his shoulders heaved.

"To be perfectly frank I was completely taken aback by the profound, insoluble chaos of life. What was all this? How were all those words connected to laughter and weeping? What had one thing to do with another—the letter with the photograph of the dog, the photograph with the two green bone buttons, and all of them with the guard? Was it madness, or precisely the opposite, the healthy, human bursting-out of feeling? And had the whole business any meaning, in Bulgarian or anything else? Despair was all around me.

"I took a firm grip on the guard's shoulders to instill some spirit into him, and I shouted into his ear three times, in Bulgarian, 'No, no, no.' Choking in his tears, he stammered another monosyllable which could have meant, 'Thank you for being so kind,' but also, perhaps, 'You revolting phony, you cheating swine.'

"Slowly he recovered himself. His gasps became quieter. He wiped his wet face with his handkerchief. He spoke. Now, however, his voice was quite different. He addressed short, sharp questions to me. Such as, I imagine, 'If you said "yes" in the first place, why did you say "no" straight afterwards? Why did you correct what you'd approved? Let's have an end to this dubious game. Make your choice: yes or no?' He rapped out questions like a machine gun, faster and faster, more and more determinedly, poking me in the chest. There was no way that I could evade them.

"It seemed as if I was caught and that my luck had deserted me. But my superiority came to my rescue. I stood up straight and looked the guard up and down with cutting frigidity, and like one that considered it beneath his dignity to reply, turned on my heel and strode into my compartment.

"There I laid my head on my pillow. I went to sleep with the speed of a man dropping dead from a heart attack. I woke about noon to blazing sunshine. Somebody tapped at the window of my compartment. The guard came in. He advised me that I was to get off at the next station. But he didn't move. He just stood there faithfully at my side like a dog. Once more he spoke—quietly, continuously, unstoppably. Perhaps he was offering an apology, perhaps accusing me over the painful nocturnal scene, I don't know, but his face showed profound distress, heartbreak. I behaved coolly. I just let him pick up my bags and take them out into the corridor.

"At the last moment, however, I took pity on him. When he had given my bags to the porter and I was getting down, I glanced at him wordlessly as if to say 'What you did wasn't nice, but to err is human, and this once I forgive you.' And I said in Bulgarian only, 'Yes.'

"That word had a magical effect. The guard softened, cheered up, became his old self. A smile of gratitude stole onto his face. He saluted me, standing stiffly at attention. He remained there at the window, rigid with happiness, until the train moved off and he vanished forever from my sight."

X

In which Zsuzsika, daughter of a wealthy Bácska* peasant,
jumps into the well and gets married.

KORNÉL ESTI ARRIVED HOME FROM PORTUGAL. HE HAD BEEN
over to the Iberian peninsula just for a month, to have a rest. This
rest had consisted of speaking exclusively to the natives during that
time, and in Portuguese, the "language of flowers."

It was late at night when he appeared at my door, dusty and
travel-stained, on his way from the station. The Lisbon breeze was
still on his raincoat, the gravel of the Tagus on his shoes.

He dragged me out to a bar in Buda. I thought that he was going
to give me a lengthy account of his experiences on the journey, but
he wasn't disposed to talk about them. The conversation turned to
affairs in Hungary, our native town, our student years, people and
events of prewar days.

That night I came to know a new side of him. I admit that previously I had often thought of him as just a kind of dyspeptic international globetrotter, a half-baked literary freak. Now I saw that he
was a man from head to foot, and from my part of the world. How
typical of the Bácska was his every breath, his still irresponsible
tomfoolery, and his breezy boastfulness. The Bácska is the Gascony

---

* Kosztolányi's native area, a region of the Alföld southwest of Szeged, mostly now
in Serbia.

131

of Hungary. There is a provincial quality in all eccentric behavior.

He guzzled wine. He began with Badacsony, moved on to Csopak, then turned to a heavy, perfumed golden nectar which had reached the age of thirty on the racks of the cellars of the priests of Arács.* He stayed with that.

Toward dawn, when empty bottles of *kéknyelű*† and sundry other varieties were ranged in serried ranks on our table and we still had things to talk about, because by that time we had killed off most of our living friends and resurrected those who had died, he asked me:

"Now, do you remember little Zsuzsa? You know, Zsuzsa Szücs. The daughter of that peasant, that rich peasant. He used to live by the fire station, in a tumbledown cottage like any other peasant. But he had pots of money.

"When I was a boy I heard that he kept gold in the drawers of his chest and that he stuffed his mattresses with thousand-korona notes. How much of that was true I don't know, but it was a fact that he was made of money. He lived like a typical cottager. He wore a blue *guba*, a *pörge* hat, and boots.‡ Smoked foul tobacco in a clay pipe, lit it with matches that made a terrible smell. In winter he would sit dozing on the bench of the *banyakemence*, wrapped in his *suba*, like a bear sleeping its winter sleep.§ Then when spring came he would settle down outside the house, on the wooden bench, and sit there until autumn. He didn't say a word to anybody. Just sat in silence. Sat there as if he were sitting on his money.

"The old man was dreadfully mean. For all he cared, the whole world could rot. True, he spent money on his daughter. But she was

---

* Badacsony and Csopak are celebrated white-wine regions on the north shore of Lake Balaton, as is (Balaton) Arács too. This latter is now joined to Balatonfüred and the monastery is no more.

† *Kéknyelű*, "blue-stemmed," is a traditional Hungarian grape variety, grown mostly in Badacsony.

‡ The *guba* is a cloaklike garment, often of rough woollen cloth; the *pörge*, "upturned," hat is that traditionally worn by Hungarian shepherds, low-crowned with an upturned brim, somewhat similar to a bowler.

§ *Banyakemence* is a big, rick-shaped earthenware stove found in peasant houses. *Suba* is a sheepskin coat, worn with the fleece inside.

his only child. Apart from her he had nobody. He'd buried his wife a long time before.

"Young Zsuzsa went to the convent school, learned French, and played the piano. She wore a hat, like all our girls. She was pretty and unhappy. There was no way that she could find her place in our accursed society, which had so much artifice and so many unfathomable rules and regulations that no schooling or etiquette could list them or even adequately cover the subject. If anyone spoke to her she blushed to the ears, and if anyone offered his hand she turned pale and withdrew hers in alarm. She would smile when she should have been solemn, and vice versa. But what did that matter? Despite it all, she was gorgeous.

"You say you only saw her once or twice? She didn't really go anywhere. She lived with her silent father and became as silent as him. For the most part she hid indoors. If she went into town she avoided people. She was permanently embarrassed. For instance, not for all the tea in China could you have got her to go into a *cukrászda* and eat a *szerecsenfánk.*

"For a long time she didn't marry. Yet she had so many suitors that she could scarcely manage to turn them down. The problem was that she didn't know where she belonged. She looked down on peasant boys and they didn't dare to approach her, while in the young men of the so-called gentry she saw gold diggers and in their company she was ill at ease—overcome by respectfulness and disdain together, like a sort of stage fright. Actually, do you know what it was? It was the historic stage fright of her emergent social class, which had not previously played a leading role on the stage of history, whose name wasn't even in the program, because it had always approved or disapproved only in the background, and always anonymously.

"On Sundays she used to go to the *szagosmise*† at half past eleven in the ancient Franciscan church. I saw her there several times. Oh, she

---

* "Saracen doughnut," a doughnut coated with chocolate.
† "Perfumed Mass," that attended by society ladies.

was such a lovely creature! In summer she wore a white dress with a red leather belt and carried a red silk parasol through which the burning Alföld sun would filter, tinting her pale little face. She was like a lily under a Bengal light, like a posy of wild flowers, white and red, cowbane and poppies, white and red all together. Like a young noblewoman going incognito or a young duchess in disguise as a peasant. I wonder, was I in love with her too?

"Anyway, one Sunday, when the gilded youth of the town were standing in a semicircle outside the church, dangling their slender canes and brand new kid gloves, polishing their monocles in lordly fashion, and observing the ladies as they emerged, Pista Boros caught sight of her and fell fatally in love. He rushed after her and spoke to her. Zsuzsa screwed up her face in horror. But Pista went on talking. At that, Zsuzsa took her hands from her ears, began to pay attention, looked at him, and smiled—when she actually should have, for once.

"So how did Pista score that success which none of the rest of us had been able to claim? Well, you see, he was a wonderful fellow, an absolute marvel. First of all he was a handsome man, with curly hair and an aquiline nose. He dressed like Imre Lubloy, the famous actor, when he was playing a filthy rich count. Even in summer he wore spats. And then he had such an impressive natural air of culture, the kind that can't be acquired, you have to be born with it.

"He knew everything. He knew at least a thousand Hungarian folk songs, all the words and tunes, he could handle Gypsies, give them instructions and keep them in order, check their familiarity with the flicker of an eyelid, then win their affection with a lordly, condescending, and yet fraternal-playful sidelong glance, he could call 'ácsi'* perfectly, shout at the first violin when he didn't strike up *Csendesen, csak csendesen* quietly enough and at the cimbalomist when the padded sticks didn't make the steel strings thunder and rumble sufficiently in *Hullámzó Balaton,*† he could kiss the viola player's pock-

---

* "Silence!" A Romany word.
† "Quietly, just quietly" and "Waves of Balaton" are well-known folk songs.

marked face, give the double bass a kick, break glasses and mirrors, drink wine, beer, and marc brandy for three days on end out of tumblers, smack his lips at the sight of cabbage soup and cold pork stew, take ages inspecting his cards (with relish, one eye closed), dance a quick *csárdás* for a whole half-hour, urging and driving himself on to stamp and shout and toss his partner high in the air and catch her, light as a feather, with one arm: so, as I said, he could do everything that raises Man from his animal condition and makes him truly Man.

"He could also speak Zsuzsa's language. He'd been brought up on Csantavér puszta. He remained a peasant at heart, a son of the puszta. If he opened his mouth the people itself spoke. He was a living collection of folk poetry bound in human skin.

"Quite how he made a conquest of Zsuzsa I don't know. As I imagine it, however, within five or six minutes he was wooing her with 'Zsuzsika, I kiss your hands, your dear little hands, for you I'd be a sheepdog for two years.' He must have expressed himself even more astutely, more spontaneously than that, however. Our imaginations aren't really up to such things. But whatever the case, by the time he'd walked her home, Zsuzsa was in love with him and almost fatally.

"Things were certainly not easy for them. They could only meet after Mass on Sunday, and for a short time. The old man watched his daughter like a savage *kuvasz*. Here I must mention that there were two real savage *kuvasz* in their yard. They were let off their chains in the evening, and the moment there was a sound at the fence they would rush to the gate with eyes rolling, suffused with blood, and rouse the neighborhood with their din. It was impossible even to make signals with them around. For a while Pista was gloomy, drank, had himself serenaded. Then he decided to ask for her hand in proper form and order.

"He put on his *ferencjóska*,* stuck a panama hat on his head, borrowed Tóni Vermes's gold watch and chain, and called on the wealthy peasant. His hopes were not high. He was at the time a mere assistant

---

* A style of frock coat popularized by Emperor Franz Josef.

notary, twenty-three years of age, and his salary was only enough to hold his importunate creditors at bay. At most he could have cited his various fine and lengthy styles of nobility, but he was aware that he would achieve little with that sort of thing.

"On that sweltering summer morning the old man had been sitting in his weed-ridden yard since early dawn, bundled up from head to foot and wearing boots and hat. He looked at Pista. But only once. He sized him up with his eye and found him a frivolous, thin, overdressed dandy—a useless scrounger unfit to be a husband. He immediately turned his head away, as if to say 'there's more room in the street.' He didn't ask him in. They stayed in the yard. He didn't even offer him a seat. Pista sat down uninvited and spoke his piece. The old man said neither yes nor no. He said nothing. And that was a considerable difficulty. If someone opposes you, it may still be possible to talk him round him somehow. Faced with silence, everyone is powerless. Pista slunk out crestfallen. As he left he extended a hand, but the old man ignored it. He just raised an index finger—slowly, stiffly, and deliberately—to the brim of his hat.

"At that time we too lived in that weed-ridden, dusty street, obliquely opposite. Because of that I know what happened next. In actual fact, nothing happened for months, until early October. It was, I remember, a cool, clear autumn night. The full moon was so bright that one could have taken photographs or even shaved by it. It must have been almost eleven o'clock. I heard a scream followed by repeated shouts for help. Women were wailing, men shouting. Sleepers jumped out of bed. Everybody ran toward the Szücs house. By the time I got there all was quiet. Ropes and ladders lay in the yard, as did a long walnut-gathering pole. Somebody had lit a lantern. Around the well stood silent, shocked people—some bowing their heads and even kneeling—and in the middle of this dark group, dressed only in her nightgown, lay Zsuzsa, dripping wet, having been just pulled out of the well. The water had been shaken out of her and now she was just spluttering and shivering, her lips blue in the moonlight. The soaked nightgown clung to her youthful breasts. The poor girl had tried to drown herself, like Ophelia.

"She had jumped into the well. See, nature will out. It had been no good Zsuzsa's going to the convent school, no good her knowing La Fontaine's fable about the ant and the cricket in the original French, no good her practising a few of the simpler finger exercises from Köhler's piano tutor; at the decisive crux in her life she had yielded to the murky instinct and grim traditions of her ancestors and had done what so many peasant girls and women had done over the centuries, women who had conceived of suicide only as taking death into their arms one night in the icy water of a well among moss-green bricks and toads.

"Her father was standing a little apart from the group, wringing his hands. This even he had understood. If a girl jumps into the well, she loves somebody. That was a clear, meaningful, plain statement. There could be no argument about it. Nor did he raise further objections. He immediately gave his consent to the marriage, opened his heart and—in wondrous fashion—his purse too. He gave his daughter as a dowry forty crisp thousand-korona notes. Pista led her to the altar before Christmas.

"Now then. After this incident the old man began to waste away; he shrank to a shadow of his former self. He suddenly went to pieces. People thought that he would kick the bucket. What's that? No, you're wrong. Of course he hadn't gone mad because she'd jumped into the well. He wasn't even very upset that Zsuzsa'd left him alone in his old age. It was the money that upset him, that heap of money, those forty thousand-korona notes out of which—he himself couldn't understand how—he'd been diddled. That he never forgave.

"So he vanished from public view, was no more to be seen even on the wooden bench in the street. He huddled in his earth-floored room in boots and hat, stick in hand, like any peasant waiting for a train in the third-class waiting room. He jabbed at the floor with the tip of his stick and spat. By evening he had spat a whole nice little puddle. A man who spits is thinking. I grant you that Immanuel Kant didn't do his thinking quite like that when he was writing the *Critique of Pure Reason*. But we all have our ways. With old Szücs, spitting always meant intense contemplation. He was contemplating his son-in-law, that good-for-nothing gold digger, who had so craftily trapped and robbed him.

"Pista, however, was not a gold digger. He would have married that girl without the forty thousand just the same, without a thing to her name, in the nightgown in which she'd jumped down the well. He loved little Zsuzsa, and grew to love her even more. I've never seen a husband so worship his wife. He didn't swear a vow to himself or to her, but from that day on he was dead as far as the world of debauchery was concerned; he stopped drinking and playing cards. He was just tied to her apron strings. He hid her away in his bachelor flat, which is where they moved to, and didn't rent anywhere else. They put their money in the bank. All they bought was a gig, in which they drove about. In the evening they strolled hand in hand in the deserted streets. If ever there was a love match, this was it.

"Even a love match, however, can have its other side. He that that brings love to a marriage is not much wiser than he that establishes a lovely, graceful leopard in his home to see to its tranquility. It's quite unsuitable.

"They were always arguing. Pista was possessive toward his wife, and she toward him. She was even possessive toward his thoughts. They were both very young, little more than children. After the storms came the rainbows, and they would make up in tears. So they argued and kissed, like doves.

"After one reconciliation a couple of months went by, and they fell out again over some trifle. It was a morning in spring. Pista slammed the door behind him and rushed to the office. When he came home at midday the place was empty. The kitchen fire wasn't burning. Nor had young Zsuzsa made lunch. He looked everywhere for her, even under the bed. He waited for her until three in the afternoon. Then he went to see his father-in-law.

"The old man, whom he'd met only once since the wedding—and even then they'd visited him—received him coldly. On this occasion too he didn't shake hands, and he addressed him as *maga*.* What

* The honorific form of address, implying a certain distance.

138

he heard didn't surprise him. He merely shook his head, shrugged his shoulders, hemmed and hawed; his daughter hadn't been there, goodness knows where she might be, he really didn't know. Anyway, he wasn't particularly interested.

"In the yard Pista looked into the well and then rushed home. He was hoping that by the time he arrived he'd find Zsuzsa there. But she wasn't. Now he began to worry. Where could she be, where could she have got to? Zsuzsa had no close friends. She was still too shy to go into a restaurant alone. Pista searched the town, looking down every street and alley. As evening approached he—in despair—reported her disappearance to the police. The officer advised him to take another look at her father's house.

"There was nothing else that he could do. First, however, he approached the house from behind, up the other street. There he saw a light in the window. Never in all his life had the old man lit the lamp—he begrudged the expense. So Zsuzsa must be hiding there. Pista tapped on the window. At that the lamp inside was blown out. It was she, it was she.

"He did not dare resort to force. He knew her. She was as obstinate as her father. She met force with greater force. He rang at the gate.* After a lengthy interval the old man opened it. Pista informed him that his wife was hiding there. The old man didn't deny it, but neither did he confirm it. Pista resorted to pleas, begged him to soften his daughter's heart, reconcile her to him, he would be grateful, promised him all sorts of things. The old man pondered. Then he spat out that it would cost him a cool five hundred koronas.

"Pista thought that it was all a joke—even laughed—but it was no joke. Next day too his father-in-law would not let him in, merely spoke briefly through the window, and when he saw that Pista had come empty-handed he shut it. Pista couldn't get near Zsuzsa, nor did she accept his letters. So Pista didn't get his wife back until he withdrew from the bank the five hundred korona and counted every

---

* The gate, not the house door, because of the *kuvasz*. This is standard Hungarian practice.

one of them out into the old man's hand.

"Thus he blackmailed Pista the first time. Then it happened twice more. The second time it was more expensive—fifteen thousand korona were extorted from him. The most serious, however, was the third occasion, which happened one Whitsun, in the second year of their marriage.

"This time there was a lot at stake. They had come home from a masked ball—the first to which her husband had taken Zsuzsa— and had argued so badly in the street that when they reached home Pista gave his wife two quick slaps in the face in the hall. Zsuzsa turned on her heel, and in her thin patent leather shoes and her Tündér Ilona costume, ran out into the street and went weeping through the freezing winter night to her father's. Pista, who was by that time tired of all the arguments and reconciliations, and also of the ransoms which were more exorbitant every time, decided on a new tactic: he would ignore the whole thing, his wife would simply relent, get tired of sulking, and come back of her own accord. Days went by, weeks too. Three long weeks passed without any sign of life from his wife. He didn't even know whether she had in fact gone home on that bitter night, or even whether she was alive or dead. One evening he took a walk past his father-in-law's. The house was shut up, dark and gloomy as a castle.

"Pista drank until dawn. At dawn he returned with the gypsy band, to assault the fortress with violins. Until morning came he made them play his wife's song—*Hány csillagból áll a szemed, Zsuzsikám?**—under her window. Until morning came he sang it at the top of his voice toward the window, toward the snow clouds in the sky, toward the stars, as if expecting from somewhere an objective reply to that rhetorical question, that excusable poetic exaggeration. Nobody replied. Only the two *kuvasz* howled in opposition.

"The fourth week passed too. Now a whole month had gone by. Pista's patience was exhausted. He engaged a lawyer to go and hold talks on his behalf. Zsuzsa told him that she absolutely wanted a di-

---

* How many stars are your eyes made of, my Zsuzsika?

vorce and asked her husband to agree to it peacefully. The lawyer continued talks for a further week. Then he brought the old man's reply, that peace would cost a round twenty thousand koronas.

"Why drag the story out? Pista hurried to the bank, withdrew what remained of his dowry, nineteen thousand, seven hundred and sixty koronas—the rest he had to scrape together from his friends—and paid up. Then, after almost six weeks of absence, he brought his wife out in his arms, placed her triumphantly in the gig and drove home with her.

"I heard this from people who swear that, word for word, that's exactly what happened. And I believe them. There's just one thing that I don't understand. Was she in league with the old miser, who had recouped his daughter's dowry to the last krajcár? Possibly so. But it's also possible that she was a mere tool in his hands, and that she only wanted her husband back but wanted to sell her love dear. That too is possible.

"Something else that's odd—after that they never quarreled again. That's strange. That I could not begin to explain. Perhaps you can.

"Yes, yes. As soon as they had nothing they were happy and content. But they were often hard up. True, they knew that they had mighty expectations when the old man closed his eyes. That could have happened any day. But he wouldn't die. His financial success really galvanized him, he took a new lease on life. Once more he sat on the bench saying nothing.

"He lived for years, hale and hearty. Why is it that misers are all long-lived? Some say that meanness itself is an indication of an indomitable joie de vivre, and like every true passion, doesn't kill but keeps one alive. Some say that this long-term, constant greed is what's missing in puny individuals who die young. Some say that misers are steeled, filled with obstinacy, by the antipathy that surrounds them, it's the burning hatred of their dependents that keeps them alive, just as the enthusiastic adoration of their children sustains the good. Finally, there are those who say that the earth keeps them here, won't let them go, clasps them to its dirty, muddy bosom, because misers are dirty and muddy like their relative, the earth. These are theories, and nothing can be settled by theories. Everything, however, is settled by a severe brain hemorrhage in the night. That killed even the old man. Pista and his wife then inherited more than they had hoped for, almost half a million prewar gold koronas.

"Believe me, I would love to end this newfangled folk tale happily, to show in glowing colors how Zsuzsa and Pista finally obtained their reward and lived happily ever after. Unfortunately, I can't. The old man died on the second of June 1914, and on the twenty-eighth— as I'm sure you've heard—war broke out. As a lieutenant in the reserve, Pista was called up into the First Honvéd Hussars. Before joining them he decided to invest all his money in war bonds. Zsuzsa, a peasant girl of limited outlook who clung to the soil, at first would not approve of this. She proposed that with part of it at least they should buy gold and land. She changed her mind only when her husband, who being a man had a better understanding of politics, explained that when the war was over they would get their money back with interest from the great syndicate which would have become a grateful posterity. Pista was never able to learn that this didn't quite work out. The fault, it must be said, wasn't his own. That is to say, in the first cavalry charge a shell so hit him that not so much as a kneecap or a brass button was left—even his horse vanished without a trace. It was as if the earth had swallowed the two of them up, or as if they had galloped up fully armed to the Milky Way, that golden roadway in the sky, and from there rushed into some wonderful and splendid military heaven. Young Zsuzsa waited for him for a while. She slowly used up what money she had. Then she languished on her war widow's pension and eventually left town. The last time I went down there I heard that she'd found employment as a maid on a farm and had become a complete peasant, setting hens and fattening geese.

"So life has its ups and downs, doesn't it? No, we really can't complain. But let's add that not only has it ups and downs, it also has deep meaning. Quite. Now, aren't we ever going to have another drink?"

XI

In which is an account
of the most excellent hotel in the world.

"ARE YOU AWARE OF THE RICH RANGE OF HOTELS?" KORNÉL
Esti turned to us. "I could find a lot to say about it.

"There are family hotels, in which we feel more comfortable than
at home, free from domestic tensions in addition to being independent. There are pleasant, intimate, nice hotels. There are dismal hotels, especially in the country, which have something in common
with out-of-tune pianos, inducing melancholia with their dull mirrors and damp quilt covers, and then there are hotels that drive one
to despair, accursed, deadly hotels, where on a November evening
one might easily commit suicide. There are cheerful hotels, where
even the taps laugh out loud. There are stiff, ceremonious, silent hotels, chatty hotels, boozy hotels, cheeky hotels, showy, loud, worthless hotels, reliable, calm, lordly hotels, noble with the rust of the
past, frivolous hotels, ponderous hotels, healthy hotels, in which
the sun shines even from the drains, and sick hotels in which the table limps and the chair wobbles, the chest of drawers is on crutches,
the sofa is consumptive, and the pillows lie on the bed breathing
their last. So there are very many kinds of hotels.

"The last time I went abroad I passed through a small country on
my way home. There I came across a hotel which I have to remember specially.

"This hotel was excellent. It was so excellent that I've never seen the like anywhere. I have no qualms about saying that it was the most excellent hotel in the world.

"My car had been racing along in the dust of twilight among decrepit, single-story hovels when it came to a halt outside a thirteen-story skyscraper complete with plaster roses and a dome, which contrasted sharply with its lowly surroundings and was obviously intended for the accommodation of distinguished foreigners who strayed that way.

"I immediately realized that I had come upon no ordinary place.

"The horn of my car had scarcely sounded than staff emerged from the revolving door of the hotel. There must have been fifteen or twenty of them—a veritable small army.

"One member of staff opened the door of my car, a second helped me out, a third took off my English dust coat, a fourth took my American traveling trunk, a fifth my two suitcases, a sixth my crocodile leather briefcase, and a seventh my French newspaper, which I'd left on the passenger seat. All this happened in the twinkling of an eye, fast, smoothly.

"Those who had no part to play in this stood on the asphalt in a relaxed line, not in military fashion, but none the less in disciplined, silent readiness.

"All of them wore braided hats and curious, violet-colored uniforms that might have come from some operetta. When I walked past them as if inspecting a parade, the braided hats—at no audible word of command—were doffed to reveal well-brushed heads.

"This was how guests arriving from afar were greeted, with that assured, sincere, almost puerile respect which must always have been stored in the very depths of their hearts, where no change in fickle fortune could ever eradicate it, and the only reason that such respect hadn't previously been shown to me must have been simply that until that day they just hadn't known me.

"I looked for a long time at my tiny army. I gained the impression that should need arise they were even prepared to shed their blood for me. Tears came to my eyes. A king could not have been received with greater fealty.

"The army, all the more heroic for its small size, dispersed, without trumpet call or drumroll, at a sign from the clean-shaven, graying gentleman who, until then in the background, was directing them. This was the bell captain. He addressed me in English, and bore a striking resemblance to Edison.

"With ineffable tact Edison escorted me through the foyer, which was decorated with exotic plants. He ushered me into a capacious room. He indicated a chesterfield and requested me 'to be so good as to be seated.' When I had obeyed he pressed a button.

"The capacious room, without a sound, began to rise. I then realized that it was the elevator.

"It was a wonderfully equipped elevator. Apple-green bulbs shed a muted green light so that the sensitive eyes of guests should not be upset. In addition to the chesterfield, other leather-upholstered armchairs stood on the silk Persian rugs, while here and there in corners could be seen little tables with cigarettes and lighters, illustrated magazines, and chessboards on which the pieces were set out so that guests might dispel the ennui of their sojourn there with a little profitable, refreshing entertainment. Unfortunately, I had no time for these delights, as a few seconds later the elevator stopped with a melodious chime at its appointed destination on the second floor.

"Here I was received by a second detachment of staff, dressed in coffee-colored uniforms. At the bell captain's bidding they opened the double doors opposite the elevator.

"Passing through the foyer I entered a large room, which on account of its dimensions I could rather call a throne room. Artistically draped brocade curtains poured from the Empire windows, which gave a view onto a swiftly flowing stream of blue water. Off this room opened a reception room, with white, gilded chairs, a dining room, a bedroom, and a smaller sitting room, together with a bathroom with a sunken marble bath and Venetian mirrors, in front of which glittered a countless profusion of perfume sprays, nail files, and small scissors. In every room—even the bathroom— three telephones were at the guest's disposal. The first connected to the hotel switchboard, the second to the outside world, and the third—which had a pink handset—to I know not what.

"I could hardly believe my eyes as I stood in that suite, and then I inquired of the bell captain approximately how much it cost per diem.

"The bell captain didn't reply. It seemed that he was hard of hearing. In that too he resembled Edison. By this time I was absolutely convinced that he didn't just resemble him but that he was actually Edison himself.

"I therefore repeated my question loudly, as one usually speaks to the deaf. The aged inventor did hear that. But it seemed that he was shocked and somewhat distressed. He closed his eyes.

"The staff, ranged before us in a position of relaxed attention, likewise closed their eyes, modestly. Their spirits, which surely moved in higher spheres—in realms of thought unaffected by sordid material considerations—had been cut to the quick by my worldliness. It was as if a poet, in the blazing fire of inspiration, had been asked the price of potatoes.

"They all remained silent.

"I was about to apologize, to offer the explanation that I was a poet who earned his bread by the bitter toil of writing, and that therefore I regarded money as important and had a deep respect for it, when the bell captain gave expression to his disappointment by coldly, dispassionately letting fall a number—in dollars—such as all but laid me flat on my back.

"I asked to see another room.

"Thomas Alva Edison nodded courteously. He took me to the third floor, where egg-yellow uniforms awaited us. As I didn't find the price of rooms suitable there either, we went to the fourth floor, among lackeys in blue and white, then to the fifth and sixth, ever up and up.

"Finally we reached the eleventh floor. Here very handsome blond pageboys in red were on duty.

"The bell captain was becoming worn out, but led me with a still respectful guard of honor along an endless corridor. Here and there a colored light was burning above the lintel of a door. I inquired what those were for.

"He didn't reply at once.

146

"At first he seemed amazed at my unsophisticated curiosity, at the fact that there was still on the earth anyone unaware of the purpose of such lights, and then with dignified brevity informed me that those lights took the place of bells and were meant for various members of the staff, with whom guests could make contact without disturbing one another's tranquility and the perfect silence of the hotel.

"At the back, in a secluded corner, I found a room which more or less answered my 'requirements.'

"But it was so luxurious, so splendid, that I don't dare describe it.

"All that I'll tell you is that I found on a little malachite table a longish wooden box shaped like a spinet, on which eighty-five black-and-white buttons presented me with a keyboard of an unknown kind.

"As I'm a keen musician and play the piano whenever possible, I immediately sat down and began to play Beethoven, the *Pathétique* sonata. Scarcely had I reached the Allegretto when I heard a quiet knock on my door.

"A flunky in evening dress appeared. Behind him a darkling crowd of staff awaited my orders. I immediately counted them. There were exactly eighty-five. From that I deduced that the longish, spinet-shaped instrument was the keyboard for the system that called the staff, and that by my playing I had—quite unthinkingly—summoned them all. I apologized.

"The more important of them took advantage of the occasion to introduce themselves one by one.

"I was a little surprised. My daytime room waiter resembled Chopin, and the night man, on the other hand, was like Shakespeare himself. My surprise increased immediately because I discovered that there was a certain system in this. The first chambermaid was like Cléo de Mérode,* the second like Marie Antoinette, and the cleaner was the image of Annie Besant,† the well-known theosophist.

"My amazement reached its peak, however, when among the

* Cléopatra Diane de Mérode (1875–1966), much-portrayed beauty and celebrated dancer.

† English theosophist (1847–1933) who followed Madame Blavatsky as high priestess of that movement.

large cohort of lesser servants I saw one after the other Eckener, the heroic oceanic pilot,[*] Rodin, Bismarck, and Murillo, and then a bearded, shy gentleman who reminded me of the late lamented Tsar of Russia much more than his actual portraits.

"That wasn't all. The hotel secretary looked like Schopenhauer, the chefs in charge of cold and hot menus resembled respectively Torricelli[†] and Einstein, the stockroom manager Caruso, and a pale, sickly errand boy resembled the unhappy Dauphin, the son of Louis XVI who mysteriously disappeared.

"A glittering historical portrait gallery of international notables had come back to life in those worthy members of staff.

"What part the hotel management had in this, and whether they had selected them by virtue of resemblance, as a feature, a delightful idea with which to attract guests, or whether those living wax figures had come together by chance, I had no time to decide.

"I swear, however, by all that is holy, that it was absolutely as I describe. Here everyone resembled someone, and everything resembled something.

"Schopenhauer asked how he might be of service. I asked him to have my dusty shoes cleaned, because I would like to go out into the town and bathe in that swift, blue-watered stream as I had so wished to do from the very first moment I saw it.

"The grim Frankfurt philosopher took my desire as quite natural and human, and assured me that it would be satisfied forthwith.

"As he left he pointed out to me that all the staff spoke several European languages, the least well educated among them at least five, but the night porter spoke fifteen, not to mention Latin and Classical Greek, and so, should I chance to return home in the early hours, I could talk with him about the enjoyable experiences that I had had in my nocturnal excursions.

---

[*] Hugo Eckener (1868–1954), aeronautical engineer, who in 1924 piloted the airship ZR3 on the first transatlantic airship flight.

[†] Evangelista Torricelli (1608–47), mathematician and physicist, associate of and successor to Galileo.

"With that he left. After that someone knocked. In came Nicholas II. He bowed very low with Slavonic humility, looked into my face, and then subjected my shoes to his spectacles without touching them with his royal fingers.

"The examination continued much as when a general medical practitioner examines a patient and in the process can see that it is a case of a specific and complex disease of some organ which he could in fact treat on the basis of his general medical training, but which it would be much more correct to refer to a specialist who deals exclusively with that sort of thing.

"He did not reveal that train of thought by a single word. He bowed low again and withdrew.

"After a brief interval Bismarck came back with Murillo, Eckener, and Rodin. They also stared at my shoes. It seemed that all five were preparing a diagnosis and recommended treatment. The whole thing was like a conference of doctors at the bedside of a very sick patient.

"They summoned a chambermaid, a new one whom I had not previously met—Fanny Elssler, if I remember correctly.* She announced in ringing tones that this did not "fall within my sphere of influence."

"Once more everyone left me. Only the faithful Bismarck remained at my side.

"A few moments later, four of the very handsome blond pageboys in red assigned to service in that corridor came into my room and trundled in an ingenious, electrically driven contraption on wheels, which each of them was steering with just the tip of his little finger. Under Bismarck's expert supervision, my shoes were placed on the contraption with the aid of a tiny crane and, to the accompaniment of deep bows, removed.

"Scarcely an hour and a half had elapsed when the ingenious machine was trundled back. My shoes were now brilliantly clean.

---

* The Viennese sisters Fanny (1810–84) and Therese (1808–78) Elssler were celebrated dancers.

"Stimulated by this excellence, this unaccustomed attention, I went to bathe. I splashed in the stream until evening, returning only for dinner.

"There were a few remaining guests in the dining room. For me a very long table had been laid, such as one would find at a banquet. Naturally I sat in the middle, the place of honor, alone.

"The delicious twelve-course meal was served at once. Most of all I wish to extol the crab, which swam with its marbled pink flesh in a thick, light gray sauce. Otherwise I rather drank. First, my favorite drink, a light beer, the golden nectar whose bitter foam, reminiscent of freshly baked rye bread, and nourishing scent of hops I have adored since childhood. I followed that with wine, Rhine wine and Greek *aszú*. Finally I settled on champagne. Bottle after bottle came to the ice-bucket, sweet and brut, and cooled slowly among the crystals of artificial snow.

"The fish was brought from the fish kitchen, the coffee from the coffee kitchen. Fresh bouquets were placed in the vases several times so that they should not wither while my eye and nose took pleasure in them.

"After dinner I asked for the bill. The staff clasped their hands and smiled. All meals went like that. They appeared altogether exceptionally willing. If I had asked them to set fire to the town for my pleasure, or to kill their beloved prince and place his head on my table in a silver tureen, cooked as Irish stew, I really believe that they would have done so without the least objection.

"Their courtesy grew and grew. So, however, did their number. This I sometimes estimated at four hundred, sometimes eight hundred. As, however, in my whole stay in the hotel I saw only eight guests, including myself, there were approximately a hundred staff to each guest.

"As I went down the corridor with its sound-absorbent carpet, they stood like silent caryatids along the walls. I only became aware of their existence when they raised their hats and greeted me quietly. Modesty and good manners were second nature to them. They were machines, not people.

"Just once it happened that a waiter was holding a cigarette furtively in his palm and exhaling smoke, but after glancing at me he was embarrassed at succumbing to so vile a passion, and his cigarette vanished at once. Where it vanished to, I do not know to this day. Perhaps he threw it into one of the ubiquitous asbestos-lined airtight ashtrays, or perhaps, pricked by conscience, he took it into his mouth, chewed it up, and swallowed it, burning tip and all. The latter seems the more likely.

"I repeat, the staff were without equal. Every day they favored me with something. They pressed into my hand announcements printed on wood-free Japanese paper and worthy of consideration as works of art, and marvelously edited and wonderfully informative catalogues. With unflagging zeal they brought to my attention the hotel's Dalcroze dance school* and its Mensendik gymnasia, its bacteriological laboratory, its copying, shorthand, and typing office, its elegant swimming pool for dogs, its private car tire store, and indeed its lavishly equipped psychiatric institution, in which distinguished psychiatrists gave devoted attention at all hours of the day or night to the hotel's deeply respected nervous and mental patients.

"I don't wish to bore you all with further details, and will only say that I lived for ten days in that delightful, refined milieu.

"One morning I said into the recording machine at my bedside that the next afternoon I would be leaving for home on the two-fourteen electric train, and therefore they were to forward my trunk and suitcases—with the exception of my crocodile leather briefcase, in which I keep my manuscripts—to my Budapest address. I had the wax cylinder of the recording machine taken down to my friend Edison by Nicholas II. The Tsar brought a wax cylinder back. On placing this in the machine I was informed that the porter 'had taken the necessary steps.'

"From this point the attention of the staff was redoubled, and minute by minute, hour by hour, increased by geometrical progression. Annie Besant, the cleaner, greeted me with sighs. Cléo de

---

* Émile Jaques-Dalcroze (1865–1941), the Swiss inventor of eurhythmics.

Mérode, Fanny Elssler, and Marie Antoinette came and went sorrowfully around me, as if they would scarcely survive my departure, and in their grief would end their young lives with poison. Chopin, Einstein, Murillo, Bismarck, Schopenhauer, Torricelli, Nicholas II, Caruso, Rodin, and the hapless little Dauphin too greeted me passionately with 'Good morning' or 'Good evening' every time that we met in the corridor. It sounded like the reminder of the Carthusians in the monastery: *Memento mori*.

"What were they reminding me of, in fact? Sometimes I thought that perhaps it was of the tip which they certainly deserved. It was enough, however, for me to glance into their faces, which reflected the pain caused by my imminent departure, enough for me to look into their eyes, red with weeping and which they tried in vain to hide, for me to be convinced of the contrary.

"That evening, after dinner, Edison and the headwaiter placed before me a slip of paper on a silver salver. It was a railway receipt showing that the train would take all my luggage home as express freight, and that the hotel had—in advance, naturally—'settled' the bill.

"I nodded in approval and made for my room.

"Before I could get to sleep I was startled by a terrible din. A raucous chorus of male voices was howling 'Good night' into my ear from close range. I leapt out of bed. There was no one in my room. What was happening was that the hotel's enthusiastic and attentive male staff, who, as everyone knew, had a private reception and transmission set, were calling on me by radio.

"The same thing happened in the morning too, the difference being that on this occasion I was awoken by the dulcet tones of the female staff wishing me a good morning.

"Early in the morning of that final day I called on Edison at the reception desk, as I wished to pay. At the mention of money there appeared on his face that disparaging, world-weary smile. He assured me that I would still have time to 'settle up,' as my train did not leave until after two and I would still be taking lunch with them. In any case, my bill was mostly ready, and the finishing touches were being made to it even then in the Central Accounts office.

"With my crocodile leather briefcase in hand, I strolled slowly out into the palm grove at the end of the town, where I had previously worked every day on my garland of love songs, worthily famous on account of its immediacy and warm spontaneity, entitled *Inhibitions and Transpositions*.

"I sat down on the marble rim of the fountain. I daydreamed for a while. Then I attempted in my old established way to evoke the creative urge. I struck my forehead several times, one after the other, on the marble rim. I can only create if I completely switch off my intelligence.

"Unfortunately, this was not immediately successful. Intelligence is an extraordinarily stupid thing. On this occasion too it persisted in forcing itself upon me.

"Then others also drew my attention to the fact that there is intelligence on earth. Among them, the staff of the hotel.

"When I sneezed, the male and female staff of the hotel conveyed to me from a radio installed up a fifteen-foot palm tree and equipped with a loudspeaker, their wishes for my health.

"Nevertheless, in a couple of hours I succeeded in writing one of my major works—a two-line poem telling of the prescient hatred felt toward me by Elinor, my most recent inamorata.

"This exceedingly spiritual work quite wore me out. Afterwards I stared into space for a further two hours and waited for my intelligence to return.

"I was astonished to see an airplane land, as lightly and elegantly as a dragonfly, in a nearby clearing.

"It was making for my home. I myself don't know why, but I got in and ordered the airplane to take me home at full speed.

"Up in the air, when the altimeter was reading twenty thousand feet and that swift, blue-watered stream looked as big as the platinum bracelet that Elinor wore on her wrist, above the clouds, above the snowy mountains, I suddenly realized that I'd forgotten to pay my hotel bill and had unintentionally not given tips to the staff who had so good-heartedly watched over me for almost two weeks.

"As a man phenomenally well trained in psychology, I know that there is no such thing as 'unintentional' and that we don't 'forget' anything without cause. I immediately viewed my lapse as suspicious.

"I began to analyze myself with lightning speed. While the airplane looped the loop with a daring rush and I hung with my head upside-down, I continued my psychological analysis, which I quickly brought to a successful conclusion.

"I realized that my action had been subconsciously conscious, or rather consciously subconscious. But it had been astute, very astute. Nor could I have acted otherwise.

"When all was said and done, it would have been unthinkable to insult so excellent a hotel, such excellent staff, by offering them money. That would have been tactlessness, gross tactlessness."

XII

In which the president, Baron Wilhelm Eduard von Wüstenfeld,
immortal figure of his student years in Germany
and his mentor and preceptor,
sleeps through the entire chapter.

MY DATE WAS FOR A QUARTER TO TWO IN THE MORNING AT the Torpedo coffeehouse.

I tried to be precisely on time. But I couldn't get a cab straightaway. Then it started to rain cats and dogs. The cab could go only very cautiously, at walking pace. It was approaching a quarter past two when I opened the door of the private room in the Torpedo.

My arrival was greeted by a frantic hushing. Kornél Esti, who had been in full flow, glanced disparagingly in my direction and fell silent.

Around him was his usual motley company, nine or ten writers of various sorts and a woman or two. In front of him was a glass of Bull's Blood* and a silver dish on which lay the fabulously delicate skeleton of a trout and the remains of a light green sauce.

In the unfriendly silence I threw down my fur coat and lit a cigarette. Someone informed me in a whisper of the preliminaries of the story which had begun.

He had been telling them about his student years in Germany and about a distinguished, refined elderly gentleman, prominent in public life in Darmstadt—his full name was Baron Wilhelm Friedrich Eduard von Wüstenfeld—who had been president of Germania,

---

* A dry red Hungarian wine, by law a blend of at least three grapes.

the local cultural association, and also president and director of numerous other political, literary, and scientific associations, societies, clubs, unions, conferences, committees, and subcommittees.

"So," Kornél went on, "it always happened as I said. The president would open the session and go to sleep. The lecturer wouldn't even have reached the table and he'd be asleep. He'd go off quickly, like lightning, the way little children do. He'd plunge from the brink of wakefulness straight into the bottomless abyss of sleep. He'd close his eyes and sleep deeply and sweetly.

"The lecturer would step to the table, acknowledge the applause, bow, sit down, shuffle his ominously high pile of script, clear his throat, and set about his lecture on something like *The Observation of the Essence of Dynamic Existence* or *Plant and Animal Names in the Erotic Poetry of Heinrich von Morungen*, but that no longer concerned the president, who had slipped discreetly from the world of consciousness by an invisible secret door, leaving behind only his body as a token in the presidential chair.

"When the lecturer had finished, the president would call the second and then the third to the rostrum from the printed program, and when they had performed their duties he too performed his.

"Understand me: the lecturers and the president's briefly interrupted sleep, which could yet be called uninterrupted and continuous, interacted, were in close contact, almost in a causal relationship. The president opened the session and closed his eyes. The president closed the session and opened his eyes. At first this was a mystery to me.

"I was young and inexperienced when I went to Germany. At the time I'd been drifting around among the lighthearted, easygoing French, but in Paris I received a stern telegram from my father telling me to go at once to Germany and there continue my studies, and work only at my studies, not at creating literature as I had been doing. In his telegram he emphasized that if I didn't do as I was told he'd cut off my monthly allowance. Whether for that reason, or because of my measureless love for him, I complied with his request right away. And to this day I'm grateful to him for making me go.

Otherwise I'd hardly have gotten to know the Germans.

"Naturally, I'd heard a thing or two about them. I knew that they were one of the world's greatest peoples and had given humanity music and abstract thought. They were *Cloudy and burdened with thought*, as their divine Hölderlin has it. When I'm really down in the dumps I hum Bach fugues and say lines of Goethe to myself. 'Among pine forests and hills lives an earnest, industrious people,' I thought, 'with the starry sky and the moral world order above their heads.' So I had a great respect for the Germans. Perhaps I respected them more than any other people. But I didn't know them. The French, however, I loved.

"What a loss it would have been had I missed this close acquaintance. A new world opened before me. As soon as my train had rolled onto German soil, one surprise followed another. My mouth, so to speak, was constantly agape, from which my fellow-travelers deduced that I was a half-wit. Order and cleanliness were everywhere, in things and, indeed, in people alike.

"I got off first at a small spa, to wash the dust off. I didn't have to ask anyone where the sea was. There were elegant pillars at precise ten-yard intervals in the clean, swept streets, bearing white enamel signs showing a pointing hand with the words *To the Sea* beneath. The stranger could not have been given clearer directions. I reached the sea. There, however, I was rather taken aback. On the pebble beach, a yard from the water, another pillar drew my attention; it was identical to the rest, but the white enamel sign was rather larger and bore the words: *The Sea*.

"Having come from among the Latin races, I felt at first that this was exceedingly superfluous. Before me foamed restless infinity, and it was obvious that no one could mistake the Baltic for a spittoon or a steam laundry. Later I realized that I had been wrong in my youthful superiority. This was where the true greatness of the Germans lay. This was perfection itself. Their philosophical tendency demanded that the argument be concluded and the outcome demonstrated, as the mathematician often writes in the course of a deduction that $1 = 1$, or as is often stated in logical proofs, Peter = Peter (and not Paul).

"In Darmstadt I rented a modest little student's room in the house of a master cooper. There too a series of surprises awaited me. The family was pleasant, considerate, and very clean. The cooper's father, an old man who seemed to be simple, treated me, a nobody who had been tossed ashore there from abroad, with kindly, human affection. In the evening, when I came in, he always questioned me: *Well, young man, tell me, what have you experienced today, 1. humanly, 2. literarily, 3. philosophically?* I couldn't answer this question at first. Not only because I could as yet hardly speak German. This profundity, this classification so normal to the German mind but to which I was not accustomed, confused me. My unrefined brain all but exploded. It came to my mind that that morning I had read Hegel in the library, then had some dill sauce in the refectory, and in the afternoon strolled with Minna in the town park. Was the library a human experience, the dill sauce a literary experience, and Minna a philosophical experience, or vice versa? To me these three had been one until then. I mixed up the library with the dill sauce and Minna, experiences human, literary, and philosophical. It was quite some time—and required constant mental gymnastics—before I was able to separate them.

"They're an enigmatic people, I can tell you. There's no people so enigmatic. They think all the time. One after another I met eccentrics who 'on principle' ate only things that were raw, who every morning 'on principle' did breathing exercises, who in the evening, 'on principle,' slept on hard beds with no quilts, even in the dead of winter. Their level of culture is astounding. They go from school to university but don't finish their studies even then, and I suspect that after that all of them enroll in the universe. The universe with its myriad stars is there in their calculations, indeed in their appointment diaries too. Even girls and women refer to it like a popular place of entertainment. German women are, on the whole, sensitive and romantic. They're like French women. The only difference between them is perhaps that French women tend to have large eyes, whereas German women have large feet and souls which absorb at once everything that is noble and beautiful. The moment one makes their acquaintance, they describe themselves exhaustingly, cleverly, and abstractly. They reveal the length and breadth of their spiritual lives, two or three of its fundamental attributes, and their basic symptoms, like a patient revealing the history of his disease to a doctor. They are terribly sincere. And they don't conceal their faults. They are not embarrassed by anything human. I had scarcely begun courting one delightful, divorced little woman, beneath the limes one sunny autumn morning, than she confessed that she had had hemorrhoids since giving birth and was suffering badly from them that very day. All that not for my interest, just because it was sincere and human. It's a bewildering world.

"One after another the doors of the best houses opened to me. They accepted me into their circle as if I were not a foreigner. What little merit there was in me they appreciated. They respect all other nations just as much as they love their own. They do not proclaim international principles—they practice them. The Germans are instinctively welcoming. There was a place for me too at their table. I'll not conceal, however, that here too I was surprised at this and that. At the end of dinner, for instance, they serve a longish, stick-shaped, dead-white, very smelly cheese, which they call 'Dead Man's Finger' (*Leichenfinger*). They filled my glass with a dark red liqueur the name of which was, according to the manufacturer's label, 'Blood Blister' (*Blutgeschwür*). As a well-brought-up person I sank my teeth into the dead man's finger and washed it down with the sticky secretion of the blood blister.

"There was one thing that I couldn't accept for a long time: their mustard pots. On the best families' tables there is a very strange mustard pot from which—as I later found out—the manufacturer had become wealthy; his product was in demand everywhere and he could not make enough. This mustard pot was in the shape of a tiny, white porcelain lavatory pedestal, with a brown wooden lid that closed, a deceptively faithful replica with only the inscription 'Mustard' (*Senft*) to betray what it was. In this they keep the yellowish-brown mustard which they put on their blood sausage during a meal. At first they didn't understand that I could only eat with limited appetite when that witty, risible little object was set playfully before me. They found it amusing. Even engaged couples looked at it with a smile and knew in advance that their future home would contain one like it. Respectable mothers of families, in whose presence it would be unthinkable to make the slightest risqué remark, passed it nonchalantly to guests. Small boys screwed up their faces as they sniffed at it and licked off the brown fragments that stuck to the porcelain bowl, and little girls, whom their doting parents had photographed with hands clasped in prayer, took a delight in scraping at the paste that had congealed in it and, like enthusiastic mudlarks, softening it with vinegar.

"I confess that for a while I found that healthily studentish good humor repulsive. Previously, however, I'd been through the school of Paris, enjoyed all the coarse slapstick and thinly veiled double entendres of the bawdy theater of Montmartre; I'd studied decadent poetry too, which often enthrones indecency and filth. This, however, was repugnant to me. It was the openness that shocked me, the cosy sniggering at this devilment. But who can understand a people?

"I repeat, this people is unfathomably enigmatic. They are loyal, clever, and attentive. If I was unwell, my landlady herself made my bed, plumped up my pillow and smoothed it down, made up embrocations, took my temperature, made me drink linden leaf tea, and nursed me with motherly love and with such knowing skill. Only German women know how to nurse the sick. A doctor would be called too. German doctors have no equal. The least of them is worth more than a university professor in another country. Their forget-me-not-blue eyes would look at my fevered brow with inexpressible objectivity and concern. Their medicines, prepared in a million forms by the best factories on earth, cure us the moment we look at them. I've often said that I'd like to be sick and die only among the Germans. But I'd rather live somewhere else—here in Hungary, and when I'm on holiday, in France.

"However, I hadn't gone there to live, but to study. First and foremost, to study their rather difficult, harsh, tortuous, complex, but splendid and ancient language, in which as yet I could only stammer incompetently and inadequately. I frequently didn't understand what they said. They frequently didn't understand what I said. These two defects didn't cancel one another out, they increased each other. It was my sole ambition to learn German. I listened like a secret policeman. I talked to everybody. Living grammars and dictionaries were all around me. I tried hard to turn the pages. I even spoke to three-year-old children, as they spoke better German than I did although I had read and understood Kant's *Prolegomena* in the original. If I failed to understand a snatch of conversation in the street, my pride was injured. Once I almost felt disposed to commit suicide when a shopkeeper noticed the foreign accent of my otherwise tolerable speech and didn't answer my questions but—no doubt out of consideration—made signs like a deaf-mute or a savage would. I worked with indefatigable industry and lost no opportunity to ensure progress. Unfortunately, numerous disasters befell me. I went home by cab late one night after a student feast. I asked the driver what I owed him. I presumably misunderstood him and didn't give him enough. He began to shout, called me a lousy villain, even threatened me with his whip, but all that I could do was admire his wonderful command of strong verbs, the masterly way that he maneuvered subject and predicate, his rich and varied vocabulary, and took out a pencil with which to make notes of it all. At that the cabby too was amazed, but at the patient way I had borne his filthy tirade. He thought that I was either the founder of a religion or mad. But I was only being a linguist.

"And so I went everywhere that German was spoken, publicly or privately. There were few visitors at the Germania and other cultural institutions as keen as I. At all costs I meant to hear spoken German, the more the merrier, and I didn't care what.

"Allow me, after this long but necessary digression, to return to Baron Wüstenfeld, the president, who was asleep when we left him, and I assure you is still asleep. What did the people of Darmstadt have to say about this? Well, they were used to it. So was I eventually. At first, however, I recall, at one lecture I turned to a citizen of Darmstadt who was sitting beside me and asked him why the president was always sleeping. He was surprised at my question. He looked at me, then at the president, and replied—dispassionately—

that he was in fact asleep, but he was, after all, the president, and he shrugged as if I'd asked why the sun was shining. The president was president in order to sleep. It was accepted at that time, and they went on with the agenda regardless.

"I apologized for my inquisitiveness. As time went by I realized that they were right. The president was an old man. A very old man. Very old and very tired. Clearly, that was why he was always known as the 'tireless fighter for public education.' He was also called 'the watchman of public education,' and not out of weary contempt or without good reason. He was a man of great culture and great breadth of vision, with a long career behind him, who functioned actively from morning to night in public life. He would open an extraordinary meeting early in the forenoon, convene a preparatory subcommittee at noon, chair a political council in the afternoon, and in the evening propose the toast to the guest of honor at a banquet. In general he presided everywhere, rang the bell everywhere, spoke the introductory or closing words everywhere. In the meanwhile he appeared everywhere that he had to, and his name was never missing from the list of those present. Was it any wonder that the burden of the years weighed on him and he was worn out with so much feverish and useful activity?

"No, indeed. Gradually I too came to regard as natural what all of Darmstadt, all Hesse, all Germany did. When as a scatterbrained student I rushed headlong into the distinguished, paneled hall of the Germania and wanted to be certain that I had arrived in time, I didn't look at the table or at the audience, only at the presidential dais. If the president was asleep, I knew that the session had begun. If he was not, I knew that the session had not yet begun, and stepped outside for a cigarette or two. I became firmly assured that the sleeping of the president was at the same time the beginning of intellectual work and an infallible indicator and scientific measure of it.

"The lecturers themselves thought so too. Didn't this habit of the president disturb or offend them? On the contrary. As the first word of their paper rocked the president to sleep with irresistible force, they too derived courage and inspiration from his slumbers. If they noticed that he was awake, they would pause briefly, sip their water, adjust the light, but they didn't have to wait long before he was sleeping the age-old sleep of the just. Some scarcely dared speak for the first few minutes. They trembled quietly through the introductory remarks almost in a whisper, like mothers beside the cradles of their children, their thoughts and feelings coming almost on tiptoe, and only when they were convinced that the chairman's sleep had reached the required depth and that nothing could now wake him did they raise and develop their voices, abandon themselves to flights of oratory. Need I remark that this touching, childlike attention on the part of the lecturers, this caution which sprang from profound respect, was in all cases superfluous?

"Yes, my friends, that man could certainly sleep. Never have I seen a president sleep like that, and I've seen many a president sleep in Germany and in other European countries, big and small. By that time I could get along quite well in German, and I only went to the Germania and elsewhere in order to admire him. And I wasn't the only one that had a similar aim in view. Zwetschke was actually studying him—he was a slender, quick-witted young psychiatrist with whom I became friendly over this common interest. Foreigners came too—Norwegians, English, and Danes—presidents, for the most part, who despite their advanced ages made the pilgrimage to Darmstadt in order to spy out the modus operandi of their remarkable colleague, his secret, his stratagem, and to turn their experience to fruitful advantage in their demanding and responsible careers.

"But how did he sleep? In masterful fashion, remarkably, perfectly, with inimitable artistry. This was quite understandable. Even as a young man—at the age of twenty-eight—he had attained high office, and since then—for generations—had borne it constantly in the Germania and in other cultural organizations. He had vast experience. On each side of him on the dais sat a vice president, like the thieves on the right and the left. They were Professor Dr. Hubertus von Zeilenzig and Professor Dr. Eugen Ludwig von Wuttke. I'm not saying that they too nodded, dozed, snoozed, indeed actually slept, but they did it with only one eye, like hares, uneasily, like dogs do. A single glance at them was enough for the keen observer to appreciate at once the difference between master and apprentice, to realize that these were mere disciples, only vice presidents, and would never become presidents. He, however, who slept between them with profound conviction and expertise was a president, the real thing. God had created him such. I heard from Darmstadt people that this rare ability of his had shown itself even in boyhood, and while his frolicsome companions noisily played soccer in the field he would sit apart on a dais-like mound and preside.

"Significantly he slept, sternly and importantly, with indescribable dignity and pride. By that I don't at all mean to imply that when he was awake he lacked any of these desirable qualities. Awake too he was a man of standing. He was likable, but ice cold; fair, but grave. If he appeared anywhere, with his frock coat buttoned to the chin, his freshly tied black cravat, and his trousers with their knifelike crease, smiles froze on faces. Our friends told us that one summer, when he was entertaining some German naturalists and escorting them officially in the Darmstadt woods, the thrushes, tits, and all the songbirds together suddenly stopped their singing, which was out of keeping with the gravity of the situation. His importance grew, however, when he was asleep. At such times he changed into an enigmatic statue of himself. Sleep drew a sort of superficial, improvised death mask over his face. He looked a little like Beethoven.

"Furthermore he slept refinedly, choicely, in gentlemanly fashion so to speak, aristocratically and chivalrously. For example, he never snored, never dribbled. He could exercise restraint. After all, he was a baron, a nobleman. He would hang his head slightly between his shoulders. He shut his eyes, and it seemed that by cutting off his sense of sight he merely intended to increase his attentiveness, as if in this way he meant only to render homage to science and literature. His face too was transfigured by inner absorption; a sort of church-like piety came over it. Certainly, next moment, the aged head, which the sinews of the neck now supported only laxly, sank lower and lower toward the green baize under the remorseless laws of gravity, and the head drew after itself the chest and then the torso. Many a time I was afraid that his face was going to fall onto the presidential bell, the bronze of which drew it like a magnet, and that his lips would kiss it. I can, however, assure you—that never happened.

"The amazing thing was this. He slept self-assuredly and masterfully. As soon as his nodding head reached the azimuth, it rose of its own accord, the torso became erect, and so the whole process began again. He was in command of himself. He recognized the territory marked out for him in infinite space in which he could range freely without contravening decorum and etiquette. Even in his sleep he knew that he was doing something illicit, and only conditionally allowed himself this trifling foible of old age, as pleasant and understandable as the taking of snuff. His discipline set a limit just when need arose.

"Nor did it ever happen that he overslept a lecturer. He would wake up of himself, just a couple of seconds before the end. How did he manage it? I could never make it out. According to my psychiatrist friend Zwetschke, the lecturers themselves must have warned him by speaking more loudly, with greater verve, as they were coming to a close. I didn't accept that explanation. The delicate final lines of lyric verses, their sweetly allusive dying fall, had just as stimulating an effect on him as the stirring spirit of science and literature, and on all occasions he was alert, on watch in his lookout post, like one who had long been awake, and he would rise to his feet and with enviable knowledge of the subject express thanks in well-rounded sentences, as was his presidential right and duty, for the 'elevated, thought-provoking, and still entertaining exposition' or 'brilliant, high-minded, and yet moving poetry.'

"Zwetschke observed that he slept according to types of subject. He said that he slept most soundly during philosophical discourses and most superficially during lyric poetry. It was his considered opinion that the president relied on his great experience and adjusted his sleep to match the characteristics of each category. That explanation I couldn't accept either. I rather inclined to the thesis which several experts have recently upheld, that in the depths of our consciousness we are constantly aware of the passage of time while we sleep, and in particular follow the rotation of the earth by our ancient instincts, and this serves us as a time-measuring mechanism, so that when we really mean to wake up by a certain time we always do, and when we are to leave on a journey and set our alarm clocks for five we wake a few minutes before five. That instinct must have been at work in our president too.

"It happened—I won't deny it—that now and then even he made mistakes in this and that, unimportant things. After all, extraordinary spirit and peerless intellect that he was, he was only human. He only made two mistakes. The privy councillor Dr. Max Reindfleisch was reading an excerpt from his historical novel in verse about Friedrich Barbarossa. He had not been reading for ten minutes when the president opened his eyes. This gave rise to a general sensation and consternation. The audience began to whisper. Some stood up to get a better look. He himself was horrified too. The suspicion flashed through his soul that perhaps his dozing had been noticed, and he was a little embarrassed. At that he deceived the audience and perpetrated a devilish trick. He decided to close his eyes again straightaway, and also to open them again several times one after another, indicating thereby that he had been keeping his eyes closed deliberately because that way he could pay better attention. And he shut his eyes. But he didn't open them again. His eyelids were instantly gummed together by the sweet, warm honey of sleep and his head set off on its usual flight path toward the table and back, and thus he wavered to and fro until Privy Councillor Dr. Max Reindfleisch had finished the informative and learned excerpt from his novel.

"What was the second occasion? Oh, yes. The second was even more startling. You need to know that in that cultural organization a lecture would last at least an hour and a half. Professor Dr. Blutholz, privy councillor and well-known philosopher, was lecturing on his favorite topic, a very popular one in Germany, *On the First-Order Metaphysical Roots of the Intelligible World and Their Four Metaphysical Determinants*; he was warming a little to his excitingly attractive exposition and had been speaking for two whole hours without pause. At that point the president opened his misty eyes. Like a man rising from the deepest metaphysical depths, he didn't know where he was, didn't know whether the concluding speech came next, and just looked at the lecturer and the audience like visions in a nightmare. Fortunately, however, Professor Dr. Blutholz announced at that moment that after that brief introduction he would at last move on to his subject proper. That sentence had the effect on the president of the chloroform that merciful anesthetists promptly drip onto the mask of the restlessly moaning patient, strapped down on the operating table, who regains consciousness in the course of the operation. He too instantly subsided, he too 'moved on to his subject proper': he slept on, nice and evenly.

"What did he dream of at such times? On this point opinions differed. The German women, who—as I've hinted—are sensitive and romantic, said that in his dreams he obviously saw little roe deer, and ran about in the meadows of his long-past childhood, butterfly net in hand. Zwetschke, who was interested in psychoanalysis at the time, considered it likely that the president was weaving a dream which would advance his sleeping, and as his sole desire was to sleep, according to him the dream could only reflect the fulfilment of that desire in alluring little images: the lecturer would crash down from the rostrum, split his skull, and die horribly, the audience would rush upon one another in blind panic, a war of extermination would break out among them, they would shriek and die, covered in blood, the chandeliers would go out, darkness would enfold it all, the walls of the Germania would collapse, and the president would finally close the session and go home to sleep in his feather bed. In principle I agreed with this interpretation. The only thing that hurt me was that the distinguished psychiatrist had such a role in mind for the president, whom I knew to be one of the gentlest men in the world. I suggested that even in his dream he would refrain from thoughts of murder and violence. I put it to my friend that the president's interest was not in the closing of the session but its continuation. I rather imagined, therefore, that in his dream the president constantly saw Count Leo Tolstoy visiting his humble Darmstadt society, there to read the three fat volumes of *War and Peace* from beginning to end, which in the first place would be a great honor to German culture, and second would guarantee the president of the Germania at least a week of uninterrupted slumber. To this day I feel proud that the excellent Zwetschke accepted my explanation.

"I repeat, the president was a kindly man, noble, tolerant, and broad-minded. It was because of his broad-mindedness that he slept. What else could he have done? I, a young man of twenty, fit as a fiddle, with nerves of steel, who had listened only for nine months, day after day, to those lectures which he as president must have listened to for fifty-seven years, I went to pieces and developed alarming symptoms. As a result of the nauseating stupidity and eccentric bragging generally called lyric poetry, the dull and insipid nonsense which generally passed for science, that man-pleasing hairsplitting, that hodgepodge of theories generally called politics, one night in my student room I suffered a fit of rage, suddenly began to go cross-eyed and shout, and bellowed at the top of my voice for two hours until the faithful Zwetschke hurried to my bedside and administered scopolamine, which—as you will know—is usually used to calm raving lunatics. Imagine what would happen to that respectable president, who truly deserved a better fate, if he had not discovered in early life the sole solution, and his healthy spirit had not taken the stand that it had against injury. It must have been simply his instinct for self-preservation that suggested it to him. By it, however, he saved not only himself but also culture, science, and literature too, saved his nation, and also humanity as it strove toward progress.

"Yes, his sleep was the very fulfillment of national and human obligation. As he slept objectively, impartially, apolitically and without bias, to left and right equally, toward men as toward women, toward Christians and Jews alike, in brief, as he slept without regard to distinctions of age, sex, or religion, it appeared that he closed his eyes to all human failings, and not only did it 'appear,' but it was in fact so. Believe me, that sleep was veritable approval. The sleeper nods, thereby approving everything. I'll venture to state that at times in the honorable paneled lecture hall of the Germania, even the most forbearing member of the audience wished the lecturer to Hell, wished that he might have a seizure, that cancer of the tongue might render him dumb, distend his revolting mouth—and only one single person showed himself at all times tolerant toward him, the president, who was always asleep. Like outspread angelic wings, his sleep fluttered above millions upon millions of foolishnesses and vanities of the human spirit, above sterile ambition and paltry attention-seeking, the St. Vitus' dance of envy and meanness, all the nastiness and futility that is public life, science, and literature. *Qui tacet consentire videtur.** He that is silent agrees to everything. But is there so true an agreement as sleep? His sleep was a bulwark against vandalism, it was reassurance, the saving of society; it was understanding itself, forgiveness itself.

"My friends, a sleeper is always understanding and forgiving. A sleeper can never be hostile to us. The moment he goes to sleep he turns his back on the world, and all hatred, all wickedness cease to be as far as he is concerned, as they cease for the dead. The French have a saying, 'To go away is to die a little.' That I've never believed, because I love traveling, and every time that I get on a train I feel revitalized. To sleep, however, is certainly to die a little, and not a little but a lot, as much as departing life (which, when all's said and done, is nothing more than awareness of the self), as much as dying completely for a short time. This is precisely why the person who is asleep leaves the field, turns his will—with its sharp, damaging point—inward, and behaves toward us with the indifference of one who began long ago to decay. Who wants a greater benevolence on this earth? I have always insisted on respect for those who are asleep, and will not allow them to be disturbed in my presence. 'Nothing but good of the sleeper' has been my slogan. Frankly, I don't understand why we don't occasionally celebrate sleepers, why we don't

* Attributed to Pope Boniface VIII.

toss onto their beds at least a flower, why we don't organize a minor, heartwarming wake after they go off, because we are for a while free of their often burdensome, often dull company, and why, when they wake, we don't play children's toy trumpets and so proclaim our daily resurrection. That's the least they deserve.

"He would have deserved more, much more. Most of humanity, however, are incorrigible blockheads, full of fussy prejudice and false modesty. After a while even he was attacked. It was mainly the poets who plotted against him, those cantankerous crackpots who pretend to be apostles, but if two get together they flay the hide off a third; the poets, who sing of purity but avoid even the vicinity of the bathroom; the poets, who beg everyone, even beggars, at street-corners for just a little fame, just a little affection, just a little statue, beg mortals for immortality; those light-minded, jealous, wan exhibitionists who will sell their souls for a rhyme or an epithet, set out their innermost secrets for sale, turn to profit the deaths of their fathers, mothers, and children and in later years, in the 'night of inspiration,' dig up their graves, open their coffins, and rummage for 'experiences' by the dark lantern of vanity like grave robbers after gold teeth and jewels, then confess and snivel, those necrophiles, those fishwives. Forgive me, but I loathe them. There in Darmstadt, in my youth, I came to loathe them. They couldn't abide that elevated president. And they had reason. They, who in their nauseating verse described themselves, without any basis, as 'knights of dreams' and 'dreamers of dreams,' envied that noble old man who was a dreamer in the strict sense of the word. They played interminable tasteless, malicious jokes on him. They said that after all those years he was satisfying his need for sleep in front of the biggest audience that he could find, like a hunger artist starving in an officially sealed glass cage in the public view. They said that he never took off his pince-nez during sessions just so as to be able to see the images more clearly in his dreams, because he was so shortsighted that he wouldn't even be able to see dream images and would wake up out of boredom. They said that since he'd been active in the sphere of public life, that fine proverb 'Life is a brief dream' had lost its meaning, because life now seemed a very long dream. I clasped my hands together and begged them for mercy and clemency. I emphasized that even the most outstanding persons have some little shortcoming which we must disregard because of their other qualities. I quoted Horace at them too. *Quandoque bonus dormitat Homerus.** To which they replied that that was quite right, but the president didn't just nod but slept all the time, and was incapable of anything else.

"I struggled desperately. The rising flood, however, soon threatened to cover everything. Sometimes the poets' anger would appear publicly in a humorous publication or in a hostile article. They hated him. What was the reason? Well, probably their pompous-mawkish outlook. The very ones who deliberately lived their lives on a dunghill just so a few colorful toadstools should grow there could not endure that purity, that mighty, peerless quality of leadership, that irreproachable genius. While he was peacefully asleep in the presidential chair they saw all kinds of nightmares—without reason, naturally, because their view was always distorted, their judgment always clouded. They thought of the helmsman of a ship, overcome by sleep at the wheel while the ship ran onto an iceberg. They thought of the railwayman snoring beside the switch box while behind his back the skeleton grinned as it directed the train to thunder to its fate on the wrong track. What false perceptions, what lame comparisons. The ship and the train must of course be taken care of. They are physical entities. Harm could result if they collided with others. But I ask you, what harm could come to science and literature? I ask you, whom or what did that harmless, honorable president injure by sleeping, worn out by his manifold activities? I ask you, wasn't he rather beneficial to everything and everybody? I think I'm right.

"It has been my experience, at least, that in public life peace and harmony can be maintained only if we let things take their course and don't interfere with the eternal laws of life. These don't depend on our wishes, so we can do virtually nothing to alter them. The

* Sometimes even the worthy Homer nods. Horace, *Ars Poetica 359*

president's high-minded sleep, overarching opposition, gave expression to this. All the disorder on this earth has arisen from the desire of some to create order, all the filth from the fact that some have swept up. Make no mistake, the real curse in this world is planning, and true happiness the lack of it, the spontaneous, the capricious. I'll give you an example. I was the first to arrive here. For a few minutes I was all alone in the private room of the Torpedo. In came Berta, the bakery girl. I bought a *császárzsemle** from her and kissed her on the lips. A second before I had no idea that I would do that. Nor had she. So it was beautiful. Nobody had planned that kiss. If kisses are planned they turn into marriage and duties, become sour and insipid. Wars and revolutions too are planned, and that's why they're so dreadfully hideous and vile. A stabbing in the street, the murder of a wife or husband, the massacre of a whole family, is much more humane. Planning kills literature too—the formation of cliques, the guild system, in-house criticism which writes 'a few warm lines' about the in-house sacred cow. Whereas the writer that scribbles his never-to-be-published verses on an iron table by the washroom in the coffeehouse is always a saint. Examples show that those who have dragged mankind into misfortune, blood, and filth have been those who were enthusiastic about public affairs, took their mission seriously, burned the midnight oil passionately and respectably, whereas the benefactors of humanity have been those who minded their own business, shunned responsibility, took no interest, and slept. The trouble's not that the world has been guided with too little wisdom. The trouble is that it has been guided at all.

"Don't be surprised, my friends, at hearing such profound philosophizing from me on this occasion, because I'm much happier with frivolous talk. I learned it from the man from whom I've learnt more than from anyone else in my life, my loved and respected mentor and preceptor, but he never taught me anything, merely slept all the time. He was wisdom itself. Those piffling, snotty, unkempt poets, who spoke of him so disparagingly, had no idea how wise he was.

---

* A flattish roll, marked on the top with a radial pattern of grooves.

What had he not seen, what did he not know! He'd seen tendencies appear and disappear without trace. He'd seen the greatest writers in Germany become the least overnight and new poets suddenly go out of fashion—for no apparent reason, in just a few minutes, while they were shaving at home, not suspecting a thing. He'd welcomed geniuses who later rotted on straw in stables, and he'd condemned and officially denounced the false doctrines of charlatans in the cultural association under his direction, then a couple of years later endorsed those doctrines in the cultural association under his direction, and consequently later even taught them at the university. He knew that everything was hopelessly relative, and that there was no reliable means of assessment. He also knew that people generally disagreed through conflicts of interest, protested solemnly against things, but then generally solemnly retracted, made peace, and that the deadly enemies of yesteryear walked arm-in-arm in the corridors of the Germania and sat whispering on velvet couches in alcoves. Once he'd discovered that, nothing surprised him again. He had a wonderful knowledge of people and life, which would always sort itself out somehow, one should just not worry about it. What else can anyone so wise do but sleep? Put your hands on your hearts and tell me, can there be a better place for sleeping than in public, on the presidential dais, on which, like a bier, candles flicker, and there is a comfortable, imposing, presidential armchair? I tell you, he did indeed sleep out of wisdom, patience, insight, mature, manly contemplation, and therefore relied on the capricious and unexpected, and permitted the ship or train of science and literature to speed freely ahead.

"Unfortunately, those poets whom I mentioned earlier were also active. Gradually the old, reliable generation died out. The privy councillors and distinguished lawyers who had declaimed regular ballads, epic poetry, and philosophical analyses went one after another beneath the weeping willows in Darmstadt cemetery. A new generation grew up who no longer respected the boundaries of art forms, and in due course forced an entry into the Germania halls. One callow youth stepped onto the dais and announced that he was going to read his *synthetic-exotic* novel, but this consisted of only a single word, and a tasteless, obscene word at that. Another similar wretch introduced his loose and disjointed *neoclassic-metapsychic* dialogues, the content of which the human mind could neither grasp nor anticipate. A futuristic prodigy extolled in his fanciful verse war, the twilight of the universe, the annihilation of the Earth, and its simultaneous reconstitution too. The president clutched his head nervously. At the ends of lines this bloodthirsty futurist either crowed or imitated the explosions of an assortment of weapons—*bangbangbang, dagadagadaga* and the like. At every crow the president was obliged to open his eyes as if dawn had suddenly broken. That was the first time I saw that coolheaded man aroused. He assessed those immature figures indignantly. He didn't find fault with their literary tendency, nor yet with their views of the world. He approved them just like any other literary tendency and worldview. He merely dubbed them tactless and ill bred, and—let's admit it—he was right.

"Such things were certainly a strain on his nerves. He often looked pale and worn out. But—as I've said—he wasn't president only there. If he'd had three or four lecture sessions in a day, he was fresh again and went home as if he'd emerged from a tempering steel-bath to start work again next day with renewed vigor. Furthermore, he was never put out. He made good his deficiency anywhere. Should need arise, he could sleep anywhere at all, in the theater, during gala performances, during the noisiest revolutionary scenes, when the masses, freed from their chains, were howling and cheering freedom, equality, and fraternity, in the Opera, during the *Twilight of the Gods*, to the sound of kettledrums and trumpets, indeed, even when exhibitions were being opened, if for no more than a couple of minutes, in the standing position like the soldiers that were driven to death in the Russo-Japanese war. Once I saw him at a reception given by the duke of Hessen, where I'd sneaked in as the representative of a Hungarian paper. The duke came up and greeted him. He was an admirer of his. He immediately brought over his enchanting young wife, who with her bare neck and bare shoulders floated among the glittering flood of light from the chandeliers like a bittersweet swan.

The Duchess took the president's arm and got him to take her to a rococo divan embroidered with pink roses and with a gilded back. She sat him down and sat beside him. She began to chat to him. The president closed his eyes. The Duchess chattered on, laughing from time to time in her ringing contralto voice from behind her diamond-studded feather fan. Baron Wüstenfeld, who was an aristocrat and a recognized witty conversationalist, nodded. By then, however, he was asleep. The most beautiful and most décolleté young women had the same effect on that veteran philosopher as the strongest narcotic. He took every opportunity to recover from the exertions of public life, even the receptions which he likewise held as a matter of conscience at home. Many of the city's poor also called on him because of his great influence. He received and listened to everyone. In this likewise he had his own system. The widow dressed in mourning, tear-soaked handkerchief at the ready, would plead for his support, implore him to help her, and ask his permission to state the facts of her situation. When the Baron, with a cold and gracious nod, had given his consent, the widow would excuse herself and emphasize that 'I'll be brief, very brief,' and he, who knew that in all cases that meant 'I'll be long, very long,' would close his eyes and then in his sleep, thanks to his tremendous experience, would nod frequently at the right places, sometimes even simulate attention, and sleep quietly for as long as was necessary, so that when he awoke, refreshed and rejuvenated, at almost the final word, he was able charmingly to reassure the grieving, prostrate widow that 'he would do all that was possible on her behalf,' knowing beforehand that he would do nothing. This, however, was not bad faith on his part, because the president also knew that those who were so foolish as to canvass the support of others were always doomed, under sentence of death, couldn't be helped, weren't even worth helping, because they were nothing but self-deceivers, so feeble that they weren't even capable of self-deceit and went to others to deceive them instead of themselves, and that they only expected humbug, delusion, and opium, with which the president was not ungenerous. Nor were they ever disappointed. He was respected more and more, his reputation grew and grew, he was considered a charitable man, a gentleman from head to toe, and was loved everywhere.

"How much I loved him can't be expressed in human words. I only emphasize that so that you can understand what comes next. Slowly the year went by. Summer came. Every theater, school, and cultural association closed its doors, including the Germania. No lectures were given anywhere. Lecturers rested on their laurels and read one another's works in order to give out as their own the ideas that they found there, in brief, to gather strength. I put my knapsack on my back and went walking in the wild, romantic country around Darmstadt. One morning in July I had just set off for the Ludwigshöhe to see the view from the tower there, and was tramping briskly through the Luisenplatz with my genial fellow students, singing the *Wacht am Rhein* and other stirring patriotic songs, when suddenly a truly disturbing sight met my eyes. Two Red Cross nurses in uniform were leading a human wreck along the sidewalk, or rather dragging him, holding him up, like a cripple who could do nothing for himself, who lacked even the strength to walk. I won't tell you to guess who it must have been. That's what stupid narrators do who seem to think that their readers are equally stupid. You, quick-witted as you are, have probably guessed straightaway that it was Baron Wüstenfeld, of whom I've been speaking, the president, our president. I swear to you, however, that for a moment I didn't recognize him. That otherwise robust, sprightly, resilient old man had become dreadfully emaciated, a shadow of his former self. His legs were giving way under him like the slender rods of a photographic tripod. He looked like a ghost. What more can I say? He was a pitiful sight.

"The president was suffering from insomnia. Those who are ignorant of this complaint make light of it. They think that if someone can't sleep, let him stay awake and sooner or later he will go to sleep. The same goes for lack of appetite too. If anyone has no appetite, let him not eat and he's sure to become hungry. The only thing is, both conditions can have a fatal outcome. Such was the president's malady. For weeks he'd been fidgeting in fevered wakefulness, tossing and turning on his pillows without sleep ever coming to his eyes. And so German medicine was confronted with a serious, incomparably awkward case and for the time being could do nothing about it.

"As you can imagine, all the doctors in Darmstadt and Germany flocked to the patient's bedside. Dr. Weyprecht, the celebrated general practitioner, attributed the president's insomnia simply to nervous exhaustion brought on by years of unremitting intensive work. He prescribed that for the time being he should abstain strictly from all excitement, all forms of intellectual stimulus, even forbidding him to read the papers, and recommended that he should relax, listen to cheerful music, take a longish drive every day in his four-horse carriage, and for seven minutes daily—and no longer—take a little stroll in Luisenplatz, near his mansion, on the arms of those scientifically trained and absolutely reliable nurses in whose company I saw him that July day. Professor Dr. Finger, lecturer on gastroenterology at Heidelburg University, prescribed a diet of raw food—rye bread, fruit, and yogurt—with once a day (at seven in the morning) a gentle purgative and once a day (at seven in the evening) an infusion of camomile at 90 degrees, flavored with a couple of drops of lemon juice. Professor Dr. Gersfeld—the famous Gersfeld, who was summoned by telegram from Berlin University—spent several days examining the patient and only then reached a decision and made a statement. He ordered warm hip baths, which he prepared himself in the presence of the nurses. These had to be gradually cooled, then heated again, then cooled once more, but this time suddenly. Meanwhile a cold compress was applied to the head and changed every three minutes. The patient performed gentle exercises before retiring, and as soon as he was in bed a modern head-cooler of German manufacture was put on him, in which cool water ran through tubes, pleasantly chilling the bones of the skull and the agitated brain. After explaining these operations in great detail several times and causing the nurses to repeat them, the professor returned calmly to Berlin, but the patient still got no sleep. Dr. H. L. Schmidt, who was a neurologist, tried with narcotics—sodium bromide, veronal, chloral hydrate, and trianol, at first in small doses, later huge ones—but change the drugs and mix them though he might, he achieved no result. Dr. Zwiedineck, Dr. Reichensberg, and Dr. Wittingen, Jr., all three neurologists of high renown, made some use of psychoanalysis, likewise with no effect. The president became weaker and weaker. By now it was whispered in Darmstadt that the doctors had given up.

"Imagine my condition on hearing this news. I couldn't allow that irreplaceable treasure, that benefactor of humanity, to be lost. One day I called on him at his luxurious palace. When I stepped into the huge bedroom, which was completely darkened except for a single green electric light, I glanced at the president and my heart sank. There he lay in the bed, propped up on pillows piled high, his head clamped in the cooling helmet, like the wounded soldier of science and literature. I caught a heavy scent of poppy seed, wafted toward him by an automatic electric apparatus at his bedside. Facing the bed—clearly on medical instructions—could be seen the colored image of a magic lantern projected on a screen, a calm lake surface, for the purpose of evoking sleep, the redeemer, long desired in vain. All the time, however, the president was trying to jump out of bed. Two nurses were holding his hands. His face was as white as chalk.

"He was pleased to see me, for he knew me and once or twice had actually spoken to me after lectures—an unforgettable distinction for me. Now his deathly pale hand took mine and squeezed my fingers nervously. I recommended him to call in my young friend Zwetschke, who had opened his practice only recently but whom I knew to be a clever man and trusted implicitly. His apathetic entourage—an old lady, a retired colonel, and a legal adviser—seized upon my proposal. They sent for him, and a few minutes later he appeared.

"First of all Zwetschke opened the shutters and turned out the electric light and the magic lantern. The light of noon flooded the bedroom. He sat down at the patient's bedside and smiled at him. He didn't examine him. Like me, he knew him very well from the Germania lecture sessions. He didn't sound his chest, didn't look studiously at his pupils or take his pulse, nor tap his knee with the little steel hammer that he had. He took the ridiculous cooling gadget off his head and advised him not to worry about a thing, to go on living as before, not to spare himself at all. He would have thought it best if he could call an extraordinary session at once, or a special committee, but because of the summer recess that was not possible. Zwetschke shook his head and bit his lip. Suddenly he got up. He told me to get the president dressed, then turned on his heel and on the way out whispered to me to stay with him.

"We had scarcely given him his frock coat, his black cravat, and his sharply creased trousers when from outside, from the next room, from behind the closed double door, we heard Zwetschke's distinctive voice. He was giving orders in a somewhat Prussian tone: left, right, forward, forward. We all listened in astonishment. Even the president himself raised his gray head inquisitively. The double door of the bedroom opened. Then we saw six footmen, under the personal supervision of Zwetschke, slowly but surely bringing in the familiar massive oak table from the Germania. Another servant carried the presidential chair. Zwetschke watched the scene without saying a word. He gave a nod of approval. From his pocket he took the presidential bell and placed it on the table. At that he led the president to the table with infinite tact and delicacy, sat him in the chair, and asked him to ring and open the session. The president rang. 'I declare the session open,' he said. And then there took place the miracle which medical science and anxious public opinion had been awaiting in vain for a month: the president's eyelids closed and he sank into a deep, healthy sleep.

"My friend and I stood side by side in excitement and watched—he with the understanding of the expert, I with only the curiosity of the writer. Zwetschke took out his pocket watch, started the timer, and measured his rate of respiration. He glanced at me triumphantly. The chest was rising and falling rhythmically, the pale face was slowly gaining color, filling out almost visibly. The organs that had so long been driven were at rest. Blessed Mother Nature herself had taken over the cure. The president was now asleep, as he could only be in the lecture hall, within a framework of decorum and etiquette. His head sank down and rose again. That circumstance increased my admiration for him even more, because it indicated that he behaved at home as elsewhere, that he was a real gentleman. He slept for twelve hours without a break. Zwetschke, who didn't leave his side for a moment, even taking his lunch and dinner beside him, was surprised to see as midnight approached that the president picked up the bell, shook it, and declared 'the session is closed,' which meant that he'd had his sleep out, but also that we'd saved his life.

"The president wouldn't even allow Zwetschke to leave the mansion. He opened a separate wing for him, and he had to stay with him for a fortnight until he was back on his feet. Actually, the matter was hardly any trouble. If the president wanted to sleep—always fully dressed and buttoned up to the chin—he would sit in the presidential chair, ring the bell, and when he woke up ring it again. He only made use of this remarkably simple treatment (which the German medical professional journals didn't record) until the start of the season. Then, once the lectures had begun again, there was no need of it. He didn't, however, forget Zwetschke. He appointed him his doctor, and as Zwetschke had excellent connections despite his youth—he was still only just twenty-six—he was appointed doctor in charge of the nervous and mental department of the local hospital, and six months later was awarded the title of privy councillor.

"So that was my German adventure. The bill, please. Dinner, Bull's Blood, four coffees, twenty-five Mirjáms. Goodness me. I've been talking all this time. I've only just realized. Look, dawn's breaking in the January mist on the streets of Pest and smiling in at the window of the Torpedo. Dawn, rosy-fingered with dirty nails. Well, let's go and get some sleep. Or are you staying? In that case I'll have another coffee and tell you how it ended. My only entertainment these days is the sound of my own voice.

"I didn't hear anything about the president for a long time. War broke out, and I lost touch with everyone. Last year I was traveling in Germany. By a roundabout route I called at Darmstadt. I was changing trains and went to see Zwetschke. Oh, it was strange. I found my old friend there in the nervous and mental department, where I'd left him fifteen years before. He came to meet me in his white coat and embraced me. He was wearing a pince-nez with ivory frames and he'd acquired a beer belly, like the rest of the German scientists whom we'd made fun of in the old days. I just stared at him. He no longer had the tempestuous, impudent chuckle of his young days. Instead, however, he laughed all the time, slowly and prolongedly. Do you know the sort of people who laugh after every sentence, whether they've got something happy to tell us or something sad? That's how he told me that he'd got married—hahaha—had a little girl—hahaha—then she'd died at the age of four from meningitis—hahaha. I wasn't shocked at this. I knew that all psychiatrists had their personal peculiarities.

"He kept perfect order in the department. The corridors gleamed, as did the windows and the floors. Every spittoon was in place. The nurses were more frightened of him than of the raving lunatics. He had prepared demonstrations, charts, illustrative graphs. He was engaged in the study of brain tissue. In the laboratory diseased brains floated in formaldehyde, and he cut them with a machine like a bacon slicer, but much finer, into slices no thicker than skin, and from those he tried to make out the secret of the human soul and intellect. He took me round the department. Such a thing was not new to me. I've been irresistibly drawn to such places since my childhood. At all points on the earth mental departments are uniform, like parliaments. It seems that in all peoples of every clime, nature wants to pass the same message through the medium of mental disorder. The female ward dances and shrieks, the male ward is sunk in gloomy and meaningful cares. Outside in the garden, the idiots daydreamed beneath the trees, deep in their infantile foolishness. A stonemason's assistant blew his nose like a trumpet day and night, because his body was full of air, but his efforts—such was his boast—were having good results. Seventeen years previously, when he'd been admitted, the air went up as far as his forehead, but now it had gone down to the level of his chest. We worked out together that if, in the meantime, no untoward event interfered with his activity, he would be completely free of air by the time he was seventy. Even there everyone has his occupation and amusement.

"I was at first intrigued by the sharp contrast between two groups which represent the whole of mankind. Paranoiacs are cheeky, impudent, prone to exaggeration, suspicious and suspecting, dissatisfied, and eager to act, like utopian politicians. They watched me from corners, their eyes dark slits, and I could feel that they had their doubts about me. They would have been ready to haul me off to the gallows at a moment's notice in the interest of the well-being of society. They couldn't abide themselves, and their spirits were bursting to get out into the world, and they wanted to split in two. Schizophrenics are strange, original, surprising, self-accusing, incalculable, and unknowable, like born writers. Their speech is full of allusions that we can't understand. For me, the latter are the more agreeable. Two young men were standing like statues at the corner of a grassy bank, rigid. A third young man, the chalk-white-faced son of a Würzburg banker, was walking round and round, and every time he passed in front of me he greeted me with extraordinary civility, and I returned the greeting with similar respect. However, as he was passing me for the eighth time and I was returning his greeting again, he suddenly spat in my face—which pleased me immensely, as it verified and confirmed the opinion that I had long held of that disorder.

"The mentally ill didn't interest Zwetschke. He said, with his strangely prolonged, slow laugh, that they were completely mad, not even worth bothering with, only their brain sections after dissection were of interest. He invited me to tea. He introduced me to his wife, a blonde, Madonna-like woman who wore her hair drawn tightly back from her prominent forehead, shook hands with me in silence, offered me things in silence, and didn't say a single word the whole time. We ate liver pâté and drank beer. Finally I discovered what had become of the president. He'd survived everybody, even the war and the revolution. Generations had perished around him; futurists, expressionists, simultanists, neoclassicists, and construc-

tivists alike had fallen on the battlefield or been ruined, but he had
gone on working. He had the stamina of the sleeper. When he was
ending his ninetieth year, he undertook even more presidencies on
the advice of his general practitioner. In his final years he was pre-
siding in seventeen places, uninterruptedly from morning to night.
He'd died the previous winter at the age of ninety-nine. Poor fellow,
he'd failed to see his century.

"I took leave of my friend to make a pilgrimage to his grave, there
to discharge a debt of gratitude and piety. Zwetschke embraced
me with a laugh. He stuffed a wrapped-up book into my raincoat
pocket and commented that I would possibly need it. I took a car to
the cemetery, leaving the company of the mad for that of the dead. I
found the president's grave right away. He lay in a grim family crypt,
decorated with his family arms. On a marble column there was a
single sentence: *Sleep in peace.* That man, whom in life nobody had
dared to address by the familiar second person singular, was now
thus unilaterally ordered about by the impudent living. 'Be so good
as to sleep in peace,' I whispered with filial reverence, and thought
with feeling of his memory and the vanished years of my youth. I
brushed a tear from my eye.

"Sadly, I'd come empty-handed, in a great hurry, and hadn't
brought him so much as a single flower. But perhaps flowers would
have been out of place on that severe tomb. In annoyance I began
to search my pockets. I came across the book which Zwetschke
had given me for the journey and unwrapped it. It was Klopstock's
*Messiah,** that heroic poem in hexameters which—in the unani-
mous opinion of generations—is the dullest book in the world, so
dull that nobody's ever read it all, neither those who have praised
it nor those who have belittled it. I've heard it said that Klopstock
himself couldn't read it, only write it. I opened the book and leafed
pensively though it. What part should I read? It didn't matter. Since

---

* Friederich Gottlieb Klopstock (1724–1803), regarded in his time as a great religious
poet, began *The Messiah* in 1745, completing it in 1773. Much influenced by Virgil and
Milton, his odes and lyric verse helped inaugurate the golden age of German literature.

I was aware that the departed had valued repose most highly when he'd been alive, and that it must have been his wish, as it is everyone's, to sleep in peace when dead, I began to read the first canto in a monotone. The effect was astounding. A convolvulus on a neighboring tomb quivered and closed its petals as if night were descending upon it. A beetle plopped onto its back in the dust and stayed there, hypnotized. A butterfly which had been circling above the crypt fell from the air onto the stone, folded its wings, and went to sleep. I had the feeling that the hexameters were piercing the granite of the crypt, stealing their way into the mortal remains of the departed, and that his sleep in the grave—that eternal slumber—was all the deeper for them.

I awoke to feel somebody shaking me by both shoulders. It was my watchful taxi driver, whom I'd left outside at the cemetery gate. About halfway through the first canto, sleep had overcome me too. Quickly I rushed to the car. We made a frantic dash for the station. I only just had time to jump, at the very last minute, into the D-train, by then already moving, which raced with me—sparks and steam and much whistling—at sixty miles an hour toward Berlin."

XIII

In which he appears as a benefactor.
He takes the part of an afflicted widow, but is finally obliged to strike her
because he is so sorry for her that he can do nothing else.

AT ELEVEN IN THE MORNING HE WAS ABOUT TO TAKE A BATH.

He ran toward the bathroom just as he'd jumped out of bed, wearing short underpants, his chest and arms bare, no nightshirt, just pushing his feet into his green leather slippers.

In that old-fashioned apartment he had to pass through three rooms on the way.

In the third, which was a sort of reception room, stood a woman dressed from head to foot in black, heavily veiled.

At the sight of the total stranger Esti recoiled. He did not know how she could have gotten there.

His first thought was of his undressed condition. He pressed both hands to his hairy chest out of politeness.

The lady gave a squeal of alarm. She stepped back, bowing. She was appalled at meeting in this way the person whom she had called on so often and was now seeing in the flesh for the first time. She thought that this had ruined everything.

"I beg your pardon," she apologized, embarrassed.

"What do you want?" asked Esti.

"Please," she stammered, "if you don't mind ... perhaps I'd better come back later ... I don't know ... I beg your pardon."

"Please go into the hall."

"This way?"

"That way," said Esti brusquely, "in there."

The woman floated off, like a black cloud that had been filling the room, and Esti went into the bathroom, where his lukewarm morning bath awaited him.

He rang the bell in a rage.

Along came the maid. She stopped at the bathroom door.

"Jolán," he shouted in that direction, "Jolán! Have you all gone quite mad? You're letting everybody in."

"I didn't let her in. It was Viktor."

"Where did he put her?"

"In the hall."

"But she was here, in here, I walked straight into her. It's outrageous. What does she want?"

"She's asking for you, sir. She's been here several times."

"What's she after?"

"I don't know. Something to do with literature, perhaps," the maid added, naively.

"Something to do with literature," repeated Esti. "Wants to sell her collected works. Scrounging. Some kind of swindler. Or a sneak thief. She could have taken her pick. Cleaned the place out. I've told you a thousand times, give beggars something and let them go and God bless. I only see people on Sundays from twelve to one. Never any other time. Understand? And then people who come have to be announced. I'm not in now. To anyone. I've died."

"Yes, sir," said the maid.

"What's that?" asked Esti, somewhat startled at her accepting this so quickly and naturally. "So get rid of her. Tell her to come back Sunday. Between twelve and one."

When she heard the water splashing as her master took his bath the maid went away. Her quiet steps rustled in the next room. Esti called after her:

"Jolán!"

"Yes, sir?"

"Tell her to wait."

186

"Yes, sir."

"I'll be ready directly."

He did not even soap himself but got out of the bath, dressed, and called into the anteroom.

The black-clad woman came in. Once more the reception room became full of her. The white glass chandelier, with all its bulbs burning on that overcast winter morning, dimmed because of her; she was like a black cloud.

Outside snow was falling softly.

"What can I do for you?" asked Esti.

The lady did not answer. She merely burst out weeping. She choked down her tears with a thin, whining, old woman's whimper.

All that could be made out was "Help ... help ... help ..."

So: assistance.

Meanwhile she lifted her veil to wipe her wet face. She had dark green eyes. Dark green eyes surrounded by frosted curls, which had not yet had time to become gray. Disordered, almost frenzied, these tresses burst from beneath the black rim of her hat.

"The widow," thought Esti, "the widow brought down into the dust. Ghastly."

The woman blew her nose loudly, paying no attention to the fact that this disfigured her, made her seem ridiculous. In her confusion she had brought her umbrella in with her, as if she dared not leave it outside. It was dripping a whole little pond onto the mirrorlike varnish of the floor.

Her shoes and clothes were soaking wet.

But where had she come from, from what quarter of the inhabited zone, what lousy prison, what suburban slum or wooden shack? And why to him, him of all people, without any introduction or letter of recommendation?

Because she knew him. Not personally. She knew his writing.

Esti realized that.

He could tell people that knew his writing.

The widow spoke. It was impossible for so good a man as he not to understand her.

"I'm not a good man," Esti protested inwardly. "I'm a bad man. Well, not a bad man. Just like anybody else. The fact that I retain my old, pure feelings—only and exclusively for purposes of expression—is a trick of the trade, a piece of technical wizardry, like that of the anatomist who can keep a heart or a section of brain tissue that hasn't had a feeling or a thought for ages in formaldehyde for years and years. Life has left me numb, like it does everybody who reaches a certain age."

The caller alluded to the fact that she had read several of his books of verse.

"That's different," Esti continued his silent argument. "Let's not confuse the issue. That's literature. It'd be dreadful if everything I've written were true. I once wrote that I was a gas lamp, but I'd object strongly to being changed into one. And I mentioned somewhere how much I'd like to go to sea. When I'm in ten feet of water in a swimming pool, however, I never stop thinking that I'm out of my depth, and I feel definitely relieved when I reach the shallow end."

And such a refined spirituality shone from those pages, a quite extraordinarily refined spirituality.

"Refined as Hell," Esti continued to weave his thoughts, probably disturbed by the word "spirituality." "If people knew how hard, how cruel, how crudely healthy you have to be to deal with feelings. Anybody that's gentle has to be rough as well. Gentleness is just roughness in disguise, and roughness, on the other hand, is gentleness in disguise. Really, goodness and badness, mercy and cruelty have that kind of strange mutual relationship. They go together inseparably, you can't even imagine the one without the other, it'd be like someone with excellent eyes being unable to tell blue from red, or the butterfly from the larva. They are opposites, two opposing poles, but they're in constant natural interaction and change places according to circumstances, they take one another's names, fluctuate, change shape, like alternating electric current. Well, let's leave it. What feels 'refined' on paper, however, is only so because it's precise, finely tooled, and I am behind it, I—curse it!—who write for hours, work my stubborn fingers every day, come rain come shine, whether I'm in the mood or not, hissing and grinding my teeth. I'm supposed to be refined? In that case, so's the blacksmith. I'm more like a blacksmith, madam. I pound the anvil with a hammer, make shoes for my horse, fine steel shoes, so that it can gallop faster on the highway. Because take note, the griffin can't fly, it only looks as if it does, it gallops on the ground, and how! So I'm a craftsman. Look at these bones, this wrist, this chest, which you saw naked just now as it emerged from the creative workshop. Tell me the truth, do I look like a nasty, finicky poet, or more like a blacksmith?"

Esti actually stood up, showed himself as he really was, went over to the caller, so that his rough proximity might influence her to come to the point.

Slowly she came round to it.

She unbosomed her complaints, brought them out one by one as if from an open drawer.

And that had a good effect on her. She stopped weeping.

Pain, in its abstract entirety, seen at a distance, is always more terrible than close up: attention to detail sobers us up, disarms us, at least demands our concentration, self-discipline, makes us produce order from chaos. At such times we find a wheel, a screw, a hinge, which does the trick. All is now a question of detail, an easy matter. Small things reassure us.

Esti was ready for anything. He expected death and famine, prison and plague, scarlet fever, meningitis, madness.

The particular, objective data followed:

The woman's late husband had been a headmaster in a provincial town and had died the previous summer after a long battle with cancer at the age of fifty-two.

"Quite," said Esti, as if approving of cancer.

They had moved from the country, the five of them, and were now in an apartment consisting of one room and a kitchen. She had four children, that was to say. Large family, small pension, as was nowadays the fashion. The smallest boy was twelve, and had been operated on for inflammation of the middle ear, and the wound was still open and discharging.

"Quite."

His elder brother had gone to a factory and was learning to be an electrician, but was not being paid yet.

"Quite."

The elder girl was a seamstress, but could not go out of doors because now, in the winter, she had no shoes.

"Quite."

Esti was expecting consumption, and—speak of the Devil—the widow said the word: *consumption.* The smaller girl had consumption.

As for herself, the woman would like to find work, anything, because she could still work, she was thinking in particular of a tobacconist's or at least a newspaper kiosk in which she could sit, summer and winter, from morning to night.

"Quite, quite."

Esti was hearing a lot less than he had braced himself for.

After all, these were those modest—and uninteresting—complaints that life produces, for the most part with industrial, frightening uniformity. Mass production doesn't permit anything original.

But perhaps it was just that lack of imagination that surprised him, this grayness and banality: the fact that such shoddy goods were set before him, and yet certain people to whom they were shared out tolerated them as destiny.

And he thought:

"Is that all?"

And he waited.

But there was no more. It was all gone.

Esti sat down. He turned to the woman:

"How can I help you?"

With a sum of money, which was not large—to him, really, nothing at all—but with which the whole unfortunate family, which deserved a better fate, could be put on its feet for the time being. He should not misunderstand all this. She and her hapless, sick children were not asking for this as alms or a gift, only as a loan which they would redeem by their hard work, or if necessary repay in kind, here or elsewhere, but in any case they would repay to the last fillér, the very last fillér, in precise monthly installments which could be fixed in advance.

This infuriated Esti. All these people offered deals, hinted at alluring profit on capital. They were all strictly based on capital. So reliable were they that the Bank of England seemed untrustworthy by comparison.

"Indeed," he muttered, "the Bank of England," and all but burst out laughing at the silly idea.

He liked idiotic things like that.

He was afraid that, faced by all that suffering, he was about to roar with laughter. He bit his lip so that physical pain should prevent anything so disgraceful, and began to speak rapidly and lightly, because he also knew that when we keep our lips and minds busy we find it easier to refrain from laughter.

"So that's what you'd like, is it now? I understand about this money, temporarily, just to tide you over. Look, my dear lady. I myself have obligations of my own." That was a phrase that he had heard years before from a banker from whom he had begged money no less desperately (though in more prepossessing circumstances), and as he vividly saw and heard that scene he went on even more rapidly. "I have relations and friends. My staff. Etc., etc. I too work. Like a slave. Quite enough. Every letter means a bit of bread." "You mean cake," whispered something inside him. "Cake, cake, you liar."

The widow did not reply. She looked calmly into his eyes.

Esti could still hear the whispering voice. He jumped up. Hurried out into the next room.

From there he returned a little more slowly. He was holding his left fist clenched. He put down on the table a bank note. He did not look at it.

The widow, however, although she did not mean to, glanced at it at once, and amazement lit her face; it was distinctly more than she had asked for, he had rounded the amount up.

The frost which had held her almost rigid when she came in had melted, fallen away, like the melted snow on the floor. She did not know whether she could accept it. Of course, of course, just put it away.

She clutched the money in her hand. She expressed her gratitude.

Expressed it with the greatest word, than which there is none greater.

"My God."

"Good," Esti interrupted. "Write down your address. So you live in Kispest. By the way, how old's the younger girl?"

"Sixteen."

"Is she feverish?"

"Only in the evening. Never in the morning."

"Right. I'll see what I can do. Perhaps I'll manage to get her into the sanatorium. Can't say yet. Anyway, I'll try. Give me a call next week. Any time. Here's my phone number."

Next day he received a letter from them, which all five had signed. It was a long letter. It began *Your Lordship!*

According to that salutation he had been granted a new title, promoted, elevated in their sphere of influence.

They had written "*Your Lordship's heart …*" Esti laid a hand on his heart. His noble heart.

He himself had not taken seriously his promise perhaps to get the younger girl into some hospital or somewhere. He had done that rather by way of tact, for appearances, obeying his polished sense of style, to divert the widow's attention from the money in the moment of parting as she slipped it into her battered handbag, and by steering her thoughts toward a future kindness to stem the unceasing flow of her constantly repeated gratitude, which he could really no longer endure.

In the morning when he woke up Esti had the telephone brought to him in bed. He put it by his pillow, under his warm quilt, like other people put the cat. He liked that electric animal.

While he stretched out in the wide bed, feeling refreshed after his rest, he picked up the receiver and asked for a number. The city came into his bed. Still half asleep, he could hear the attentive voices of officials at the other end of the line, the background morning din of a distant TB sanatorium. He asked for the doctor in charge, an old friend of his.

"I wonder if you've got a free bed?" "Really, that's something we've never got, but we can always manage somehow. Tell the little girl and her mother to come in and bring their papers, and we'll see what we can do."

A couple of days later the doctor called him back. He informed him that his protégée had been admitted.

Now all that remained was the newspaper kiosk.

He felt that it was his duty to take this step too. And not a human duty, but one of kinship. Since he had spoken to the widow it was as if he had become related to her.

First he visited the family.

In the room where they lived, a bare wire dangled from the ceiling, and on it a single unshaded bulb shed a garish light.

Margitka, the younger girl, was by then in the sanatorium. The older girl was called Angela, and was not pretty. She looked dull. She spoke in a singsong. She had a straight, white nose, which might have been carved out of chalk. Lacika, the schoolboy with the bad ear, was hunched over his Latin grammar. The electrician had come home after a fruitless search for work, scarcely spoke to them, and with proletarian cheerlessness withdrew to a corner, from where he eyed the visitor with such gloomy and searching attention that he might well have wanted to sketch him. Esti had no idea what to make of him.

Finding a newspaper kiosk proved difficult.

At the office where that kind of licence was issued, the official informed him with a smile that in Hungary it was easier to get a ministerial post than one of those glass cages. There was absolutely no prospect of a vacancy in the foreseeable future.

Esti took note of that. As, however, there was no likelihood of a ministerial post for the widow either—some people at least would have found that strange—he held out for the glass cage. He knew that there were laws, clauses, and resolutions which were hard and remorseless, but behind every law, clause, and resolution was a mortal man who was corrupt, and with the necessary expertise could be circumvented. Nothing is impossible when it is only from men that we want it. And so he smiled, lied, flattered, crawled, browbeat, and importuned as necessary. In one place he called the widow a close relative, a dependent, and a fervent Catholic; in a second a staunch Calvinist and a refugee under the peace treaty;* and in a third a victim of the White Terror, a refugee returning from Vienna.

Esti had no scruples over such matters.

What gave him strength? He himself wondered about that.

When the family came to mind at night, or when he sometimes got up early in order to catch someone whom he needed at the office, he asked himself that question.

Perhaps he was deluding himself with the possibility of saving someone?

Was he enjoying the role of patron, living out a secret desire for power? Was his mawkish readiness to be a sacrifice influencing him? Was he atoning for something? Or was it just the excitement of the chase, of seeing the results of his amusing experiment or the extent to which people could be influenced?

Esti weighed the reasons and was compelled to answer each question in the negative.

He was after something else. Simply because he had tossed out that money in a moment of stress. It had been the direct consequence of that that he had obtained a free bed in the sanatorium for the girl, and from that it had followed that he had also had to guarantee the mother's means of support. His one action ineluctably gave rise to the other. Now, however, he would have been sorry if his work was wasted. He wanted to see a little more perfectly, a little more roundly.

As they say in business, in technical jargon, "he wanted to protect his investment."

At length the widow got her newspaper kiosk, in an excellent position at a busy corner on the Ring Road.

September sunshine gleamed on the glass, gilding the foreign magazines, drawing Dekobra and Bettauer into a wreath of rays. She came and went among them with a convalescent smile as on

* That of Trianon (1920), under which much of the territory of Greater Hungary was lost to its neighbors. Many ethnic minority Hungarians fled into into what is now Hungary.

the stage, isolated and yet part of the life of the street, in the full glare of the limelight.

As the kiosk was on his way, Esti would sometimes stop there, no longer as a patron but just as a customer. He would buy a paper but did not even need it. He inquired how Margitka was.

"Thank you," the widow would gesture, as she straightened the papers with a half-gloved hand, "thank you very much. She's not too bad. Only the food's poor. They don't give them enough," she whispered confidentially. "We have to make it up. We take her a little butter every day or two. We walk, because I can't afford the tram."

Then she spoke of the schoolboy.

"Poor little chap's had to repeat the year. He failed three subjects last year. You know, it's because of his ears. He can't hear. Can't hear what the teacher's saying. He's gone deaf in his left ear."

Esti did not believe that anything on earth could be put right. He could see that as soon as he patched up misery in one place it immediately broke out somewhere else. Secretly, however, he hoped for at least a speck of improvement, some evident relief, some relative calm, a kind word, which would cheer him, reward him. Now he was the one looking for charity.

In winter the rain poured down. The kiosk was like a lighthouse in the universal floods. Instead of the widow the seamstress was serving. She sang out with nervous gaiety:

"Mum's caught a chill. Her legs are bad. I'm standing in for her."

On his way home Esti thought of the kiosk, in which—it seemed—the elder girl too was cold, and of the widow, lying sick in bed. He sat down at his fireside. The embers cast a ruddy glow on the light brown curtains.

He stood up in irritation.

"I'm tired of this," he sighed, "really tired."

After that he watched the kiosk halfheartedly, from a distance, while he waited for the omnibus. He was sick of them. If he possibly could, he avoided them.

"Let them die," he muttered. "I shall die as well, just as miserably. Everybody does."

The widow and her family were not importunate. After repeatedly saying that they owed everything—all these things—to him and him alone, they went their way. They did not want to burden him further.

He did not see them, did not hear of them.

One restless May evening the wind was blowing up dust in the road. Esti had been drinking chocolate in a café. As he left he bumped into the widow.

She had not noticed him.

Esti spoke to her. "What's new?" said he, "I haven't seen you in ages."

For a while she did not speak.

"My little Laci," she stammered, "my little Laci," and her voice choked.

The little schoolboy had died two months previously.

Esti lowered his eyes to the ground, in which the boy was crumbling.

The widow told him everything bit by bit. Margitka was having fevers in the morning too, and they wanted to send her home from the sanatorium as they could keep her no longer. Angela had lost her job at the dressmaker's because she had had to stand in for her mother so often. The kiosk had been given up. She herself had not been able to stand about there with her bad legs. Perhaps it was just as well.

Esti nodded.

"Quite, quite."

He was standing under a gas lamp. He looked at the widow's face. She was no longer as ravaged and disheveled as when he had first met her. She was numb and calm.

If she had not been so much like his mother and those female relations of his who had likewise become dull, gone into a decline, all would have been well. But there was a look of accusation about her. An aching, almost insolent reproach.

That incensed him.

"So what can I do about it?" he raged inwardly. "Perhaps you think that I personally am doing all these dreadful things to you? What the Hell do you want from me, always from me?"

He made a gesture of refusal. He grabbed at the widow. Held her arm. Shook the thin old woman in her black clothes, struggled with her.

"Stop it," he shouted, "stop it."

Then he rushed down a side street.

"What have I done?" he gasped. "Oh, what a mess I am! A woman. A weak, miserable woman. I'm out of my mind."

He leaned against the wall. He was still gasping from the outburst. And yet he was happy. Inexpressibly happy that at last he had well and truly gotten over her.

XIV

In which are disclosed the mysterious doings of Gallus,
the cultured translator who came to no good.

WE WERE TALKING ABOUT POETS AND WRITERS, OLD FRIENDS
of ours, who had once set out with us but then had fallen away and
vanished without a trace. From time to time we would toss a name
into the air. Who could still remember him? We would nod, and
faint smiles would flicker on our lips. The image of a face that we
thought forgotten was mirrored in our eyes, a missing career and
life. Who knew anything about him? Silence answered the question, a silence in which the desiccated wreath of his fame rustled
like leaves in a cemetery. We said nothing.

We had been sitting in silence like that for some minutes when
somebody mentioned Gallus.

"Poor chap," said Kornél. "I still used to see him a few years ago—
it must be eight or nine years now—in very sorry circumstances.
Something happened to him then—something to do with a thriller,
and something of a thriller itself, the most exciting and most painful thing I've ever been through.

"Well, you all knew him, after a fashion anyway. He was a capable
man, lively, spontaneous, and conscientious and cultured as well.
Spoke several languages. Spoke English so well that it was said that
even the Prince of Wales took lessons from him. Lived over there for
four years, in Cambridge.

"He had, however, one fatal shortcoming. No, he didn't drink. But everything that came within reach he picked up. He thieved like a magpie. It didn't matter to him whether it was a pocket watch, a pair of slippers, or a great big stovepipe. He never bothered about the value of the things he stole or how big they were. He often hadn't any use for them. His enjoyment consisted simply in doing as he pleased—stealing. We, his closest friends, tried to make him see sense. We appealed to his better nature, pleasantly. We gave him a hard time and threatened him. He used to agree that we were right, he'd promise to struggle against his nature. But his mind struggled to no purpose, his nature was the stronger. He lapsed time and time again.

"Other people embarrassed and shamed him countless times, in public, caught him in the act, and at such times we had to make incredible efforts somehow to smooth over the consequences of what he'd done. On one occasion, however, on the Vienna express, he stole the wallet of a Moravian businessman who collared him then and there and handed him over to the police at the next station. He was brought back to Budapest in handcuffs.

"Once more we tried to save him. You, who are writers, know that everything turns on words, whether it's a poem or a man's fate. We gave evidence that he was a kleptomaniac, not a thief. The man we know is a kleptomaniac; the man we don't know is a thief. The court didn't know him, and so classified him as a thief and sentenced him to two years in jail.

"When he came out, one dark morning in December just before Christmas, he came straight round to me, hungry and in rags. He went down on his knees to me. Pleaded with me not to desert him, to help him, find him work. For the time being there could be no question of his writing under his own name. On the other hand, all he could do was write. So I called on a decent, kindly publisher and recommended him, and next day the publisher gave him an English thriller to translate—the sort of rubbish we wouldn't soil our hands with. We wouldn't read it. The most we'd do is translate it, and even then we'd wear gloves. The title was—to this day I can remember—

The Mysterious Mansion of Count Vicislav. But what did that matter? I was pleased to be able to do something, he was pleased to earn some money, and he cheerfully set to work. He worked so hard that he beat the deadline and delivered the translation in three weeks.

"I was infinitely amazed when a couple of days later the publisher phoned and told me that my protégé's translation was completely unusable, and so he wasn't prepared to pay him a thing for it. I couldn't make it out. I got into a taxi and went round to the publishing house.

"The publisher said not a word but put the typescript in my hand. Our friend had typed it out beautifully, numbered the pages, and tied them together with ribbon in the national colors. That was typical of him, because—as I think I've said—in literary terms he was reliable, scrupulously precise. I began to read it. I cried out in delight. Well-formed sentences, apt turns of phrase, clever linguistic devices came one after another—more, perhaps, than that drivel deserved. I was amazed and asked the publisher what he found unacceptable. He now gave me the English original, still without comment, and asked me to compare the two. I spent half an hour dipping into the book and the translation in turn. Finally I stood up in astonishment. I declared that the publisher was perfectly right.

"Why? Don't try to guess. You'll be wrong. He hadn't plagiarized something else. It really was a translation of *The Mysterious Mansion of Count Vicislav*—fluent, artistic, in places poetic in spirit. Once again, you'd be wrong. There wasn't a single mistranslation to be found in it. After all, his knowledge of English was perfect, as was his Hungarian. Stop guessing. It's something the like of which you've never heard. The problem was something different. Completely different.

"I myself came to it only slowly, bit by bit. Look here. The first sentence of the English original went like this: *All thirty-six windows in the ancient, weather-beaten mansion were gleaming. Up in the ballroom on the second floor, four crystal chandeliers shed a brilliant light.* In the Hungarian it said: *All twelve windows in the ancient, weather-beaten mansion were gleaming. Up in the ballroom on the second floor, two crystal chandeliers shed a brilliant light.* Eyes wide, I read on. On the third page the English author had written: *With a scornful smile Count Vicislav took out his bulging wallet and flung down the sum required, five thousand pounds.* This the Hungarian translator had made into: *With a scornful smile Count Vicislav took out his bulging wallet and flung down the sum required, a hundred and fifty pounds.* I was now filled with an ominous suspicion which in the following minutes—alas—was confirmed into lamentable certainty. Farther down, at the bottom of the third page of the English edition, I read: *Countess Eleonora was sitting in a corner of the ballroom in evening dress and wearing the old family jewels: on her head was the diamond tiara which she had inherited from her great-grandmother, wife of the German Elector, on her white bosom was the opalescent gleam of a necklace of real pearls, and her fingers were almost stiff with rings set with diamonds, sapphires, and emeralds.* The Hungarian, to my no small surprise, rendered this glowing description: *Countess Eleonora was sitting in a corner of the ballroom in evening dress.* That was all. Gone were the diamond tiara, the pearl necklace, the diamond, sapphire, and emerald rings.

"Do you see what he'd done, our unfortunate fellow-writer who deserved a better fate? He'd simply pilfered Countess Eleonora's family jewels, and with similar inexcusable frivolity robbed Count Vicislav too, who was such a nice man, leaving him only a hundred and fifty out of his five thousand pounds, and at the same time he'd made off with two of the four crystal chandeliers in the ballroom and disposed of twenty-four of the windows in the ancient, weather-beaten mansion. My world was going topsy-turvy, and my dismay reached its peak when I established beyond all doubt that this continued with deadly persistence throughout the book. Wherever the translator's pen went it always plundered the characters, whom he had only just met, and spared property neither personal nor real, violating the scarcely debatable sanctity of private ownership. He worked in a variety of ways. Most often items simply disappeared entirely. In the Hungarian text I found looted wholesale the carpets, safes, and silverware which are called upon to raise the tone in English literature. At other times he had filched a part of them, half or two-thirds. If a character told his servant to put five suitcases into his railway compartment, there was mention of only two and a dishonest silence about the other three. For me, at least, the most damaging detail—because it definitely spoke of bad faith and unmanliness—was that he frequently substituted worthless and inferior materials for noble metals and precious stones, replacing platinum with tinplate, gold with brass, and diamonds with quartz crystals or glass.

"I took my leave of the publisher with hanging head. Out of curiosity I asked for the typescript and the English original. As the real mystery of this thriller intrigued me, I continued my detective work at home and prepared a complete inventory of the stolen goods. I worked without a break from one in the afternoon until half past six. In the end I calculated that in the course of the translation our misguided colleague had, illegally and improperly, appropriated from the English text £1,579,251, together with 177 gold rings, 947 pearl necklaces, 181 pocket watches, 309 earrings, and 435 suitcases, not to mention land—field and forest alike—ducal and baronial mansions, and sundry other items, e.g. handkerchiefs, pocket pistols, and pendants, the listing of which would have been tedious and perhaps futile.

"Where did he put these chattels and real estate, which, after all, existed only on paper, in the realm of the imagination, and what was his purpose in stealing them? The investigation of that would lead us far afield, and I won't dwell on it. It all convinced me, however, that he was still a slave to his sinful passion or sickness, that there was no hope of a cure, and that he didn't even deserve the support of decent society. In my moral indignation I washed my hands of him, I abandoned him to his fate. Since then I've heard nothing of him."

XV

In which Pataki is anxious about his little boy,
whereas he is concerned for his poem.

ONE WINTER EVENING HE WAS IN HIS STUDY, WRITING TO HIS
publisher. His pen was flying over the paper, but suddenly he became aware that he could no longer pay attention to what he was
saying. He could hear other voices:

> *Why do I look into the night? Because I hear the thunder*
> *of the planets as they roll, see the distant roving gleam*
> *of the star . . .*

He tossed his letter aside. Wrote down those words. Then waited
to see if anything would come of it, or whether—as was often the
case—the celestial telegraph had broken off, as if there were some
remote fault in the transmitter.

This time, however, the lines kept pouring out, completing and
illuminating one another. He opened his ears wide. He could hear
other voices. He turned his gaze to the green curtain that covered the
window. Even through that he could see the starry vault of heaven.

For a long time he jotted down one thing after another. He knew
precisely what he meant to say when he'd finished.

He was simply astonished.

He read it over several times. Crossed out three lines in the middle. But had to put them back in. There was not a letter of it that could be altered. It was fine as it was.

He went to his typewriter and made a clean copy.

As he was tapping out the final lines there came a ring at the door. The maid showed in Pataki.

"Hello," he called from the typewriter without looking round. "Grab a chair. I'll just be a moment."

Pataki was standing in the half-light. His face could not be seen.

He could see Esti at the desk, his tousled hair in the golden light of the standard lamp, wreathed in tobacco smoke, as he hammered on at the keys.

Pataki didn't sit down. Just stood there.

They hadn't seen much of each other for a while.

His arrival must have been quite a surprise. Esti didn't speak, however, he hadn't the time. He went on tapping. After at last typing in his name he pulled the sheet out of the typewriter. He said:

"I've been writing a poem. Care to hear it? Two pages of typing."

Pataki sat in an armchair in the far corner of the room. Esti read slowly, syllable by syllable, so that he should understand every letter of the poem:

> *Why do I look into the night? Because I hear the thunder*
> *of the planets as they roll …*

The poem had a great arc, rising surely, smoothly, and descending slowly, gently. He was convinced that this piece of work would stand the test of time, and that years hence he would think happily of that winter evening when he had conjured it out of nothing. The concluding section, in which everything was consummated—just a few atmospheric words, a few exclamations—pleased him especially.

He laid the typescript on his desk.

"It's beautiful," came Pataki's voice out of the gloom after a brief pause.

"You like it?" Esti queried, because as soon as he was praised he assumed the role of the doubter. "You really like it?"

"Very much," replied Pataki.

He got up from the armchair. He came, slowly, into the pool of light from the standard lamp. He took hold of both of Esti's hands. He said solemnly:

"Look, I've come to see you because I've never before been so close to suicide."

"What?" Esti was startled.

"It's young Laci," Pataki stammered. "Young Laci."

Esti switched on the chandelier. He saw that his friend was deathly pale and trembling from head to foot.

"What's happened?" he asked. "What's the matter with him?"

"They're operating within the hour."

"What for?"

"Appendicitis."

"Oh, that's nothing. Sit down, Elek, come and sit here. Don't be silly. Would you like a glass of water?"

Pataki took a gulp.

"Oh, I'm finished," he sighed. "I know I'm done for. But there was no way I could stay in the hospital. We took him in this morning. Now they're getting the poor boy ready. I couldn't bear to watch. His mother's with him. The taxi's outside. I'll go in a minute."

"How long's he been ill?"

"Well, I'll tell you all about it. How did it all go, now?" he said, pressing a sweaty, white hand to his face. "Laci complained a week ago that his stomach was hurting. Always had a stomachache, etc. We thought it was indigestion after Christmas. He'd had a lot to eat over the holiday, etc., etc. So we gave him something for it. Purgatives, not too much food, etc. But it got no better. Then this morning he was sick. We called Rátz straightaway, then Vargha, then the professor, Elzász. Turned out it was appendicitis. They're operating at nine o'clock."

"Right. So is that all?"

"He's got a high temperature. Hundred and four. A temperature like that could mean that the appendix is septic."

"There's always a high temperature with appendicitis."

"What worries us is that it might be perforated."

"That'd bring on the shivers. Has he been shaking with cold? There you are. Don't worry. There's no perforation."

"You think so?"

"Yes, yes."

"But they're going to give him a general anaesthetic."

"Get them to use a local."

"Can't be done. Simple as that. Elzász says it's out of the question."

"Then they'll use a general."

"Only thing is, he's got a weak heart. Ever since he had scarlet fever his heart's been so weak he's had to take it easy all the time, he's even been excused from gym class. Oh, if anything happens to that boy I won't survive it. You know what I mean, I wouldn't survive for a moment."

"How old is he?"

"Nine."

"Nine? He's quite a big boy. Elzász operates on children of two and three, and even then nothing goes wrong. And what's more, the life force in children is nothing short of miraculous. Those young cells, those unused organs, bursting with life, they don't even catch things that grown men die of. You can feel perfectly safe. They'll whip the appendix out, and he'll be perfectly all right. Up and about inside a week. Tomorrow, no, today even, in an hour and a half, you'll be laughing about the whole thing. Both of us will."

Pataki calmed down. After pouring out his terror he had become empty, and looked in amazement round that untidy, stuffy study.

"Disgraceful," said Esti suddenly, and grimaced. "It's disgraceful. There I was, boring you."

"With what?"

"With this trash."

"What trash?"

"This poem."

"Oh. No, you didn't."

"Of course I did. When you, my poor friend, were in such a state—

without any cause, I'll observe—I treated you to my latest brainchild. Well, that's hellish, really hellish."

"No. Honestly, it still did me good to hear it. At least it took my mind off things a bit."

"Were you able to pay attention?"

"Yes."

"Did it interest you?"

"Of course."

"And what's your considered opinion of it?"

"That it's excellent. One of your significant poems."

"Only significant?"

"Very significant."

"Look here, I'm not fishing for compliments. You know I've always loathed that sort of thing. But I need you to give me an honest opinion. Whenever I write something I always think it's my very best work. Can't do otherwise. I expect you're the same. Then I gradually get used to it being there, begin to tire of it, start to have my doubts as to whether it was worth bothering with. For that matter, our whole profession's a waste of time. Who the hell cares about our heads aching when everybody's head's aching? So tell me."

"Like I said, it's magnificent."

"I'm sure myself about the first part: *Because I see the distant roving gleam of the star* … That was inspiration, pure inspiration. But later on—about the middle—it struck me—I felt it before, when I was reading it out—that it's not so good."

"Whereabouts?"

"Where the shorter lines come in. You don't remember? *Carbuncle, you glowing* … Isn't that false? Isn't it pompous and verbose? Isn't there a kind of discontinuity there?"

"None whatever."

"That's what you think?"

"Absolutely."

"And the whole thing, Elek, to your ear, isn't it a bit rhetorical?"

"Rhetorical? Personally, now, I really like a lovely rise and fall, and I'd never keep rhetoric out of poetry altogether."

"I see. Well, I have a thorough dislike of all forms of rhetoric. That's not poetry, it's sugarcoating. Be honest, tell me the truth. I'd rather tear the whole thing up and never write another line if this is rhetorical."

"You're always getting things wrong. It isn't rhetorical. Not at all. And then, what a splendid ending. *To live, to live.* That's marvelous. You'll see, others will like it just as much. Have you shown it to Werner?"

"Not yet."

"Well, do. He'll be delighted with it. I know him. I bet he'll print it on the front page in bold Garamond. You'll never have had such a success. The whole thing's masterly, masterly."

Esti rustled the typewritten sheets in his hands. Pataki took out his pocket watch.

"It's ten to nine."

"I'll go with you."

They got into the car which was waiting outside the house. They raced through the dark, snowy streets. The father was thinking whether his son would survive, the poet whether his poem would.

At a bend Pataki said:

"If it *is* septic, it can go wrong."

Esti nodded.

Later he spoke:

"I *will* take out those three lines in the middle, it'll be simpler."

Pataki approved.

After that they said no more.

Each was thinking of the other:

"How petty, how selfish."

When they reached the hospital, Pataki raced up to the second floor. Esti went after him.

Young Laci had been sedated, was drowsy, and was just being rolled to the brilliantly lit operating theater on a tall, narrow trolley.

XVI

In which Elinger pulls him out of the water,
but he pushes Elinger in.

THE BATHERS SWAM OUT TO THE MIDDLE OF THE DANUBE,
into the wake of the Vienna boat, squealing as they were rocked and
tossed by the huge waves. Esti sprawled on the shore every morning in his swimsuit and envied the lively company. He could swim
better than anyone there, but his imagination also functioned better than theirs. Therefore he was a coward.

One day he made up his mind that, come what may, he was going to swim to the other bank.

His muscular arms flailed the water. He had reached the middle
of the Danube before he realized it. There he stopped for a moment.
He took stock of himself. He wasn't out of breath, his heartbeat was
normal. He could have gone on for a long time. It crossed his mind,
however, that he wasn't afraid, and that thought, that he wasn't
afraid, frightened him so much that he immediately became afraid.

He turned round. The bank from which he had set out, however,
looked farther away than the other. And so he struck out for the far
side. In this direction the water seemed unfamiliar, deep and cold. He
got a cramp in his left leg. When he kicked out his right leg, its muscles knotted too. As was his custom, he tried to turn onto his back,
but only wallowed, rolled, went under, drank a couple of gulps, vanished for a moment or two, and then sank downward, enveloped in

the dark veils of the water. His hands beat in desperation.

This was seen on the bank. The shout went up that someone was drowning in mid-river.

A young man in blue trousers, who had been leaning on the rail by the changing rooms, flung himself into the waves and swam powerfully toward the drowning man.

He arrived in the nick of time.

Esti's head had just emerged above the water. The lifesaver took a grip on his long hair and dragged him ashore.

There he quickly regained consciousness.

When he opened his eyes he looked at the sky, then the sand, then the people who were standing there in the golden sunlight, their unclothed bodies gleaming silver. Another gentleman, similarly unclothed and wearing dark glasses, was kneeling beside him and taking his pulse. Evidently a doctor.

The group that had formed around him was looking with keen interest at the young man in blue trousers, the one who—as he discovered—had recently snatched him from the jaws of death amid frenzied public curiosity.

He came up, extended his hand and said:

"Elinger."

"Esti," Esti introduced himself.

"Oh, maestro," the young man was deferential, " who wouldn't know the maestro?"

Esti tried to conduct himself like a person that "everyone knew."

He was in some perplexity.

In the past he'd been given all sorts of things. As a boy a splendid stamp album, a gold ring as a present from his godparents, later a number of appreciative reviews, even an academic prize, but more than this he had never before received at one time. Only once, from his father and mother.

This new acquaintance had given him back his life. If he hadn't happened to come bathing that afternoon, or if at the crucial moment he'd been lighting a cigarette instead of immediately diving in headfirst, Esti would by now have been down among the fish on the riverbed ... in some unknown place ... goodness knows where ... Yes, he was reborn. He had now been born a second time, at the age of thirty-two.*

He got up and gripped the young man's hand.

He mumbled:

"Thank you."

"Oh, don't mention it."

"Thank you," he said, as if by way of acknowledging receipt of a light from someone in the street, and because he sensed the inadequacy of words he gave emphasis to his feeling by stress, and repeated warmly "Thank you."

"Think nothing of it."

'My life?' thought Esti, then said aloud: "What you did, sir, was magnificent. It was heroic. It was human."

"Only too pleased."

"But I can't express ... can't express," Esti stammered, and at that took the young man's other hand too and shook both vigorously.

"Oh, not at all," stammered the young man.

"After all this, we ought to get to know one another. I don't know if you'd be free?"

"Any time, maestro."

"Today? No, not today. Come round for a coffee tomorrow. Wait a minute, let's say the evening. You know, the roof terrace of the Glasgow. Nine o'clock."

"You do me a very great honor."

"So you'll come?"

"Certainly."

"Good-bye."

"Good-bye."

---

* Perhaps an autobiographical allusion. Kosztolányi was thirty-two in March 1917; this story dates from 1929. In his untitled poem *Most harminckét éves vagyok* (published in 1924) he says, "Now I am thirty-two. It is summer. Perhaps this is what I have been waiting for. The sun beats with golden light upon my healthy, bronzed face ..." The second stanza begins "When I am dying I shall whisper 'It was summer. Alas, happiness betook itself elsewhere. The sun beat with golden light upon my healthy, bronzed face ...'"

The young man bowed. Esti embraced his soaking form and left. As he made for the changing room, he looked back at him more than once and waved several times.

At nine precisely he appeared on the roof terrace of the Glasgow. He looked for his man. At first he couldn't find him anywhere. At the tables, grass widows were cooling themselves in front of electric fans, drinking Buck's Fizz with other women.

At half past nine Esti began to feel anxious. He had a spiritual need for this meeting. It would have grieved him if they were to miss each other, if he were never again to see his greatest benefactor as the result of a misunderstanding. One after another he called the waiters and asked about Elinger.

It then turned out that he couldn't even describe him. All that he could remember was that he wore blue trousers and had a gold front tooth.

Finally, right by the elevator, where the waiters went in and out by the potted plants, he caught sight of someone sitting with his back to the public and waiting modestly. He went over to him.

"Excuse me, Mr. Elinger?"

"That's right."

"So here you are then? How long have you been here?"

"Since half past eight."

"Didn't you see me?"

"Of course."

"Why didn't you come over?"

"I was afraid of disturbing the maestro."

"What an idea! We don't know each other, do we. That's very interesting. My dear fellow, come along. Over here, over here. Leave that. The waiter will bring your things over."

He was half a head shorter than Esti, thinner, less muscular. His reddish-blond hair was parted in the middle. He was wearing a white summer shirt, a belt, and a silk tie.

Esti stared into his face. So this was he. This was what a hero was like, a real hero. He looked at him long and closely. His brow was firm, gleaming, evincing determination and decisiveness. Esti felt life around him, real life, which he had forsaken in favor of literature. The thought flashed through his mind of how many interesting spirits lived in obscurity, unknown to the world, and that he ought to get out and about more. It was principally Elinger's simplicity that charmed him, that great simplicity that he had never had at his disposal, because evidently even in his cradle he had been labyrinthine and complex.

"Let's have something to eat first of all," he proposed lightly. "I'm ravenous. I hope you are as well."

"No, I had tea not long ago."

"That's a shame," replied Esti absently as he studied the menu. "A great shame. Well, you'll have some dinner. Now then, what is there? Pike-perch as a starter, right. Green peas, just the thing, as well. Fried chicken, cucumber salad. Gateau. Strawberries and cream. Excellent. Beer, wine afterwards. Badacsonyi. Mineral water. Everything, please," he added expansively.

Elinger sat in front of him, eyes closed, like someone who had done something wrong.

The roof garden with its electric lights blazed up into the sweltering sky. Down below, the city with its dusty houses and bridges panted in the black African darkness. Only the line of the Danube gleamed dully.

"Undo your collar," Esti advised, "it's still as hot as hell. I've been writing all day wearing nothing. All I had on was my fountain pen."

Elinger said nothing.

Esti laid a hand on his and said with warm interest:

"Now tell me something about yourself. What do you do?"

"I work in an office."

"Where?"

"First Hungarian Oil."

"Well, fancy that," said Esti, and didn't know why himself, "fancy that. Married?"

"No."

"Neither am I," Esti laughed to the heavens, which on that elevated roof garden seemed somewhat closer to him.

"My life," said Elinger mysteriously and significantly, "has been a real tragedy," and he showed anemic gums above his gold tooth. "I lost my father very early, I wasn't yet three. My poor widowed mother was left alone with five children, whom she raised by the work of her two hands."

"All this is raw material," thought Esti, "uninteresting and lacking in content. Only that which has form has interest and content."

"Thank God," Elinger went on, "since then we've all been successful. My sisters have married well. And I've got a bit of a job. I can't complain."

They both ate heartily. After telling the story of his life Elinger had nothing else to say. Esti tried now and then to revive the flagging conversation. He asked Elinger when and how he'd learned to swim so very well. He replied with laconic objectivity, then sank into uncomfortable silence.

After the strawberries the French champagne was brought in an ice bucket.

"Have some," Esti urged. "Come along. How old are you?"

"Thirty-one."

"Then I'm the elder. If you'll permit ..."*

At the end of the meal Esti announced:

"I'll be at your disposal at any time—understand that—at any time. Not like people that say 'any time'—I mean now, this minute, tomorrow, in a year's time, in twenty years' time, as long as I live. Any way that I can. Heart and soul. What you did is something I'll never forget. I'll be eternally grateful."

"You embarrass me."

"No, no. If it hadn't been for you I'd certainly not be dining here today. So feel free to call on me."

When the time came to pay, Elinger reached for his wallet.

"Now put that away," Esti stopped him.

Once again he expressed his good will.

* Up till now the conversation has used *maga*, the honorific form of address. Hungarian custom is that the elder of the pair may initiate the use of the familiar *te*, as Esti now proposes and does.

"You absolutely must come and see me. Give me a call first. Make a note of my number."

Elinger wrote down Esti's number. He gave him the number of First Hungarian Oil. Esti wrote it down.

"Why did I do that?" he wondered as they parted. "Never mind. Next time there's any lifesaving to be done I may be able to call him."

The telephone number lay unused on his desk for a long time, then vanished. He didn't call him. Nor did Elinger call. Months went by without any sign of life from him.

Esti, however, often thought of Elinger.

People that we've long been expecting mostly show up just when we're having a shave, are cross at having broken a new gramophone record, or have been getting a splinter out of a finger and our hand is still bleeding. The petty circumstances of life never permit ceremonious, decorous meetings.

Before Christmas it was freezing hard. Esti's mind was on anything but swimming and drowning. It was a Sunday, about half past eleven. He was getting ready for a lecture which began at one.

Then Elinger was shown in.

"Glad you've come at last!" Esti exclaimed. "What's new, Elinger?"

"I would have come before," said Elinger, "only my mother's been ill. Seriously ill. Last week she was taken into hospital with a brain hemorrhage. I'd be grateful if you could ..."

"How much do you need?"

"Two hundred pengős."*

"Two hundred?" said Esti. "I haven't got that much on me. Here's a hundred and fifty. I'll send fifty round in the morning."

Esti sent the other fifty round that same day. He knew that this was a debt of honor which he had to discharge. After all, he had received his life from Elinger on credit, and he was entitled to that much interest.

As his mother's illness continued, he gave Elinger in lesser and greater amounts a further two hundred pengős, and then, when she

---

* *Pengő*, "tinkler," was the unit of currency replacing the korona on January 1, 1927.

died, three hundred and fifty more after the funeral, which he himself raised on credit.

After that Elinger called several times. He got from him, on various pretexts, on his word of honor, small, trifling amounts. Sometimes twenty pengős, sometimes just five.

Esti paid out with a certain delight. Afterward his feeling was one of relief. He simply couldn't stand his presence, those bloodless gums, his gold tooth, and his boring chatter.

"This fellow," thought Esti, waking up to the truth, "is one of the biggest idiots in the world. It took somebody like him to save my life. If he were any brighter he'd surely have left me to drown."

One day, when Esti came home in the small hours, there was Elinger sitting in his study.

He informed Esti cheerfully:

"Just imagine, I've been given the sack. Without notice or severance. And I've had nowhere to live since the first. I thought I'd come here for tonight and sleep here. If you'll let me."

"Naturally," replied Esti, handing him a clean nightshirt. "You can sleep here on the couch."

Next day, however, he inquired:

"Well, what're you planning to do now?"

"I really don't know. It wasn't much of a job. Pen-pushing from eight in the morning till eight at night. For a miserable hundred and twenty pengős a month. It wasn't really worth it."

"You'll have to look for something better," Esti remarked.

Elinger spent several days going around and then announced despondently that there were no openings.

"You mustn't let it get you down," Esti consoled him. "You can live with me until you find something suitable. And I'll give you some pocket money every first of the month."

He was a quiet, unassuming young man. He went out with him to the artists' circle for lunch and dinner, and sometimes to dress rehearsals too. In the apartment he sprawled full-length on his couch. He seemed to be out of luck. He had obviously used up the last of his strength in saving Esti's life.

Only one thing was unpleasant.

When Esti was writing, in torment, screwing up his face, Elinger would sit opposite him and watch him curiously as he would an exotic animal in a cage.

"Elinger," said Esti, putting his fountain pen down, "I'm very fond of you, but for God's sake don't stare at me. If you do, I can't write. I write with my nerves. Take yourself into the other room."

For several months they lived on without anything special happening. Elinger made himself quite at home. At Easter he spent his whole month's pocket money on a new kind of cologne atomizer with a rubber tube, and sprayed all his friends.* In his spare time he read theater magazines with extraordinary attention.

One day he put a theater magazine, on the cover of which was a film actress, under Esti's nose. He said:

"I bet she knows all about it."

"Knows about what?"

"Well, you know, carrying on." And Elinger gave a sly wink.

Esti was furious. He stormed into his study and thought:

"Filth is filth. I know he saved my life. But the question is, for whom did he save it—for himself or for me? If things go on like this I won't want my life, I'll send it back to him postage-paid, like a sample, no value, and he can do what he likes with it. Anyway, by law the finder is only entitled to ten percent of lost property. I repaid that ten percent long ago, in money, time, and peace. I don't owe him anything."

He put his foot down at once.

"Elinger," he said, "this cannot go on. You've got to pull yourself together. I'll support you, but only you can help yourself. Work, Elinger. Courage!"

Elinger hung his head. In his eyes was reproach, great reproach.

After that he continued to sprawl on the couch, continued to read theater magazines, and continued going to dress rehearsals—the

* A reference to the Hungarian custom of spraying (with water or eau de cologne) at Easter. The recipients are only women.

office had by then issued him with a personal ticket, as they did to the staff of the theater's hairdressers, tailors, and gynecologists. And the months went by.

One night in December they were strolling homeward along the Buda embankment.

Elinger was asking about the private lives of actresses, how old they were, who was married to whom, who had how many children, and who was getting divorced. Such stuff drove Esti mad, and he found it degrading to answer.

"You know what?" said Elinger suddenly, "I've written a poem."

"Never!"

"Shall I recite it?"

"Go on then."

"*My Life*," he began, and paused to give the italics their full effect. "That's the title. What do you think of that?"

Slowly, with feeling, he recited it. The poem was bad and long.

Esti bowed his head. He was mulling over where all this was leading to, and what he had in common with this loathsome fellow. He looked at the Danube between the steep banks, with its murky waves and floating broken ice.

"What about pushing him in?" he thought.

But he didn't just think. In he pushed him, then and there.

And ran.

XVII

In which Ürögi drops in for a chat.

IT WAS SEVEN IN THE EVENING WHEN DANI ÜRÖGI CALLED.
Unfortunately, few will know who he is nowadays. He's still
around. He works in the office of a pottery factory, and his sideline
is teaching ladies to play bridge. He writes hardly anything. In the
old days, however, he wrote a lot and talked about it a great deal.

In the time when the coffeehouses of Budapest were differenti-
ated not by their price lists, their coffee, and their cold meats but
exclusively by their "literary" tendencies, he too used to sit with his
pale face in the baroque gallery of the New York like a faint but ever
more brilliant star in the literary firmament.

Ürögi had one very famous sonnet and one very short piece of
blank verse in which the word "Death" occurred no fewer than
thirty-seven times, always with a different tone color, always more
surprisingly and alarmingly, and then one rhyme, a very long, thir-
teen-syllable rhyme—and no one has yet discovered a more fortunate one.

But it was sufficient for the World War and sundry revolutions
to break out, for twenty million to die on the planet (some on the
battlefield, some from Spanish flu), for a few kings to be reduced to
refugee status, a few world banks, a few countries to be completely
ruined—and people forgot those poems and him personally as if
they had never been.

Kornél Esti was not such an ingrate. He forgot nothing that happened, he remembered everything that was really important.

As soon as he heard that this infrequent visitor had arrived, his face lit up. True, more than once, a year had gone by without his seeing him. When he did see Ürögi, however, he was always pleased. At such times the colored lights of his youth blazed up, far off, behind the summer foliage of merrymakings, the ragged curtains of theaters.

Dani Ürögi was pale and bald. The poor fellow was no longer a star, only a faint, dying moon among the black storm clouds of economic world revolution. He had always had an anxious disposition. But now he too was past the age of forty, and with advancing age had become even more anxious.

"Am I disturbing you?" he asked.

"Not at all," replied Esti.

"Really?"

"That's what I said."

"I won't trouble you for many minutes," he added sternly.

"Really, please. I'm glad you've come. Sit down. Have a cigarette, Dani. Here."

Dani sat down. And lit a cigarette. But as the match flame danced above his slender fingers he glanced at Esti, threw the match into the ashtray and the cigarette after it, and jumped up.

In a calm but determined voice he declared:

"I am disturbing you."

"Idiot."

"Oh yes, yes: I am disturbing you."

"Why should you be?"

"I can tell."

"From what?"

"From everything. From your eyes, first of all. You don't usually look at me like that. Now it's as if a kind of artificial light were pouring from them, as if you'd switched them to a new circuit. It's not natural. Nor is your pleasant, encouraging, master-of-the-house smile natural, which you've stuck onto your mouth simply in my honor. Nor is your tone natural, the way you say 'Not at all'—simply not natural."

"You're an ass," Esti shrugged. "I suppose you'd prefer it if my eyes closed and I yawned? Believe me. If I tell you that you're not disturbing me, that means neither more nor less than that you're not disturbing me. If, that is to say, you were disturbing me, I'd say 'You're disturbing me,' and that would mean precisely 'You're disturbing me.' Now do you see? Is that clear? So, why aren't you answering?"

"Give me your word of honor that it's really so."

"On my word of honor."

"Once more."

"On my sacred word of honor."

Esti called for coffee, a whole water-jugful, and filled tumblers so that they could drink coffee as they used to in the old days.

Dani sat back down. He said nothing for a while. Only after that silence did he speak. He said that he'd been out for a walk there in the Buda hills on that fine moonlit evening—which was beside the point—and there he'd suddenly thought of his friend and decided to look him up, surprise him—but that too was beside the point— and he'd like to ask a favor, which he was going to tell him about shortly.

His sentences crawled along, pausing amid a thousand doubts and changes of mind, like the wheels of a train descending a mountain. In the middle of one sentence he stopped. Did not finish it. His mouth remained open. Suspicion gleamed in his dark eyes. He jumped up again. He wagged a forefinger at Esti and said, in a tone that brooked no contradiction:

"You were working."

"No, I wasn't."

"Yes, you were," he repeated darkly, like a prosecuting counsel. "And here am I round your neck, holding you up, and you secretly— and quite rightly—are wishing me to the devil."

"I hadn't the slightest intention of working."

"Are you telling the truth, Kornél?" he asked, smiling like someone who has caught out a child in some crafty fib, and while the smile spread over his face like a mask he wagged his raised forefinger slightly and began to threaten his friend. "Kornél, Kornél, don't lie to me."

"I'm not," Kornél protested. "I haven't been able to get anything done for a week now. I hate all work. Especially my own. The stuff I'm scribbling at present is so atrocious that if my enemies and the people who envy me were to find out how little I think of my talent they'd surely start to argue with me, rise in my defense, and finally accept me as a friend forever. Today I've just been sitting about and feeling bored. I was just hoping that one of my creditors would call me and take my mind off things a bit, but even they aren't speaking to me. Then I wanted to swat some flies, but there aren't even any flies in my apartment. Then I started to yawn. If someone's very bored, even yawning is an amusement of sorts. I yawned for about two hours. Finally I got tired of yawning. So I stopped yawning and just sat in this armchair where you see me now, waiting for time to pass, getting a couple of hours older, a couple of inches closer to the grave. Please get this straight: at present, the thought that that terrible acquaintance of mine, whose idea of a joke has for years consisted of calling his wife 'old girl,' would knock on my door, that some complete stranger would come in and ask me for a loan of a hundred pengős for ten months on his word of honor, or that some unappreciated writer would do me the favor of reading me the novel he's working on—that thought would have made me happy at once, but the thought that you would call, Dani, you, for whom I constantly thirst, who shared my former years of beggary and my vagrant fame, my brother in ink and passion—that thought would have rendered me ecstatic, and so enticing, so remote a thought was it, so like a fairy vision, that I didn't dare even to dream it. Excuse me, don't interrupt, I'm talking. As to my work plan for today, I'm free until nine, for two whole hours, and at your disposal. We'll drink coffee here, chat or sit in silence together, and then I'd like to go for a walk, because I haven't been out of this dump all day. If you've no objection I'll keep you company, see you home. All right?"

"All right."

Dani breathed more easily and took a gulp of his espresso. He spoke again about the circumstances of his coming, of the irrelevant Buda hills, the irrelevant idea that had whirled him to Esti's, and the request to which he would come in a moment, but with which he would not trouble Esti yet because it was important only to him, not to Esti, and therefore it too was irrelevant. Suddenly he was silent. Something had come into his mind. He said:

"Besides, I've only come for a couple of minutes. I know, I know. You're very kind to me, but you are to everyone. 'Don't take seriously the polite request to stay.' I'll stay for seven or eight minutes at the most. Did I say seven or eight? I'll stay for seven only. Exactly seven minutes. Where's your pocket watch?"

"Why?"

"Please get it out. I'll get mine out as well. There now. Thank you. Goodness knows, I always feel more relaxed if I can see the time. So—when the minute hand gets to—look, here—I'll be gone and that particular stone will fall from your heart and you'll be able to sigh 'at last he's gone,' and do whatever you feel like. Promise, however, that you'll remind me. As soon as the moment of release comes—let's call it that—you'll stand up and say to me word for word 'Dani, I've been glad to have the pleasure of your company, but even more so to be rid of it, off you go and God bless.' Yes. Throw me out so fast that my feet don't touch the ground. Or don't even say that, just look at me. It'll be enough for you to look at me, not crossly, but as you do at other times, the way you're looking at me now. I assure you, there won't be any need of that either, because in seven minutes' time—beg your pardon, six minutes' time—I shall have vanished, and only the painful memory of my presence will linger in the air of this room."

"Listen here, you lunatic," said Esti to him gently, in the confident tone of established friendship, "I don't want you to go away, I want you to stay. But if you absolutely insist on these seven minutes—or these six minutes—that too I'll accept conditionally. I'll only ask one thing of you. While you're in my apartment, don't have misgivings, don't fidget, don't make excuses, but feel at home. So tell me quickly what you want. Then we'll talk. What? You can rest assured. Yes, yes. I'll do as you wish. As soon as I'm tired of you I won't beat about the bush, I won't even look at you one way or another, but I'll get up, grab you by the collar, and throw you out—even kick you downstairs if you tell me to. I hope that makes you feel better?"

Dani accepted this unselfish promise of amicable generosity with obvious pleasure. He seemed to gather strength from it, and he gulped his espresso. But how long did the effect of Esti's calming solution last? Scarcely a minute or two. After that he began again, and had to be disarmed again. In growing waves of self-accusation and soulsearching he continued to explain why it was not his custom to steal other people's valuable time, he pondered and dithered, returning again and again to his former excuses and objections, then to Esti's arguments and remonstrations too, but as he wished to quote everything verbatim and couldn't remember the words he became confused, stared in front of him, and wiped his perspiring forehead.

Esti listened to these expositions, these allusions, these digressions, these references, these hints, these circumlocutions, these angles and aspects. By this time he too was pale and weary. Now and then he stared in exhaustion at the ceiling and at his pocket watch as it ticked away in front of him. Nine o'clock passed, as did half past nine. Then slowly, with a certain solemnity, he rose and began to speak, at first quietly, then more loudly, as follows:

"Look, my dear fellow. You told me to let you know when six minutes were up. I'm telling you that those six minutes were up a long time ago. It is now, by Central European time, nine forty-two, almost a quarter to ten, so you can see that you've been squatting here for two and three-quarter hours, but you still haven't been able to utter a single proper sentence, and you haven't been able to bring yourself to tell me what on earth I have to thank for this honor. Dani, consider, I too am a man, I too have nerves. Are you holding me up? Infinitely. Am I tired of you? Inexpressibly. There's no word for how damn tired of you I am. Just now you were so kind as to advise me how, at the right moment, I should show you the door, and, scrupulous as you are, you presented me with a script for the purpose. That script, which I have in the meantime been considering carefully, would have more or less expressed my feelings, but only an hour after you arrived, at about eight. I'll confess that at about half past eight I was already thinking of adding a dose of cyanide to your coffee and poisoning you. Then toward nine I decided instead that while you were talking there I'd get out my revolver, fire a shot or two into you, and kill you. As you can see, the situation hasn't changed at all. Your script now strikes me as pale and feeble. I can't use it, and I return it to you—do whatever you like with it. At this moment I could do with a spicier, more elaborate script, an eloquent cascade of reproaches and insults compared to which the tirades of Shakespeare's heroes would be lemonade. But I gave up the idea of exterminating you with poison, bullet, or words because I consider you such a pitiful worm that you aren't even worth it. Instead, I'm telling you like this, quietly and in friendly fashion, to get out of here. Get out, this very minute. Did you get that? Get lost. I'm not joking, I swear, take your hide out of here, because I can't stand the sight of you, and don't have the effrontery ever to come back, I'm fed up with you, sick and tired, you rotten egg, you dead loss . . ."

Esti was by this time howling so that he choked, his lips writhed, and he gesticulated. One of his gestures swept the water jug off the table, smashing it to fragments, and the black liquid that it contained soaked into a white silk Persian rug.

Dani burst out laughing. He laughed heartily and happily. Only now did he realize that he had been gladly allowed to remain and that he had been a burden to no one. He settled down comfortably, lit a cigarette and his tongue was loosened.

He explained his business.

His request was simple, indeed, extremely simple.

He was asking a favor, a huge favor, which obviously was only huge to him, but perhaps not all that huge to the person who would do it, though perhaps it was huge, or significant, though it could also be that it was nothing at all, but even so he pointed out in advance that his friend might refuse it, no need to say why, just look at him, or not look at him, just say nothing, he'd understand and wouldn't take it amiss, the friendship between them would continue just as smoothly as before, as if nothing had happened: to put it in a nutshell, the point was that he would be interested in seeing the latest number of the neoactivist-simultanist-expressionist-avantgardist literary periodical *Moments and Monuments*, and would like to borrow it for twenty-four hours on condition that on the expiration of those twenty-four hours he himself brought it back entire and undamaged—naturally, however, if Esti himself hadn't read it yet or had read it and would like to read a few things in it again, or not actually to read properly but just to skim through, merely dip into it here and there, or keep it by him on the off chance, or give it to somebody else—or if he had the least shadow of suspicion that he wasn't to be completely trusted and would lose the copy or tear it, sell it to a bookseller or goodness knows what, do or not do with it all sorts of things which it was impossible really to detail or list fully there and then—then he should not undertake this favor however much he might press him, and then he would abandon the whole idea from the start, his request would be null and void, and it should be considered that he had not said a single word.

That sentence, which was in fact much more exhaustive and exhausting than that, he finished at two minutes past eleven.

Esti thereupon went to the wastepaper basket and took from it the latest, still uncut, number of *Moments and Monuments*. Dani thanked him for it, clarified a few secondary obscure points, and made to leave. Esti escorted him to the stairs. That did not pass off quickly either. When Esti had closed, locked, and bolted the gate behind him and returned to his room, his watch said that it was seventeen minutes past twelve.

XVIII

*In which he gives an appalling description of an everyday tram journey
and takes his leave of the reader.*

"THE WIND WAS HOWLING," SAID KORNÉL ESTI. "THE DARK,
the cold, and the night were lashing at my face with icy rods.

"My nose was a dark purple, my hands blue, my fingernails li-
lac. Tears were streaming down my face as if I were weeping, or as
if such life in me as had not yet frozen into a solid mass of ice were
melting. Black side streets yawned all around.

"I just stood and waited, stamping my feet on the rock-hard asphalt and blowing on my nails, hiding my numbed fingers in the
pockets of my overcoat.

"Finally far away in the mist there appeared the yellow light-eye
of the tram.

"The tram screeched along the rails. It took a slight bend and
stopped in front of me. I was about to get on, but scarcely had I
reached for the handrail than unfriendly voices shouted at me, 'Full
up!' Bunches of people were hanging from the steps. Inside, in the
doubtful red half-light of a single-filament bulb, living beings were
moving, men, women, and children in arms.

"I hesitated for a moment, then with sudden decisiveness jumped
aboard. I couldn't afford to be fussy. I was so cold that my teeth were
chattering. And then, I was in a hurry and had a long way to go; I
simply had to get to my destination.

"My situation at first was more than desperate. I clung to the human bunch, and myself too became another indistinguishable grape. We hurtled over bridges and through tunnels at such a wild speed that had I fallen off, a terrible fate awaited me. Now and then I brushed against a wall, a wooden fence or a tree trunk. I was playing with death.

"The knowledge that my fellow passengers loathed me caused me greater suffering than the danger. Up on the platform of the tram they were laughing at me, but down on the step those to whom fate had welded me would clearly have greeted my falling off and breaking my neck with a sigh of relief—that's what it would have cost them to be rid of a nuisance.

"It was a long time before I was able to get onto the platform. I found a tiny foothold on the very edge. But I was up there, on firm ground. I clung tightly with both hands to the rear of the car. There was no longer any need to be afraid of falling off.

"True, popular feeling turned against me again, and strongly. Down below I had become more or less used to it. My existence had been noted as a sad fact, and after a heated exchange no further attention had been paid to me. Up there, however, I was the next to force an entry, the newest enemy. They all united in burning hatred toward me. They greeted me openly and covertly, aloud and silently, with complaints, humorous curses, and coarse, despicable remarks. They made no secret whatever of the fact that they'd rather see me six feet underground than there.

"I didn't give up the fight, however. 'Just hold out,' I encouraged myself. 'Take the flak, don't give in to it.'

"My obstinacy paid off. I got hold of a hand strap and hung from it. Soon someone pushed me, but I fell forward so luckily that I went farther inside. I was now no longer standing right by the exit but was wedged rock-solid in the very middle of the crowd standing on the platform. I was being crushed and kept warm on all sides. Sometimes the crush was so strong that I couldn't breathe. Sometimes an object—an umbrella handle or the corner of a suitcase—poked me in the stomach.

"Apart from annoyances of a transitory nature, however, I couldn't complain.

"Then my prospects gradually improved.

"People came and went, got on and off. Now I could move freely, unbuttoned my overcoat with my left hand, extracted my purse from my trouser pocket, and was able to satisfy the conductor's repeated and solemn, but so far fruitless, appeals to buy a ticket. What a pleasure it was at least to pay.

"After that another little trouble arose. On climbed an imposing, fat inspector, whose 250 pounds almost caused the crowded tram to overflow like a brimful coffee cup into which a lump of sugar is dropped. The inspector asked for my ticket. Once more I had to undo buttons, this time with my disengaged right hand, and feel for the purse which I had only just put into my left trouser pocket.

"I was, however, definitely in luck. As the inspector forced a passage, bored a tunnel between the live bodies into the interior of the tram, a powerful surge of humanity swept me inward too and— at first I couldn't believe my luck—I was in there, right inside the tram: I had 'arrived.'

"In the process someone hit me on the head and a couple of buttons were torn off my overcoat, but what did I care about such things then? I swelled with pride at having got so far. There could, of course, be no question of a seat. I couldn't so much as see the distinguished company of the seated. Those standing, straphanging, obscured them completely as they stood now on their own feet, now on other people's, as did the vile fug, redolent of winter mist permeated by garlic-laden gastric exhalations and the sour effluvia of damp clothing.

"At the sight of this compressed and reeking herd, devoid of all human dignity, I was so disgusted that the thought haunted me of abandoning the struggle and not continuing my journey, close as I was to its end and achievement.

"At that moment, though, I caught sight of a woman. Poorly dressed, wearing a rabbit-fur stole, she was standing in one dimly lit corner and leaning on the side of the vehicle. She looked weary and woebegone. She had a simple face, a gentle, clear forehead, and blue eyes.

"When I felt the ignominy to be unbearable, when my limbs ached and my stomach churned, I would look for her in the rags, among the bestial faces, in the foul air, and play hide-and-seek among the heads and hats. Mostly she stared in front of her. Once, however, our eyes met. From then on she didn't remain aloof. It seemed as if she too thought as I did, as if she knew what I thought of that tram and everything to do with it. This consoled me.

"She let me look at her, and I looked into her blue eyes as hospital patients look into that blue electric light which is lit at night in the ward so that they shall not be quite alone in their suffering.

"I have only her to thank that I didn't finally lose my fighting spirit.

"A quarter of an hour later I actually found a place on the bench, which was divided into four seats by brass rails. At first I only had space enough to lower myself onto one thigh while the other dangled. Those sitting around me were horrid, small-minded persons, ensconced in their thick furs and the rights they had acquired, from which they would yield nothing. I made do with what they gave me. I made no demands. I pretended not to notice their paltry arrogance. I behaved like a sack. I knew that people instinctively hate people and are much quicker to forgive a sack than a person.

"So it was. When they saw that I was indifferent, the kind of nobody and nothing that didn't count, they moved up a little and ceded a tiny bit of the seat that belonged to me. Later I was able to take my pick of the seats.

"A few stops farther on I obtained a window seat. I sat down and looked around. First I looked for the blue-eyed woman, but she wasn't there—she'd obviously gotten off somewhere while I'd been engaged in life's grim struggle. I'd lost her forever.

"I heaved a sigh. I stared through the frosted window, but all that I could see were lampposts, dirty snow, and darkly hostile closed gates.

"I sighed once more, then yawned. I consoled myself as best I could. I decided that I had 'fought a good fight.' I had achieved what

I could. Who can achieve more on a tram than a comfortable window seat? I reflected and thought back almost contentedly over certain scenes in my terrible battle, the initial charge with which I had taken hold of the tram, the agonies of the step, the fisticuffs on the platform, the unbearable atmosphere and spirit inside the car, and I reproached myself for my lack of faith in all but losing heart and nearly retreating. I looked at the buttons missing from my coat as a warrior contemplates his wounds. 'Everyone gets their turn,' I repeated with the mellow experience of a philosopher, 'you just have to wait.' Rewards are not lightly bestowed on this earth, but nevertheless we receive them in the end.

"Now the desire came over me to enjoy my triumph. I was about to stretch out my cramped legs, finally to rest and relax, at last to breathe freely and happily, when the conductor came up to my window, turned round the destination board. and called out, 'Terminus.'

"I smiled and slowly got off."